PHENOMENAL PRAISE FOR
McNALLY'S RISK
BY
LAWRENCE SANDERS

*Turn the page for more rave reviews
of Lawrence Sanders's McNALLY thrillers . . .*

McNALLY'S SECRET

The rollicking bestseller that introduced Lawrence Sanders's most wickedly charming sleuth, Archy McNally . . .

"Witty, charming . . . fine entertainment!"
—Cosmopolitan

"A page-turner!" —Associated Press

"Clever . . . witty . . . a good read!"
—Copley News Service

"A suspense writer who knows how to mix chuckles with thrills."
—Wall Street Journal

"McNally is the Nick Charles of the 90s . . ."
—Ocala Star Banner

McNALLY'S LUCK

McNally returns—and the case of a kidnapped cat leads to ransom and homicide...

"Entertaining . . . sophisticated wit . . . This is a fun book!"

—South Bend Tribune

"This whodunit's plot—and clues—are top quality and give the reader plenty to puzzle over right up to the end."

—Sacramento Bee

"It's nice to have Sanders back, twisting plots and turning phrases."

—Detroit Free Press

"McNally is a charmer!"   *—Orlando Sentinel*

Berkley Books By Lawrence Sanders

McNALLY'S RISK
PRIVATE PLEASURES
McNALLY'S LUCK
McNALLY'S SECRET
THE SEVENTH COMMANDMENT
SULLIVAN'S STING
CAPITAL CRIMES
TIMOTHY'S GAME
THE TIMOTHY FILES
THE EIGHTH COMMANDMENT
THE FOURTH DEADLY SIN
THE PASSION OF MOLLY T.
THE SEDUCTION OF PETER S.
THE CASE OF LUCY BENDING
THE THIRD DEADLY SIN
THE TENTH COMMANDMENT
THE SIXTH COMMANDMENT
THE TANGENT FACTOR
THE SECOND DEADLY SIN
THE MARLOW CHRONICLES
THE TANGENT OBJECTIVE
THE TOMORROW FILE
THE FIRST DEADLY SIN
LOVE SONGS
THE PLEASURES OF HELEN
THE ANDERSON TAPES

McNALLY'S RISK

Lawrence SANDERS

BERKLEY BOOKS, NEW YORK

McNALLY'S RISK

A Berkley Book / published by arrangement with
the author

PRINTING HISTORY
G. P. Putnam's Sons edition / February 1993
Berkley edition / July 1994

ISBN: 0-425-14286-8

BERKLEY®
Berkley Books are published by
The Berkley Publishing Group, 200 Madison Avenue,
New York, New York 10016.
BERKLEY and the "B" design are trademarks of
Berkley Publishing Corporation.

PRINTED IN THE UNITED STATES OF AMERICA

10 9 8 7 6 5 4 3 2 1

McNALLY'S
RISK

1

Occasionally my behavior reminded me of that famous apothegm of the theatre: "Good acting demands absolute sincerity—and if you can fake that you've got it made."

What brought on that introspective twitch was that at the moment I was perched on the edge of a lumpy armchair, leaning forward attentively, alert as a bird dog, exhibiting every evidence of sympathetic interest, including clucking—and bored out of my gourd.

I was listening to a lecture by Mrs. Gertrude Smythe-Hersforth, a large, imperious lady who may have been the best bridge player in the Town of Palm Beach, but whose conversation had once been described to me as "a diarrhea of words and a constipation of ideas."

Mrs. Smythe-Hersforth was expounding on the importance of family tradition and bloodlines, and how in the current mongrelized (her word) Palm Beach society it was more important than ever

1

that people of breeding circle the wagons to defend their world against the determined assault of lesser beings, many of whom didn't have a single hyphen to their name.

"After all, Archy," quoth she, "one must have pride in one's family."

Don't you just love it? This overstuffed matron was implying that if your name was Smith, DiCicco, or Rabinowitz, you were incapable of pride and probably bought your Jockey shorts at K-Mart. In Britain, family determines class. But in America, it's money. I could have explained that to her, but what was the use?

The reason I was listening to Mrs. Smythe-Hersforth's rubbish with dissembled fascination was that she was an old and valued client of McNally & Son, Attorney-at-Law. (My father is the Attorney; I am the Son.) We had inherited Gertrude after her husband, Reginald, dropped dead from cardiac arrest after missing a ten-inch putt on the fourth green at his club. It is now reverently referred to as Reggie's Hole, in his honor.

I am not an attorney myself, having been expelled from Yale Law for a minor contretemps. During a performance by the New York Philharmonic, I had streaked across the stage, naked except for a Richard M. Nixon mask. To this day it is of some satisfaction that I garnered more applause than Shostakovich's Symphony No. 9 in E-flat Major.

After I returned in disgrace from New Haven to Palm Beach, my father provided me with gainful employment by creating a section in his law

firm yclept the Department of Discreet Inquiries.
I was the sole member, and it was my task to conduct investigations requested by our moneyed clients who didn't wish to consult law enforcement
agencies and possibly see their personal problems emblazoned on the covers of those tabloids
stacked next to sliced salami in supermarkets.

This particular inquiry had been initiated with
iron determination by the aforementioned Mrs.
Gertrude Smythe-Hersforth. Her son, unmarried,
had apparently become enamored of a local lady
fifteen years his junior, and he wished to plight his
troth. In other words, Chauncey Wilson Smythe-
Hersforth yearned to get hitched, and to a woman
whose surname of Johnson seemed to his mother
distressingly plebeian and therefore suspect.

In view of mommy's prejudices, you would think,
wouldn't you, that the Smythe-Hersforths rated at
least a page in Burke's Peerage? *Au contraire.*

I happened to know that Lemuel Smythe had
founded the family fortune by selling moldy bread
to Union forces during the Civil War and had
subsequently tripled his net worth by marrying Abagail Hersforth, the only child of Isaac
Hersforth, who had made *his* pile in the slave
trade. So much for our client's family tradition. It
couldn't hold a candle stub to my own pride in my
paternal grandfather, who was known as Ready
Freddy McNally and was one of the most popular
burlesque comics on the old Minsky Circuit.

I promised Mrs. Smythe-Hersforth I would conduct a discreet but thorough investigation into
the antecedents and character of Miss Theodosia

Johnson, the young woman who had snared her son's heart.

"I wouldn't be surprised if she was just a common fortune hunter," Mrs. S-H said darkly.

That was the tip-off, of course. The old biddy was less interested in protecting the family's name than in protecting the family's bucks, which, according to gossip I had heard, amounted to Gettysburg Address millions: four score and seven. A tidy sum, to be sure, but petty cash compared to the wealth of some of her neighbors on Ocean Boulevard.

I was happy to depart the Smythe-Hersforth manse. The interior looked as if it had been decorated in the Avocado Green–Harvest Gold era of the 1950s and hadn't been dusted since. I emerged into bright August sunshine, the sea glittering and a sweet sky dotted with popcorn clouds. I vaulted into my fire-engine-red Miata and headed for the Pelican Club, desperately in need of a liquid buck-up. An hour spent with Mrs. Gertrude Smythe-Hersforth was an affront to the Eighth Amendment, the one dealing with cruel and unusual punishment.

As I tooled westward I reflected that this was not the first time I had been handed the job of establishing the bona fides of a prospective bride or groom. I recalled that on my initial assignment of this type I had expressed some misgivings. I am essentially a romantic cove—and something of a featherbrain, my father might add—and it seemed rather infra dig to investigate the personal history, bank balance, and private kinks of a potential mate with whom one is madly in love.

"Archy," the squire explained in his stodgy way, "you must understand that marriage is a legal contract, presumably for life. Would you sign a contract with a party of the second part without first making an inquiry into his or her trustworthiness? Would you sign a mortgage without inspecting the property and perhaps having it evaluated by an independent appraiser? Would you make a loan without first establishing the financial resources of the borrower? If you would do any of those things, then you are a mindless ass."

I had to acknowledge the logic of his argument, and so I surrendered and accepted the task. I must confess I am not a bloke of strong convictions, other than hot English mustard is splendid on broiled calves' liver.

The Pelican Club is a private dining and drinking establishment housed in a rather decrepit freestanding building out near the airport. It is my favorite watering hole and a popular home-away-from-home for many golden lads and lasses in the Palm Beach area. I was one of the founding members and am proud to say I helped create its most famous annual event, the Running of the Lambs—more fun than Pamplona with considerably less possibility of being gored.

It was not quite noon and the luncheon crowd had not yet come galloping in. The sole occupant of the bar area was Mr. Simon Pettibone, an elderly and dignified gentleman of color who served as club manager and bartender. At the moment, he was watching the screen of a TV set showing a running tape of stock quotations.

I swung aboard a barstool. "Is the market up or down, Mr. Pettibone?" I inquired.

"Sideways, Mr. McNally," he said. "Frozen daiquiri?"

"Excellent suggestion," I said, and watched him prepare it with the deft movements of a practiced mixologist.

"Mr. Pettibone," I said, "are you by any chance acquainted with the Smythe-Hersforth family?"

"Somewhat," he said warily. "When the mister was alive I worked a few of their soirées."

"And what was your impression?"

He chuffed a short laugh. "You could see up their nostrils," he said.

I smiled at his description of nose-in-the-air snoots. "I know the son," I mentioned. "Chauncey Wilson Smythe-Hersforth. He belongs to my golf club. I played a round with him once. Just once. He's an awful duffer. He likes to be called CW— for Chauncey Wilson, you know. So we oblige. He hasn't yet caught on that most of us mean the Chinless Wonder."

"He is that," Mr. Pettibone agreed. "I would call him a young codger."

"Well put," I said. "He must be—what would you say—about forty-five?"

"About."

"And never married?"

"Not to my knowledge. What woman would want a mama's boy?"

"Not even a rich mama's boy?" I asked.

Mr. Pettibone paused to consider that. "Um," he said finally.

I sipped my plasma and considered what might be the wisest next move in my investigation of CW's intended. I had never met the lady, never heard of her prior to that morning, knew absolutely nothing about her. I mention this because it was so unusual. Palm Beach is a small town, especially in the off-season, and everybody knows everybody. But Ms. Theodosia Johnson was, as far as I was concerned, Ms. Terra Incognita.

Ordinarily, I would have immediately consulted Consuela Garcia. She is social secretary to Lady Cynthia Horowitz, one of Palm Beach's wealthiest chatelaines. Connie is plugged in to *all* our town's gossip, rumors, and scandals. She would surely have some poop to contribute on the subject of Theodosia Johnson.

But Connie is also my light-o'-love, and has been for several years. She is a Marielito and an absolutely smashing senorita to whom I have been, I must regretfully confess, unfaithful on more than one occasion.

If Connie has one failing, it's that the green-eyed monster seems permanently perched on her soft, tanned shoulder. We have vowed, many times, to maintain an open relationship, both of us free to consort with whomever she (Connie) or he (me) chooses. I have faithfully hewed to this agreement, but occasionally Connie has been overwhelmed by her fiery Latin blood.

For instance, not too long ago I escorted a charming miss to Testa's for Sunday brunch. We entered the dining room and I immediately espied Connie alone at a distant table. Unfortunately she spotted me and my companion at the same time. She gave me a look I don't wish to describe. She rose immediately and, carrying her brunch plate, marched up to us. I attempted an awkward introduction but to no avail. Connie pulled open the waistband of my lime green linen slacks and slipped in two eggs Benedict. Then she stalked out. It is not a memory I cherish.

So, in view of that recent confrontation, I thought it best not to request Connie's assistance in investigating a nubile young woman. Instead, I went to the rear of the Pelican Club's bar area and used the public phone to call Lolly Spindrift, the social reporter for one of our local gazettes. His popular column is called "Hither and Yon," which I presume refers to the Island of Palm Beach and West Palm Beach across Lake Worth.

"Lol?" I said. "Archy McNally here."

"You swine!" he shrieked. "You don't write, you don't call. How could I possibly have offended? I've never written a word about your vulgar dalliances, although the evidence occupies a full file drawer. And did I not mention your name— spelled correctly, incidentally—in my scoop on the Gillsworth homicides? A word of thanks from you? Hah! Stony silence has been my reward. Watch your step, bucko, or I may add you to my annual list of the Island's most noxious bachelors."

"Slow down a mo, Lol," I begged, "and have lunch with me."

"Where?" he demanded.

"The Pelican Club?" I suggested hopefully.

"Surely you jest," he said. "I wouldn't dine there if I was suffering from a terminal case of malnutrition. Try again."

"The Cafe L'Europe?"

"You're on, darling," he said promptly. "But only if I can have Krug with my beluga. You obviously want something from me, and it's going to cost you, sweetie. Meet you at the bar in a half-hour."

But it was two hours later that I was finally able to muffle his volubility long enough to broach the reason for this extravagant feast. By that time we were on our second bottle of bubbly. Not smashed, you understand, but not whimpering with pain either. Lolly was a sparrow of a man, all dash and chatter. Despite his small size, his capacity for food and drink is legendary. Once, at a party, I saw him consume an entire roast chicken, belch delicately, and head for the broiled lobster.

"Theodosia Johnson," I said to him. "About thirty years old, I think. The chosen of Chauncey Wilson Smythe-Hersforth. What do you know about her?"

Spindrift looked at me sorrowfully. "Oh dear," he said, "I fear I have been dining under false pretenses. There is very little I can tell you about the lady. I like to think of her as Madam X."

"Surely you must know *something* about her," I urged. "She lives in Palm Beach? On the acceptable side of the water?"

"She does indeed. In a rented condo. With her father."

"Single? Divorced? Widowed?"

"Part of the mystery," Lol said, filling our glasses again. "She's been in residence about a year. Seems to be well-heeled. Becoming more active in local charities. That's how she met the Chinless Wonder. At a black-tie bash to save the whales or dolphins or manatees—whatever. You've never met her?"

"Never heard of her until this morning."

He gave me a pitying glance. "Be prepared to have your timbers shivered, m'lad."

"Oh?" I said. "Why is that?"

"Beautiful!" he said enthusiastically. "A corker, believe me. If I was of a different religion, I would definitely be attracted. She's half-Garbo, half-Dietrich. Careful, darling. One look and you'll lose that prune you call your heart."

"An intriguing prospect," I said, pouring the remainder of the second bottle into our glasses. "How do you suggest I might meet this lalapalooza?"

"Easiest thing in the world," he told me. "Tonight the Pristine Gallery is having an exhibit of Silas Hawkin's portraits. You know him?"

"I've met him," I said. "I think he's an idiot."

"More oaf than idiot," Lolly said. "And a *rich* oaf. You know what they say about him, don't you? As a portrait painter he's the best plastic surgeon in Palm Beach. He charges thirty grand and up—mostly up—for a genuine oil portrait of our wealthier beldames. And every matron he's painted has her bosom lifted, wattles excised, and her gin-dulled stare replaced with a youthful sparkle. The man is really a genius at pleasing his clients. Anyway, at the to-do tonight, the gallery is going to show his latest masterpiece: a portrait of Theodosia Johnson. How does that grab you? Madam X herself is sure to be there. Why don't you pop by?"

"Thank you, Lol," I said gratefully. "I think I'll do exactly that."

Eventually we tottered outside and stood in the afternoon heat grinning foolishly at each other.

"Another luncheon like that," I said, "and I'll have a liver as big as the Ritz."

"Nonsense, darling," Spindrift said, gently swaying back and forth. "It was a yummy spread, and I'm pickled tink you asked me."

He gave me a careless wave and wandered away, leaving me to wonder if his "pickled tink" was deliberate or a lurch of a champagne-loosened tongue. I stood rooted, knowing I should return to my miniature office in the McNally Building and begin an inquiry into the creditworthiness of Madam X, including bank balances, net worth, source of income, and all that. But I feared my Krugged brain might not be capable of the task.

During my brief sojourn at Yale Law I had learned an effective method of determining whether one was or was not plotched. You recited aloud the following:

"Amidst the mists and coldest frosts, with stoutest wrists and loudest boasts, he thrusts his fists against the posts and still insists he sees the ghosts."

If you can say that without slobbering all over your chin, you are definitely *not* hors de combat. So I declaimed it aloud on Worth Avenue, attracting wary glances from passing tourists. I was delighted to discover my lower mandible remained bone-dry; the McNally medulla oblongata had not lost its keen edge.

But it was then threeish or fourish, much too late to return to the salt mines. So I drove home, slowly and cautiously, and took a nap.

I roused an hour later, full of p&v, and went for my daily swim. The Atlantic is just across Ocean Boulevard from the McNally digs, and I try to do two miles each day, chugging along parallel to the shore and hoping no Portuguese man-of-war is lurking nearby, licking its chops. I returned home in time to dress and attend the cocktail hour, a family ceremony. That evening, as usual, my father did the honors, stirring up a pitcher of traditional dry martinis.

My mother, Madelaine, is one of the ditsiest of all mommies, but a lovely gentlewoman who talks to her begonias. She also drinks sauterne with meat and fish courses and is very concerned about the ozone layer, without quite knowing what ozone *is*.

My father, Prescott McNally, has been playing the part of landed gentry so long that he has become exactly that: a squire, rectitudinous attorney, and possibly the most hidebound man I know. He has a wide Guardsman's mustache, tangled as the Amazon rain forest, and I like to visualize him wearing a busby, planted outside

Buckingham Palace, staring fixedly into space.

I don't wish to imply that my parents are "characters." They, and I, would be offended by that designation. They are just very decent, loving, and lovable human beings. They have their oddities—but who does not? I happen to believe I do a marvelous imitation of Humphrey Bogart, though friends assure me I sound more like Donald Duck.

What I'm trying to convey is that I love my parents. Of course. But just as important, I *enjoy* them. How many sons and daughters can say that?

That evening I was wearing the palest of pink linen suits with a deep lavender polo shirt of Sea Island cotton. Tasseled white loafers with no socks, of course. My father raised one eyebrow (a trick I've never been able to master), and I hastened to explain the glad rags.

"I'm attending an exhibit at the Pristine Gallery tonight," I said. "Silas Hawkin's paintings. I understand the showpiece will be his latest work, a portrait of Theodosia Johnson."

"Ah," the guv said.

Mother looked up. "I've met her father," she declared. "Hector Johnson. A very fine gentleman."

The pater and I exchanged glances.

"How did you happen to meet him, Maddie?" he asked.

"Why, he joined our garden club," she said. "He's only been in South Florida a short while—about a year I think he said—and he's into orchids. He seems very knowledgeable."

"How old is he, mother?" I inquired.

"Oh, I don't know, Archy," she answered. "Mid-sixties perhaps. Shall I ask him?"

McNally père smiled. "I don't think that will be necessary," he said. "A civilized man?"

"Charming," mother said, "just charming! He said my 'Iron Cross' was the healthiest begonia he had ever seen."

Father gulped the remainder of his martini. "That was very kind of him," he said, absolutely deadpan. "Shall we go down to dinner?"

I remember well the menu that night, the way I imagine the condemned might savor their last meal before the unknown. Ursi Olson, our cook-housekeeper, had sautéed red snapper with white wine and shallots. And husband Jamie, our houseman, served the dessert: chocolate torte with cappuccino ice cream. Any wonder why the waist-bands of my slacks continue to shrink?

Before departing for the Pristine Gallery I climbed to the third floor of the McNally faux Tudor manor. There, under a leaking copper roof, I had my own aerie, a rather dilapidated but snug suite: sitting room, bedroom, bath. Not luxurious, you understand, but you couldn't beat the rent. Zip.

Since becoming chief of Discreet Inquiries at McNally & Son, I had kept a private journal in which I recorded the details of my investigations. It was an invaluable aid in keeping track of things, especially when I had two or more cases running concurrently. I jotted down facts, impressions, bits of actual dialogue, and whatever else I thought might be of value. Most of my scribblings turned out to be of no value whatsoever. But one never knows, do one?

That night I hurriedly made brief notes on my interview with Mrs. Gertrude Smythe-Hersforth, the chat with Simon Pettibone, the information learned at that bibulous luncheon with Lolly Spindrift, and what mother had mentioned about Hector, Theodosia Johnson's father. Finished, I read over what I had written and found absolutely zilch in the way of inspiration. So I closed up shop, clattered downstairs, and went to meet my fate.

It was a still, cloudless night but hot and humid as a sauna. As I drove back to Worth Avenue I hoped the owner of the Pristine Gallery, Ivan Duvalnik, would have the decency to serve something refreshing. He did: a Chilean chardonnay so cold it made my fillings ache.

It turned out to be a hugger-mugger evening, the gallery overcrowded, chatter too loud, paintings almost hidden by the billows of chiffon gown (f.) and the sheen of silk sport jackets (m.). I knew most of the guests and mingled determinedly, working my way toward the pièce de résistance: the portrait of Theodosia Johnson.

When I finally stood before it, I was simultaneously rapt and unwrapped. I mean I was totally engrossed and at the same time felt a sag of the knees and a horrible need to let my jaw droop and just gawk. Spindrift had not exaggerated; the lady was a corker. What beauty! But not of the plastic variety one sees so often in fashion ads and centerfolds. Again, Lolly had it right: she was half-Garbo, half-Dietrich, with all the mystery and promise in those two mesmerizing faces.

I am not an expert on paintings, figuring one man's "September Morn" is another man's "Les Demoiselles d'Avignon." But I defy any hot-blodded yute to look at that portrait of Madam X without saying to himself, "I *must* meet her."

I was filling my eyes when a voice at my elbow interrupted my fantasies by stating, "Awfully good, am I right, Archy? Si has caught her expression perfectly, and the colors are striking. Don't you agree?"

I turned, and there was the Chinless Wonder himself, Chauncey Wilson Smythe-Hersforth, wearing a midnight blue dinner jacket and looking like the groom on a wedding cake. His pushbroom mustache was meticulously trimmed and he was exuding a fruity cologne. That was a surprise. CW was known as a nebbishy sort of chap. Palm Beach gossips (the total population) claimed he wore a helmet while pedaling his Exercycle.

"You couldn't be righter, CW," I said. "Or more right—whichever comes first. Hawkin has done a marvelous job, and the lady is beautiful."

"My fiancée," he said with a fatuous grin. "Or soon to be."

"Congratulations!" I said, smiling, and recalling that "one may smile and smile, and be a villain."

"Well, it's not exactly official yet," he said in that pontifical way he had of speaking. "But it soon will be, I assure you."

"I'd like to meet the lucky lady," I said, perking his ego. "Is she here this evening?"

"Somewhere," he said vaguely, looking about the mobbed gallery. "Just find the biggest crowd, and she's sure to be the center."

Then he drifted away, obviously having no desire to introduce me personally. Quite understandable.

I glanced around and saw in one corner a jammed circle of men surrounding someone I presumed to be the star of the evening. Rather than join the adoring throng, I eased my way to the bar to replenish my supply of that excellent chardonnay. And there I bumped into Silas Hawkin, the famous portraitist and plastic surgeon himself.

"Hi, Si," I said, thinking how silly that sounded.

He stared. "Do I know you?" he demanded.

We had met several times; he knew very well who I was. But feigning ignorance was his particular brand of one-upmanship.

"Archy McNally," I said, as equably as I could.

"Oh yeah," he said. "The lawyer feller. Didn't know you were interested in fine art."

"Oh my yes," I said. "I have a lovely collection of Bugs Bunny cels. Good show tonight."

"I think so," he said complacently. "People know quality when they see it. You caught my latest? The portrait of Theodosia Johnson?"

"Extraordinary," I said.

"It is that," he agreed. "Took me a week to do her lips."

A ribald reply leaped to mind, but I squelched it. "By the way, Si," I said, "may I give you a call? It concerns a silly inquiry I'm making. Nothing of any great importance."

"Sure," he said casually, his eyes roving. "Anytime."

Then we were jostled away from the bar and separated. I finally decided I had to make my move—win or lose. So I joined the ring of admirers, and sure enough Theodosia Johnson was at the center, flushed but poised and accepting compliments with the graciousness of E. II. I slowly inched forward until I was standing directly in front of Madam X herself.

"Archy McNally," I said, giving her the 150-watt smile I call my Jumbocharmer.

"Theo Johnson," she said, and reached out a hand to shake. It was one of the hardest decisions of my life to let go.

"A fantastic portrait, Miss Johnson," I told her. "But it doesn't do you justice."

"Thank you," she murmured, and gave me the full blaze of azure eyes. "You're very kind."

Naturally I wanted to say more, but I was elbowed away by other victims, and regretfully departed with the feeling that I had been privileged to be in the presence of great, almost supernal beauty. For the third time, Lolly Spindrift had been right: my timbers had been shivered and I was in love.

Again.

I left the gallery and drove home singing one of my favorite songs: "When It's Apple Blossom Time in Orange, New Jersey, We'll Make a Peach of a Pair."

2

I awoke the next morning with the conviction that if Johnny Keats was right—"Beauty is truth, truth beauty."—then Mrs. Smythe-Hersforth had no reason to worry about the motives of Ms. Theodosia Johnson. How could a paragon with that mass of shimmering chestnut hair, those burning eyes, that Limoges complexion ever be guilty of even the teeniest deceit? Ridiculous! As far as I was concerned, my investigation could be canceled forthwith.

But I knew if I dared suggest such a thing to my father, he wouldn't say a word. He would merely glare at me from under those snarled eyebrows, and that would be my answer. So, sighing, I started the second day of what I later came to call The Affair of Madam X.

I was late getting downstairs, as usual, and so I breakfasted in the kitchen, served by Jamie Olson. He was working on what was probably his third mug of black coffee to which, I was sure, he had added a splash of aquavit.

Jamie is seventyish, semi-wizened, and a taci-turn bloke. He is also privy to all the backstairs gossip in Palm Beach, stuff even Lolly Spindrift isn't aware of since it's shared only by the ser-vants of the Island's nabobs. And the things these maids, chauffeurs, valets, housekeeps, and but-lers know or suspect would make a platoon of tabloid editors moan with delight.

"Jamie," I said, after I had smeared my toasted onion bagel with salmon mousse, "have you ever heard of Theodosia Johnson?"

"Yep," he said. "A looker."

"She is that," I agreed. "I understand she's been here about a year. Lives with her father, Hector, in a rented condo. Do they have any staff?"

"Don't know."

"Could you find out?"

"Mebbe."

"What about the Smythe-Hersforths? Hear any talk?"

"Tight."

"Tight? You mean stingy?"

"Uh-huh."

I seemed to be making little progress with Jamie, but I had learned from past experience that patience frequently paid off. He really was a remarkable fount of inside info. Turning on the tap was the problem.

"I can believe the gammer might have miser-ly tendencies," I said. "What about the son, Chauncey Wilson? I know he's got a good job with a local bank. All title and no work. Is he also a penny-pincher?"

"Yep," Jamie said.

"Blood will tell," I said, and poured myself another cup of coffee that had been laced with chicory. "One more: How about the painter, Silas Hawkin? Know him?"

He nodded.

"How many in his ménage?"

"Ménage?"

"Household."

"Him, wife, daughter. One live-in."

"Everything harmonious there? All peace and goodwill?"

"Nope," Jamie said.

I woke up. "What seems to be the problem?" I asked.

"Him."

"I can understand that," I said. "The man's a dolt. Know any details?"

He shook his head.

"Ask around, will you, Jamie? About Theodosia and her father, and the reason for discord in Si Hawkin's not-so-happy home."

He nodded.

I slipped him a tenner before I left. The lord of the manor would be outraged to learn that I customarily gave Jamie a pourboire for information. The Olsons drew a handsome stipend to keep the McNally family comfortable and well-nourished, but I felt revealing inside skinny to yrs. truly was not included in domestic chores and deserved an extra quid now and then.

I went into my father's study and sat in the big

armchair behind his desk, feeling like a fraudulent dauphin. I used his local telephone directory that had been bound in a leather slipcover. I swear, he would put a calfskin cozy on a teapot. I looked up the number and pecked it out.

"The Hawkins' residence," a chirpy female voice answered. I presumed this was the live-in.

"May I speak to Mr. Hawkin, please," I said. "Archy McNally calling."

"Just a moment, please, sir," she said.

It was more than a moment, more like three or four, before he came on the line.

"Yeah?" he said. It was practically a grunt.

"Good morning, Si," I said, giving him a heavy dose of the McNally cheer. "That was a wonderful show last night."

"It went okay," he said. "Ivan Duvalnik called earlier and claims we got two new clients out of it and four possibles."

"Congratulations!" I cried. "Due to that marvelous portrait of Theo Johnson, no doubt. Listen, may I pop over this morning and ask a few questions? That silly inquiry I mentioned to you last night. It won't take long."

"Well . . . all right," he said, "if you keep it short. I've got a lot of work to do."

"Just take a few minutes," I promised. "I'm on my way."

They lived in an imitation Mizner on the Intracoastal down toward South Palm Beach, and when I saw the house, really a villa, I guessed a million five. Then I saw the guest house and changed my estimate to two million five. That detached, two-story edifice looked like an enormous Nebraska barn painted white, but the upper floor seemed entirely enclosed in glass, and I mean big, openable picture windows. It had to be the artist's studio—or a solarium devoted to sunbathing in the buff.

I was greeted at the front door of the main house by the chirpy-voiced domestic who had answered the phone. I had envisioned her as young, small, lissome. She was old, large, creaky.

"Archy McNally," I said. "To see Mr. Hawkin."

"Of course," she said, and her smile won me over. "Do come in."

I followed this pleasant woman into a home decorated in what is called the Mediterranean Style, but whether that means Marseille or Beirut I've never been able to figure out. Anyway, I thought it a strident interior with a lot of rattan, jangling patterns, acidic hues, and the skins of endangered species. On the walls, to my surprise, were seascapes and paintings of Lake Worth by Silas Hawkin. I had no idea he did that kind of thing, but there was no mistaking his style; the man *was* a superb colorist.

There were two women seated in the Florida room, leafing through slick magazines, and it was the older who rose to greet me.

"You must be Archy McNally," she said, holding out a hand. "I do believe I've met your parents. I am Louise Hawkin."

"A pleasure to make your acquaintance, ma'am," I said, pressing dry, bony fingers.

"And this is my daughter, Marcia," she added.

"*Step*daughter," the younger woman said in a Freon voice, not looking up from her copy of *Vogue.*

Mrs. Hawkin made a small moue as if she had suffered that correction before.

"Glad to meet you, Miss Hawkin," I said, and was rewarded with a nod. One.

"Would you care for something to drink?" Mrs. Hawkin asked. "Coffee perhaps? Or anything else?"

"Thank you, no," I replied. "I promised your husband I'd only stay a few minutes. I know how busy he must be."

"Oh yes," she said airily, "he's always busy."

I heard a sound from the stepdaughter. It might have been a short, scornful laugh. Or maybe she was only clearing her throat.

"He's in the studio now," Louise Hawkin said. "Through that door and along the walkway. He's on the second floor."

"Thank you," I said. "I hope to meet you ladies again."

Neither replied and I left in silence. Happy to leave, as a matter of fact. Bad vibes in that room. Something bilious about the relationship between the two women. But perhaps they had merely had an early morning squabble ("Aren't you finished with the *Vogue* yet?" "No, I am *not* finished with it!"), and I thought no more about it.

The walkway to the guest house was roofed with slates. A nice touch, I acknowledged, but not very practical if you got a blowy squall coming in from the sea. The door to the Nebraska barn

was oak and etched frosted glass. It was horribly
scarred, and I judged it had been purchased from
one of those antique shops that specialize in old
saloon furnishings.

I pushed in and found myself in an enormous
space that had indeed been designed for sleep-over
guests: bedroom area, conversation pit, kitchenette. But it did have all the comforts of home:
fridge, TV set, VCR, and what appeared to be
a well-stocked bar. Everything was precisely
arranged, new and unused, awaiting guests who
never arrived.

I climbed a cast-iron staircase to the second story and entered the studio, as large and open as the
floor below. But this area was cluttered with all
the paraphernalia and detritus a working artist
might accumulate: easels, taborets, palettes, tubes
of oil, stretched blank canvases, stacks of finished
paintings leaning against the outside walls, innu-
merable cans of turps and who knows what.

There was a dais decorated like a stage set, the
floor carpeted, maroon drapes, an ornate armchair
alongside a delicate tea table. I remembered seeing those drapes and that tea table in the painting
of Theodosia Johnson, and had little doubt that the
artist used the same props in all his portraits of
Palm Beach matrons.

Oh yes, one more thing: In a far corner was
a battered sleigh bed that might have been a
charming antique at one time but was now in
such a dreadful state of disrepair that it had all
the compelling grace of an army cot. It was covered with rumpled sheets, and the wadded pillow

looked as if it had been used to smother palmetto bugs.

The artist himself was seated at a shockingly dilapidated desk, smoking a morning cigar and apparently making entries in a ledger. He slapped it shut when I entered. He rose and came forward to meet me, viewing with some distaste the madras blazer and electric blue slacks I was wearing. He made no offer to shake hands.

"Found me, did you?" he said. "Pull up a chair. That one over there. It looks ready to collapse, but it won't. You met my wife and daughter?"

"I did," I said, seating myself rather gingerly on the spindly kitchen chair he had indicated. "Lovely ladies."

"Yeah," he said, going back behind his desk. "Now what's all this bullshit about an inquiry and questions?"

It *was* bs, but it was a scam I had used before with some success, and I saw no reason why it wouldn't work on this crude man. He might have been a talented artist, but he was also, in my opinion, a vulgar pig. There. I said it and I'm glad.

"It's a project dreamed up by the Real Estate Department of McNally and Son," I said earnestly. (Hey, I can do earnest.) "We are agents for perhaps a dozen mansions in the Palm Beach area, ranging from two million to twelve. Asking price, of course. What we're planning to do is put together a list of potential buyers, people with sufficient resources to afford one of these magnificent estates. Before we send them a very expensive four-color brochure, we'd like to do a little research and make certain they're completely trustworthy and capable of making such a hefty investment. One of the names on the list is Hector Johnson, and I hoped you'd be willing to tell me a little about him. Strictly *entre nous,* of course."

He looked at me. I could see he didn't believe and he didn't *dis*believe. He finally decided to give me the benefit of the doubt. People are continually doing that—until they learn better.

Let me tell you something about Silas Hawkin. He suffered from what I called the Hemingway Syndrome—very prevalent in South Florida and particularly in the Keys. Bulky, middle-aged men cultivate a grizzled beard, wear a long-billed fishing cap, and drink nothing but Myers's Dark rum. Some go so far as to sport a small gold ring in one ear or even a ponytail. None wear bifocals or a hearing aid in public.

Hawkin was a charter member of this macho cult. I didn't know whether or not he was an obsessed fisherman, but I would have bet a farthing that he had the cap and drank rum. I could see he had the requisite pepper-and-salt beard, for at the moment he was combing it with his fingers and regarding me with a mixture of hostility and suspicion.

"Hector Johnson," he repeated. "Theo's father. I've only met the guy a couple of times. He seems okay. Knows a lot about art. Good taste."

Which meant, I presumed, that Hector said he admired Hawkin's work.

"Seems to have bucks, does he?" I asked.

The artist shrugged. "I get the feeling he ain't hurting."

"Paid your bill on time?" I pressed.

He took that badly. "None of your damned business," he snapped angrily. "As a matter of fact, I haven't sent in my bill yet."

"I have no desire to pry unnecessarily," I hastily assured him. "I'm just trying to get a handle on the man. Do you know anything about his background? What he did before he and his daughter moved to South Florida?"

"I don't really know. I think he said he was a professor."

"Oh?" I said. "Biology?"

"Biology?" He was puzzled. "Why do you say that?"

"I heard he was an expert on orchids."

"Nah," the artist said. "Maybe he knows orchids, but I think he taught electronics or computer stuff—something like that. Look, I've really got to get back to work."

"Of course," I said, rising. "Before I go I must tell you again that I think your portrait of Theodosia Johnson is the best thing you've ever done."

"Yeah," he agreed, "but I couldn't miss with a model like that. Beautifully proportioned. Classic. Incredible skin tone. That hair! And carries herself like a duchess. A complete woman. I'll never find another like her."

I was somewhat surprised by his excessive praise but made no comment—mostly because I concurred with everything he had said. Before I departed I proffered my business card.

"If you come across anything that might help my inquiry," I said, "pro or con, I'd appreciate it if you'd give me a call."

"Sure," he said, tossing my card into the litter on his desk.

And that was that. I tramped downstairs wondering what I had learned. Not much. I reached the ground level, glanced in, and there was Mrs. Louise Hawkin, a winsome lady, seated on one of the couches in the conversation pit. She beckoned, and I obeyed. Good boy! Now *heel*.

"I'm having a vodka gimlet," she said. "There's a pitcher in the fridge. Would you like one?"

I considered this invitation for a long time—possibly three seconds. "Yes," I said, "thank you."

It was an excellent gimlet, not so tart that it puckered one's lips but sharp and energizing. Mrs. Hawkin patted the cushion beside her and I obediently took my place. Good boy! Now sit up and beg.

"How did you make out with Si?" she inquired lazily, her drawl obviously an attempt to conceal a real curiosity.

"Fine," I said. "I only had a few questions. Your husband was very cooperative."

"He was?" she said, mildly astonished. "Questions about what?"

"Whom," I said. "A mutual acquaintance." I hoped she wouldn't push it. She didn't.

"You're a lawyer?" she asked suddenly.

"No, ma'am," I said. "My father is an attorney but I am not."

"Does he do divorce work? A friend of mine is

looking for a good divorce lawyer and asked if I could recommend someone."

"Sorry," I said. "McNally and Son doesn't handle divorces. But if you like, I can ask my father. I'm sure he can suggest someone who would be willing to talk to your friend. Shall I do that?"

"Yes. Let me know as soon as possible."

"Of course," I said.

She sipped her gimlet, stared at the high ceiling, and ignored me. Good boy! Now lie down and play dead.

She was a heavy-bodied woman with an attractive mastiff face: very strong, very determined. I decided I would rather have her for a friend than an enemy. That may sound simple, but there are some people, men and women, of whom you are instinctively wary, knowing they could be trouble.

I finished my drink, rose, and expressed thanks for her hospitality. She gazed at me thoughtfully but made no reply. So I slunk away, grateful to be out of her presence. I can't explain exactly why. Just that I was conscious of a very deep anger there with which I could not cope, and had no desire to.

I retraced my route and entered the main house through the door to the Florida room. I could have circled around and reclaimed my Miata on the bricked driveway, but I wanted to learn the name of the pleasant, chirpy-voiced maid who had ushered me in.

Instead, I found Marcia Hawkin wandering about, hugging her elbows. I was about to bid her a polite farewell when she accosted me—and accosted is a mild word for her attitude. She was in my face.

"Did you go to daddy's show last night?" she demanded.

"Why, yes, Miss Hawkin," I said as softly as I could. "I did attend the exhibit."

"It was a circus, wasn't it?" she challenged. "A bloody circus."

"Not really," I said cautiously. "Not much different from a hundred other similar affairs."

"And I suppose *she* was there," she said bitterly.

Complete confusion. Did she mean Mrs. Hawkin or the cynosure of the evening?

"*She?*" I repeated. "Your stepmother or Theodosia Johnson?"

"You know who I mean," she said darkly. "The *whore!*"

That was rough stuff that not only shocked but left me as flummoxed as before. To whom was she referring? All I could do at the moment was stare at her, utterly bewildered.

I cannot say she was an unattractive woman. Quite young. Tall and attenuated. But there was a brittleness about her I found a mite off-putting. She seemed assembled of piano wire and glass, ready to snap or shatter at any moment.

She stalked away from me and stood staring through an open window at her father's studio. I judged it would be wise to make a quiet and unobtrusive exit. To tell you the truth, I had enough of naked human passions for one morning. I felt like I had been wrung out hard and hung up wet. I murmured a courteous goodbye and slipped away. I don't believe she was even aware of my going.

I loitered in the entrance hallway a moment, hoping to have a few words with the live-in domestic. I was rewarded when she came bustling forward to show me out.

"You've been very kind," I told her, "and I thank you for it. You know, I must confess that I don't know your name. You know mine, and I don't know yours. That's not fair!"

She gave me that radiant smile again. "Mrs. Jane Folsby," she said.

"Mrs. Folsby," I said, reaching to shake her hand, "it's been a pleasure to meet you. Have you been with the Hawkins long?"

The smile faded. "Too long," she said.

I left that acorn academy and turned to see if there was a nameplate over the front door. Some Palm Beach mansions have cutesy titles such as "Last Resort" and "Wit's End." But the Hawkins' manse boasted no legend. I thought "Villa Bile" might be fitting.

But I'm a sunny-tempered johnny, and even the events of that gruesome morning didn't drag me down for long. I wasn't quite certain if what I had heard from the Hawkin family had anything at all to do with Theodosia Johnson, the intended bride of the Chinless Wonder.

It was time, I concluded, to inject some joy and innocent delight into my life. So as I drove northward I used my new cellular phone to call

Consuela Garcia at Lady Cynthia Horowitz's
mansion.

"Miss Garcia," I said formally, "this is Archy
McNally speaking. I wish to apologize for my
recent behavior and beg your forgiveness. I also
wish to invite you to lunch at twelve-thirty at the
Pelican Club."

"Okay," Connie said cheerfully.

Divine woman! Why I continually fall in love
with others of the female persuasion is beyond me.
If it isn't a genetic defect, it must be a compulsive-
obsessive disorder. I really should read up on it,
and I fully intend to—one of these days.

3

The Pelican Club was cranking with the noonday crowd when I entered, but fortunately most of the Pelicanites were seated at tables in the bar area or dining room. I was able to find an unoccupied barstool, and Simon Pettibone came ambling over to ask my pleasure.

Ordinarily, my favorite summer potion is a frozen daiquiri, but recently I had been browsing through a secondhand bookstore and had come across a bartender's guide published in the mid-1930s, shortly after Prohibition was repealed. (Bless you, FDR!)

Naturally I purchased this fascinating compendium and spent many enjoyable hours studying the recipes of cocktails now lost and forgotten. Of course it included such classics as Manhattan, Bronx, Rob Roy, and Sazerac. But it also listed the ingredients of such obscure mixed drinks as Sweet Patootie, Seventh Heaven, and Arise My Love. (I kid you not.)

Much to my astonishment, I discovered our publican knew, he actually *knew,* how to mix many of these antique libations. It had become a game to test his expertise, and he succeeded more often than he failed.

"Today, Mr. Pettibone," I said, "I would like a Soul Kiss." It was a request that drew a few startled glances from nearby bar patrons.

"Soul Kiss," he repeated thoughtfully, cast his eyes upward and reflected. "Ah, yes," he said finally. "Orange juice, Dubonnet, dry vermouth, and bourbon."

"Bravo!" I cried. "You've got it—and I hope to get it as soon as possible."

He set to work.

I was sipping my Soul Kiss, wondering how long it might take to work my way through the 1000-plus drinks listed in the guide, when Consuela Garcia came bouncing into the Club. She immediately looked toward the bar, spotted me, and waved. I stood up and beamed happily.

Connie is as toothsome as a charlotte russe, but that is hardly the limit of her appeal. She has a sharp wit, is extremely clever at her job, and is just naturally a jolly lady. There are those who wonder why I don't marry the girl. The answer is simple: cowardice. Not fear of Connie so much as fear of matrimony itself.

I see wedded bliss as a kind of surrender—which I agree is an immature attitude. But I think of myself as an honorable chap, and if I were married it would mean that never again could I look at a dishy woman with lust in my heart. That is what scares me: that I would be incapable of resisting temptation, and so my self-esteem would evaporate, let alone the trust of my mate.

You may possibly feel all that is blarney, and my sole reason for remaining a bachelor is that I relish the life of a rake. You may possibly be right.

Connie and I had Leroy's special hamburgers, a beef-veal-pork combination mixed with chilies. We shared a big side order of extra-thick potato chips and drank Buckler, which is a non-alcoholic beer that tastes swell but doesn't do a thing for you except quench your thirst.

Connie chattered on about a reception Lady Horowitz was planning for a visiting Russian ballerina and didn't mention a word about L'Affaire d'Oeufs Benedict, for which I was thankful. She was excited about her arrangements for the party, and it showed in her features: snappy eyes, laughing mouth, squinched-up nose to express displeasure.

Charming, no doubt about it. But different from Theodosia Johnson's beauty. Not inferior or superior, just different. Connie was earthy, open, solid. Madam X was an unsolved riddle. So far.

"Hey," Connie said over coffee, "I've been yakking up a storm and haven't asked about you. What mischief are you up to these days, Archy?"

"Oh, this and that," I said. "Nothing heavy. Right now I'm running a credit check on a man named Hector Johnson. Ever hear of him?"

"Of course," she said promptly. "He sent in a nice check for Lady Cynthia's latest project, to install Art Nouveau pissoirs on Worth Avenue. Can you imagine? Anyway, the boss asked him over for cocktails. What a doll! He's got charm coming out his ears."

"Uh-huh," I said. "Retired, is he?"

"Semi, I guess. He said he used to work for the government. He didn't say doing what, but I got the feeling it was the CIA."

"Connie, whatever gave you that idea?"

"Because he was so mysterious about it. I suppose I could have asked straight out, but I didn't want to pry. Who cares if he was a spy? He's nice and that's all that counts."

"Sure," I said.

She looked at her Swatch. "Oh, lordy, I have to get my rear in gear. Sorry to eat and run, luv, but I've got a zillion things to do. Okay?"

"Of course," I said. "You go ahead. I think I'll dawdle a bit."

She swooped to kiss my cheek, gathered up handbag and scarf, and sashayed out. I wasn't the only man, or woman, in the dining room who watched her leave. Connie radiates a healthy vigor that even strangers admire. With her robust figure and long black hair flying, she could model for the hood ornament on a turbo-charged sports coupe.

I finished a second cup of coffee, signed my tab at the bar, and wandered out. I was musing about Hector Johnson, a man who apparently was knowledgeable about orchids, had been a professor of electronics or computer stuff, and had worked for the U.S. of A., possibly as a spy. Curiouser and curiouser. I had been enlisted to investigate Theo Johnson, but now I found myself concentrating on daddy. Because, to paraphrase Willie Sutton, that's where the money was, I supposed.

I went back to my cubicle in the McNally Building on Royal Palm Way. It is a squarish structure of glass and stainless steel, so stark and modern it makes you yearn to see a Chick Sales just once more before you die.

My office was a joke: a tiny windowless room as confining as a Pullman berth. I am convinced my father banished me there to prove to other employees that there would be no nepotism at McNally & Son. But at least I had an air-conditioner vent, and I lighted my first English Oval of the day as I set to work gathering the financial skinny on Hector Johnson and his wondrous daughter.

I phoned contacts at local banks, promising my pals a dinner at the Pelican if they would reveal whatever they had on the enigmatic Hector. Then I prepared a letter to be faxed to national credit agencies to which we subscribed. Those snoops could usually deliver everything from an individual's date of birth and Social Security number to current Zip Code, hat size, and passionate preferences, such as an inordinate fondness for sun-dried tomatoes. Privacy? It doesn't exist anymore. Not even if you're lucky enough to be dead.

I finished the letter and was about to take it upstairs to Mrs. Trelawney, my father's private secretary, and have her fax it out, when my phone rang. That was such an unusual occurrence that I stared at it a moment before picking up. I was sure it would be an automatic marketing machine working through every possible telephone number in sequence and delivering a recorded spiel on the wonderful opportunity I had been granted to invest in a rhinestone mine.

"H'lo?" I said cautiously.

"Archy McNally?"

I thought I recognized that whiny voice but hoped I was wrong.

"Yes," I said. "Speaking."

"This is Chauncey Wilson Smythe-Hersforth," he said, reeling off the four names like a sergeant selecting a latrine detail.

"Hello, CW," I said, resolving to get rid of this world-class bore as fast as humanly possible.

"Archy," he said, and I thought I detected a note of desperation, "I've got to see you as soon as possible."

"Oh?" I said. "Concerning what?"

"Well . . . " he started, stopped, gave me a few "Uh's" and "Um's," and finally said, "It's a legal matter."

"Then you better speak to my father," I told him. "As you know, I am not an attorney. Would you like me to set up an appointment?"

"No!" he cried. "No, no, no! I know your father is an estimable man, but he scares me."

"Well . . . yes," I conceded. "At times he can be rather daunting. But if you need legal advice,

CW, I'm just not your man."

"It's not really a legal thing," he stammered on. "It is and it isn't. And I'd rather talk about it to you. *Please,* Archy."

Now I was intrigued; the Chinless Wonder, with an ego as big as all outdoors, was pleading for help. And it just might have something to do with the trustworthiness of Theodosia Johnson.

"All right, CW," I said. "Would you like to pop over to the office?"

"Oh no," he said immediately. "I'd probably be seen, the word would get back to mother, and she'd demand to know why I was seeing our lawyer."

"Very well. Then how about the Pelican Club? Cafe L'Europe? Testa's? Perhaps a Pizza Hut?"

"Won't do," he said despairingly. "I can't be seen huddling with you in public. You know how people talk."

"CW," I said, more than a little miffed, "you ask to meet me to discuss what is apparently a personal matter of some importance, and then you reject all my suggestions for a rendezvous. Here is my final offer, and I do mean final: The McNally Building has an underground garage. If you will drive down there, I will be pleased to meet with you, and we will have a cozy tête-à-tête."

"Is that the best you can do?" he said, the whine becoming a drone.

The McNally temper, though rarely displayed, is not totally nonexistent. "Not only the best," I said with some asperity, "but the only. Either be there within fifteen minutes or forget about the whole thing."

"All right," he said faintly.

I dropped my letter off in Mrs. Trelawney's office, asked her to fax it out, and went down to the garage. After that goofy exchange with CW, I was far from being gruntled, so I merely waved at Herb, our security guard, and lighted my second cigarette of the day. I leaned against a concrete pillar, puffed away, and awaited the arrival of the Chinless Wonder.

About ten minutes later his black Mercedes came rolling slowly down the ramp. He pulled into an empty parking slot, and I went over and slid in next to him.

"Are you certain no one will see us?" he asked nervously.

"No, I am not certain," I answered. "But the odds against it are worth a wager. Now what's this all about?"

"Mother told me she asked you to investigate Theodosia."

"That's correct."

"Well, I'm sure you'll find she's true-blue."

"I'm sure I shall. So what's the problem?"

He hesitated. "This is embarrassing," he said.

"Not for me," I said. "What is it?"

"Well . . . " he started, and I got another dose of "Uh's" and "Um's." "You see, Archy, before I met Theo, I had a, ah, fling with another young woman."

"Hardly a mortal sin, CW."

"Well, after I met Theo, I realized she was the genuine article. I fell completely in love and decided I wanted to marry her. So I broke off with the previous young woman—or attempted to."

"Oh-ho," I said, "I'm beginning to get the picture. The previous lady has raised objections?"

"Loud and clear," he said miserably. "She claims I had promised to marry *her,* and she threatens to sue me."

I laughed. "Breach of Promise? Forget it, CW. That's as common as Contempt of Congress. Everyone's guilty. The lady has no case."

"Well, uh," he continued, "she may not have a *legal* case, but there's more to it than that. I wrote her letters."

I looked at him. "You actually wrote letters to her? Promising marriage?"

"Yes."

"Told her how much you adored her, did you?"

"Yes."

"That you would be faithful for a lifetime?"

"Yes."

"That you desire no girl in the world but her?"

"Yes."

"CW, you're a fool."

"Yes," he said. "And now she's threatening to sell my letters to a tabloid. They're, um, somewhat passionate."

It was difficult to believe this lump could compose passionate prose, but I let it go. "How much does she want?" I asked.

"She doesn't mention money," he said. "She keeps saying that all she wants is to marry me."

"Who is she? What's her name? What does she do for a living besides collect letters from brainless bachelors?"

He swallowed the insult. "Her name is Shirley Feebling, and she works in a topless car wash down near Lauderdale. That's how I met her."

I wasn't surprised. Florida is the home of the topless car wash, topless restaurants, topless maid service, topless coffee shops. It is only a matter of time before we have topless funeral homes.

"And what is it you wish me to do?" I asked.

"Talk to her," he begged. "Persuade her to turn over the letters and keep quiet. If she wants money, I'll pay. Within reason, of course. Archy, if she carries out her threat, she could ruin me. Mother would disown me, Theo would give me the broom. You've got to do *something!*"

I didn't know why I should, but then the thought occurred to me that someday I might be in a similar fix myself. And after all, he was a client—or at least the son of a wealthy client.

"All right," I said finally, "I'll see what I can do. Give me her name, address, and telephone number."

He reached into his inside jacket pocket and withdrew a ballpoint pen. Typical Chinless Wonder: He drove a Mercedes and carried a Bic. He tore a page from a pocket notebook and jotted down all the vital info.

I tucked it away, started to get out of the car, then paused.

"By the way, CW," I said, "I imagine you've met Hector Johnson many times. What is your impression of him?"

"A great fellow!" he said enthusiastically. "Never knew a man who understands as much about banking as old Heck. He used to own a bank somewhere out West, you know."

"Uh-huh," I said, and started to leave again. This time he stopped me.

"Listen, Archy," he said, the whine rising in pitch, "I hope you won't mention anything about my problem to your father. I mean it's just between us, isn't it? Confidential and all that?"

"Of course," I said. "My lips are sealed."

"Good man," he said.

So that evening, after my ocean swim, the family cocktail hour and dinner, I followed the sire to his study.

"Father," I said, "may I have a word with you?"

"Can't it wait?" he said testily.

I knew what irked him; I was delaying his nighttime routine. He was looking forward to having one or more glasses of port while he continued slogging his way through the entire oeuvre of Charles Dickens. I think he was currently deep in the complexities of *Martin Chuzzlewit* but it might have been *Little Dorrit*. The amazing thing was that he stayed awake while reading.

"It'll just take a few minutes," I promised.

"Oh, very well," he said. "Come on in."

He stood erect behind his massive desk and I stood in front. As I delivered a report on my recent conversation with Chauncey Wilson

Smythe-Hersforth, his face twisted with distaste.

"A tawdry business," he pronounced when I had finished.

"Yes, sir," I said, "but troubling. Was I correct in telling him that the woman had no legal grounds for a suit against him for Breach of Promise?"

"You were quite right," he said. "Breach of Promise actions were abolished by the Florida legislature in 1945. In fact, lawmakers had such an abhorrence of the practice that they decreed that anyone initiating such a suit would be guilty of a misdemeanor in the second degree. Shortly after the statute was passed, a law review published an article on the subject entitled 'No More Torts for Tarts.'"

"Not bad," I said. "But now the question is how to handle CW's problem. I imagine the complainant will accept a cash settlement."

"A reasonable assumption," father said dryly. "But that doesn't necessarily mean the end of the affair. I can draw up a release she will be required to sign before she hands over the letters and gets paid. But a release never completely eliminates the possibility of her making another claim at some future date, especially if she's shrewd enough to keep photocopies of the letters. It could go on and on. It's really blackmail, Archy, and blackmailers rarely give up after one payoff."

"I concur," I said. "I think I better meet the young woman, get a take on her, and perhaps a rough idea of how much she expects for the letters. After that, we can decide how to deal with it."

My father was silent, mulling over my suggestion. He was a champion muller; I have seen him spend three minutes deciding whether to furl his golf umbrella clockwise or counterclockwise.

"Yes," he said finally, "I think that would be best. Interview the lady, appear to be sympathetic and understanding, and find out exactly what she wants. Then report to me, and we'll take it from there."

"Yes, sir," I said, resisting an urge to salute.

I trudged upstairs to my nest, put on the reading specs, and set to work recording the details of that eventful day. I paused while I was scribbling a précis of the Chinless Wonder's remarks about Hector Johnson: "Knows banking. Owned a Western bank." Let's see, I recapped, that made Theodosia's father an expert on orchids, electronics and/or computer stuff, government service (possibly espionage), and banking. Why, the man was a veritable polymath, and I wouldn't be a bit surprised if my next interviewee claimed that Hector was a master bialy maker.

I finished my labors, closed my journal, and was preparing to relax by sipping a dram of marc and listening to a Patricia Kaas cassette when my blasted phone blasted. I glanced at my Mickey Mouse watch (an original, not a reproduction) and saw it was almost ten-thirty.

"Archy McNally," I said, expecting the worst. It was close.

"Ah-ha!" Sgt. Al Rogoff, PBPD, said in his heavy rumble. "I have tracked the sherlock of

Palm Beach to his elegant lair. How you doing, old buddy?"

"Up to my nates in drudgery," I said. "And you?"

"Likewise," he said. "But enough of this idle chitchat. You know the painter Silas Hawkin?"

I hesitated for just the briefest. "Yes, I know him," I said. "Matter of fact, I visited him at his studio this morning."

"Interesting," Al said. "I think you better wheel your baby carriage back to his studio. Right now."

"Why on earth should I do that?"

"Because the maid just found Silas with a knife stuck in his neck."

I swallowed. "Dead?"

"Couldn't be deader," Rogoff said cheerfully.

"But why pick on me, Al?"

"Because your business card was on his desk. You coming or do I have to send a SWAT team after you?"

"On my way," I said.

I paused long enough to take one sip of marc (a gulp would have demolished me) and bounced downstairs. I trotted out to the garage to board my pride and joy. It had been a sparkling day, and the night was still dulcet. As I drove, I admired Mother Nature while I pondered who might have stuck a shiv in the throat of Father Hawkin.

People acquainted with my investigative career sometimes ask, "What was your first case?" To which I invariably reply, "A 1986 Haut Brion." Actually, my first Discreet Inquiry that involved criminal behavior turned out to be a debacle because I hadn't yet learned that in addition to lust, we all have murder in our hearts—or if not murder, at least larceny.

So now I could easily come up with a Cast of Characters who might have put down Silas Hawkin, including wife, daughter, maid, gallery agent, and any of his clients. But, as in any homicide investigation, the prime question was *Cui bono?* Or who benefited from the artist's death?

When I arrived at the Villa Bile the studio building had already been festooned with crime scene tape. The bricked driveway was crowded with official vehicles including an ambulance, indicating they had not yet removed what Al Rogoff enjoys referring to as the corpus delicious.

There was a uniformed officer standing guard at the studio door, inspecting the heavens and dreaming, no doubt, of Madonna.

"Archy McNally," I reported to this stalwart. "Sergeant Rogoff asked me to come over."

"Yeah?" he said, not very interested. "You stay here and I'll go see."

I waited patiently, and in a few minutes the sergeant himself came trundling out, a cold cigar jutting from his meaty face. Al is built like an M1-A1 tank, and when he moves I always expect to hear the clanking of treads.

"What were you doing here this morning?" he demanded, wasting no time on preliminaries.

"Good evening, Al," I said.

"Good evening," he said. "What were you doing here this morning? The maid, wife, and daughter don't know—or maybe they do and aren't saying."

"I'm doing a credit check on a man Hawkin knew," I said. "I stopped by to get his opinion on the subject."

"And who is the subject?"

I had calculated how much I could tell him and how much, in good conscience, I could withhold.

"Hector Johnson," I told him. "The father of one of the late artist's customers."

"And why are you doing a credit check on him?"

"At the request of a client of McNally and Son."

"What client?"

"Nope," I said. "Unethical. Confidentiality."

He looked at me. "You're no lawyer and you know it."

"But I represent my father who *is* an attorney," I pointed out. "And I can't divulge the information you request without his permission."

"Son," Al said heavily, "you've got more crap than a Christmas goose. All right, I won't push it—for now. Let's go up."

We entered through that oak and etched glass door. I glanced into the ground floor area. Mrs. Louise Hawkin was slumped at one end of a sailcloth-covered couch and Marcia Hawkin was at the other end, both as far apart as ever. We tramped up the cast-iron staircase and walked into the studio. The techs were busy.

Rogoff stopped me. "Wife was out playing bridge. Daughter went to a movie. They say. Silas didn't go over to the main house for dinner, but everyone says that wasn't unusual. When his work was going good he hated to stop. Finally, around nine o'clock, the maid called him to ask if he was coming over to eat or if he wanted her to bring him a plate. No answer. But she could see the lights on up here. So she came over and found him. Let's go take a look."

He was lying supine, naked on that tattered sleigh bed. His eyes were still open. The knife was still in his throat. An assistant from the ME's office was fussing over him. I knew the man. Thomas Bunion. One of the few people I've ever met who are simultaneously cantankerous and timid.

I stared down at the remains of Silas Hawkin. There was an ocean of blood. An *ocean*. I am not a total stranger to violent death and thought I had learned to view a corpse with some dispassion, without needing to scurry away and upchuck in private. But I admit I was spooked by the sight of the murdered artist. So pale. For some reason his beard looked fake, as if it had been spirit-gummed to his face.

A wooden handle protruded from his neck.

"It looks like a palette knife," I said, trying to keep my voice steady.

"Uh-huh," Rogoff said. "We already figured that."

"But a palette knife doesn't have a cutting edge," I said. "And the blade is usually thin and pliable, something like a spatula. It's difficult to believe it was driven in so deeply and killed him."

"Well, it did," Bunion said crossly. "Looks like an artery was severed, but we won't know for sure until we get him on a slab. Thin blade or not, it was a lucky hit."

"Not for Silas," Al said.

"Poor devil," I muttered, turned away, and took a deep breath.

The sergeant inspected me. "Want to go outside, Archy?" he asked quietly.

"No, I'm fine," I told him. "But thanks." I looked around the studio. A plainclothesman was seated behind the decrepit desk, slowly turning pages of the ledger Si had slammed shut when I visited him that morning.

"What is he doing?" I asked.

Rogoff answered: "Hawkin may have been a nutsy artist, but he was a helluva businessman. He kept a record of every painting he did: date started, date finished, and disposition. If it was sold, he wrote down the size of the painting, name and address of the buyer, and the price paid. What we'll do is check his ledger against those finished works stacked against the wall and see if anything is missing."

"That makes sense," I said, but then I thought about it. "Al, are you figuring Hawkin was sleeping naked on that ugly bed and a burglar broke in to grab something he could fence? Then the artist wakes up and the crook grabs the nearest deadly weapon, a palette knife, and shoves it into the victim's throat to keep him quiet?"

He shrugged. "The wife and daughter were away. The maid was in the kitchen at the far side of the maid house with her radio going full blast. She couldn't have heard or seen an intruder. The door to the studio building was unlocked. It could have been a grab-and-run scumbag. Maybe a junkie."

"Do you really believe that?" I asked him.

"No," he said.

We went downstairs together. "Excuse me a moment," I said to the sergeant. I went over to the couch where wife and daughter were still sitting, isolated from each other. "May I express my sympathy and my deepest sorrow at this horrible tragedy," I said. It came out more floridly than I had intended.

Only Mrs. Louise Hawkin looked up. "Thank you," she said faintly.

Al and I moved outside. He used a wooden kitchen match to light his cold cigar and I borrowed the flame for my third cigarette of the day, resolving it would be the last.

Rogoff jerked a thumb over his shoulder at the ground floor of the studio building. "Not much love lost there," he said.

"No," I agreed, "not much. It was a sex scene, wasn't it, Al?"

He nodded. "That's the way I see it. The guy's in bed with someone, woman or man. There's an argument. She or he grabs up the nearest tool, the palette knife. I think it was a spur-of-the-moment thing. Not planned. They started out making love and then things went sour."

"Where do you go from here?"

"Check his inventory of paintings. Check the alibis of wife, daughter, maid, agent, clients, friends, enemies, and everyone connected with him."

"When did it happen—do you know that?"

"Tom Bunion figures it was about an hour before we got the squeal. That would put the time of death around nine o'clock, give or take."

"I was home," I told him. "Upstairs in my rooms. I had just talked with my father in his study."

"We'll check it out," he said with ponderous good humor. Then, suddenly serious, he added, "You got any wild ideas?"

"Not at the moment," I said. "Except that it must have required a great deal of strength to drive a blunt blade into Hawkin's throat. That would suggest a male assailant."

"Yeah," the sergeant said. "Or a furious woman."

"One never knows, do one?"

"There you go again," he said.

I returned home that night to find the house darkened except for the bulb burning over the rear entrance. I went directly to my quarters and finished that marc I had started aeons ago. Also my fourth English Oval. Then I went to bed hoping I wouldn't have nightmares involving palette knives and oceans of blood. I didn't. Instead I had a dotty dream about Zasu Pitts. Don't ask me why.

4

I glanced at local newspapers the next morning and watched a few TV news programs. I learned nothing about the homicide I didn't already know.

But after reading the obits on Silas Hawkin, I was surprised to discover that Louise was his third wife, and Marcia his daughter by his first. She was his only child. Wife No. 1 had died of cancer. Divorce had ended Marriage No. 2.

I was even more startled to read of the professional career of the artist. He had studied at prestigious academies in New York and Paris. His work was owned and exhibited by several museums. He had been honored with awards from artists' guilds. In other words, the man had been far from a hack. I had underestimated his talents because I thought him a dunce. But then the creative juices have no relation to intelligence, personality, or character, do they?

Finally, a little before noon, I decided I needed

a change of subject and a change of venue. So I determined to wheel down to Fort Lauderdale and have a chat with Shirley Feebling, the young woman who was causing Chauncey Wilson Smythe-Hersforth to suffer an acute attack of the fantods.

In my innocence it never occurred to me the two investigations might be connected. But as A. Pope remarked, "Fools rush in . . . " Right on, Alex!

Less than two hours later I was in a minimall north of Ft. Liquordale, staring with some bemusement at a large sign that advertised in block letters: TOPLESS CAR WASH. And below, in a chaste script: "No touching allowed." The activities within were hidden from prurient passers-by by a canvas curtain slit down the middle. Customers' cars were driven through the curtain to the interior, where vehicles and drivers were presumably rejuvenated.

I decided my flag-red Miata convertible would be abashed by such intimate attention, so I parked nearby and returned on foot to push my way through the slit curtain. I was confronted by a woolly mammoth, who appeared to be either the manager or a hired sentinel assigned to halt sightseers who didn't arrive on wheels.

"I'd like to speak to Miss Shirley Feebling, please," I said.

"Yeah?" he said belligerently. "Who're you?"

"Andrew Jackson," I said, proffering a twenty-dollar bill. "Here is my business card."

"Oh yeah," he said, grabbing it. "I thought I recognized you. She's over there washing down the Tuchas."

I turned to look. "Taurus," I said.

"Whatever," he said, shrugging.

I was a bit taken aback by my first sight of Ms. Feebling. I suppose I had expected a brazen hussy and instead I saw a small, demure brunet who looked rather sweet and vulnerable. There was a waifish innocence about her that made her costume even more outré. She was wearing the bottom section of a pink thong bikini, and she was indeed topless.

It would be indelicate to describe those gifts that qualified her for employment in a topless car wash. Suffice to say that she was well-qualified.

I waited until she finished wiping the Taurus dry and had been handed what appeared to be a generous tip by the pop-eyed driver. Then I approached and offered her my business card, a legitimate one this time.

"My name is Archibald McNally," I said with a restrained 100-watt smile. "My law firm represents Mr. Smythe-Hersforth. I was hoping to have a friendly talk with you so that we might arrive at some mutually beneficial solution of your misunderstanding with our client."

"There's no misunderstanding," she said, inspecting my card. "Chauncey said he'd marry me, and I've got the letters to prove it."

"Of course," I said, "but I hope you'll be willing to discuss it. I drove down from Palm Beach specifically to meet you and learn your side of this

disagreement. Could we go somewhere reasonably private where we can chat? I would be more
than willing to recompense you or your employer
for the time you are absent from work."

She looked up at me. "Will you buy me a pizza?"
she asked.

"Delighted," I told her.

"Then I'll ask Jake," she said. She went over
to the woolly mammoth, talked a moment, then
came back. "He wants fifty for an hour. Okay?"

"Certainly," I said, imagining my father's reaction when he saw this item on my expense
account.

"That's neat," she said, and her smile sparkled.
"I'll go get dressed. Just take a minute."

She went through an unmarked door that I
presumed led to a dressing room, or rather an
undressing room. I thought she would don a volu-
minous coverup, but when she reappeared she
had added only a T-shirt that had PEACE printed on the front, an affirmation to which I heartily subscribed. But unfortunately—or fortunately,
depending on the state of one's hormones—the T-
shirt appeared to be sodden, and it clung. Lucky
T-shirt.

"The pizza joint is just two doors away," she
said. "All us girls go there. The owner don't mind
as long as our boobs are covered."

A few moments later we were seated in the pizza joint, a fancy palace with real Formica-topped
tables and real paper lace doilies under the plates.
We decided we would share a Ponderosa Delight,
which, the menu claimed, came "with everything."

Shirley ordered a Diet Cherry Coke. I asked for a Pepsi since a 1982 Mumm's Cordon Rouge was not available.

"Miss Feebling—" I started, but she interrupted.

"You can call me Shirl," she said. "Everyone in the world calls me Shirl."

"And so shall I," I said, "if you'll call me Archy. Shirl, I know that Chauncey said he loved you, but people do fall out of love, you know."

"I haven't," she promptly replied. "I still love him and want to marry him like he promised in his letters. He's such a wonderful guy."

I was about to ask if she didn't find CW somewhat dim. But I refrained, reflecting that Shirley herself might be somewhat dim and had found a soul mate in the Chinless Wonder.

"Shirl," I said, "you seem to me a very sensitive and intelligent young lady."

"Thank you, sir," she said coyly.

"And I am sure you want only the best for yourself—and for Chauncey, too, of course. He has informed you that he wishes to wed another?"

She nodded.

"I know you want him to be happy," I pleaded, "even though it might mean your own unhappiness. But a generous cash settlement would help you endure a temporary sorrow."

"Oh, I don't want any money," she said brightly. "I just want to marry Chauncey."

"Shirl, it's impossible for me to believe that a young lady of your outstanding attributes hasn't had and doesn't have the opportunity to marry any of a dozen eager young men."

"Oh sure, I've had the chance," she said, almost dreamily. "But no one like Chauncey."

That I could believe. But then our Ponderosa Delight and drinks were served, and I postponed further attempts to convince her to reach an equitable compromise.

She was starting on her second wedge of pizza when I noted she was casting furtive glances over my shoulder.

"Something wrong?" I asked.

She leaned forward across the table to speak in a low voice. "There's a man over there who keeps staring at me."

"Quite understandable," I said cheerily. "You're worth staring at, Shirl, and I'm sure you're aware of it."

"But I don't like the way he keeps smiling with a smirky grin. Like he knows something secret about me."

"Have you ever seen him before?"

"No, I'm sure I haven't."

"Shall I go over and ask him to stop smirking at you?"

"Oh no," she said quickly, "don't do that. I don't want to cause no trouble."

We finished the pizza, and I tried again to persuade her to accept cash in return for CW's mash notes. But she was adamant; she wanted only to marry the man as he had promised, not once but many times, and if he reneged she would have no choice but to make his letters public.

She was explaining all this, determinedly and

with some passion, when she suddenly broke off
and said, "Here he comes."

A man halted alongside our table. I looked up
to see a tall, saturnine bloke in raw black silk
with a white Izod. He stared down at my companion, and I could agree with what she had said: It
was a smirky grin. He didn't even glance at me.

"Hiya, Shirl," he said in a raspy baritone. "Having a good time?"

Then he sauntered away, paid his bill at the
front counter, and went outside. I noted that he
had a profile like a cleaver. I watched him get
into a gunmetal Cadillac de Ville and pull away.
I turned back to Shirley.

"You don't know him?" I asked.

She shook her head.

"He knew your name."

"I don't know how," she said, obviously troubled.

"Perhaps he was a customer," I suggested.

"No," she insisted. "I'd have remembered. I don't
like his looks. He scares me."

"Nothing to be scared about," I assured her. "I
doubt if you'll ever see him again."

But I couldn't comfort her. Her bouncy mood
had vanished; she seemed subdued. "Listen," she
said finally, "I've got to get to work."

I paid our tab and walked her back. I gave her
fifty dollars, wondering how much would go to
Jake and how much she'd be allowed to keep.

"Shirl," I said, "it's been a pleasure meeting
you. I'll relay what you've told me to our client.
But I still hope a mutually satisfactory solution

to this impasse can be arranged."

"Sure it can," she said, "if he marries me."

"Uh-huh," I said. "May I come back and talk to you again if it proves necessary?"

"Of course," she said. Then: "You're nice," she added, and stretched up to kiss my cheek. "Thanks for the pizza."

She marched through the slit canvas curtain, providing me with a final glimpse of her thong bikini, also called a shoestring bikini in South Florida, and sometimes a flosser.

I drove back to Palm Beach in a reflective mood. It had not been a totally profitless trip, although CW might think so. But I had, at least to my own satisfaction, learned something about Shirley Feebling and could guess at what might be motivating her demands. There were three possibilities, none of which would bring a gleeful smile to the puss of our distraught client.

1. My discussion with Shirl had been the opening round of what would prove to be lengthy and difficult negotiations. In other words, the lady was hanging tough in order to up the ante.

2. She was shrewd enough to forgo an immediate cash settlement, no matter how generous, in hopes of marrying the Chinless Wonder and becoming the wife of a man who would inherit millions when his mommy passed to that bourn from which no traveler returns.

3. And this was the most disquieting: Shirley Feebling was totally sincere and honest. She really did love the simp, wanted to marry him, and was determined to become a loving helpmate. His

present or potential wealth had no influence on
her decision.

Very disturbing. I don't pretend to understand
True Love. I don't know what it is or how it works.
Oh, I know all about affection, attachment, admi-
ration—stuff like that. But True Love stumps me.
I am not only ignorant of its nature but suspicious
of its effects because whenever I have observed it
in others, it has always seemed to me infernally
serious. And since my life has been sedulously
devoted to triviality, I find the seriousness of True
Love to be a fatal flaw.

Still, although I know no more about TL than
I do about Babylonian cuneiform, I cannot ignore
the testimony of poets and Tin Pan Alley tune-
smiths. It is obvious that True Love *does* exist,
and I reckoned Ms. Feebling might very well be
infected with a particularly virulent strain. If so,
it did not bode well for the Chinless Wonder.

Which led me to musing about his intended
fiancée, Theodosia Johnson, and wondering if my
own reactions to that stellar lady might be True
Love or merely gonadal twinges. I just didn't
know and decided that only another personal
meeting with the radiant Theo might provide the
answer.

I was then approaching South Palm Beach and
on a sudden whim (*the* guiding principle in my
life) resolved to stop at the Hawkin residence.
You may ask, and justly so, what on earth I
thought I was doing since I was not part of the
official homicide investigation and my assistance
had not been requested.

The answer to your question is simple: I am
nosy. I admit it and don't give a tinker's damn—
or dam, depending on your erudition—who knows
it. Also, there were several puzzling aspects about
the murder that piqued my curiosity. I could have
asked Sgt. Al Rogoff, of course, but would he have
told me? Fat chance.

Al is a closemouthed gent, even when he doesn't
have to be. He and I worked several cases together
in the past, to our mutual benefit, but he never
tells me *everything* he knows any more than I
Reveal All to him. I think that in addition to our
friendship we keep the scimitar of competitiveness
keenly honed, sensing that it contributes to our
success.

The crime scene tape still surrounded the studio building, and there was a sole uniformed officer on guard. But the main house appeared to be
open to all comers. I rang the chimes, expecting
they would be answered by Mrs. Jane Folsby, the
live-in servant I hoped to question.

And she indeed opened the door, recognized
me, and smiled warmly. "Good afternoon, Mr.
McNally," she said. "It's good to see you again."

"And it's a pleasure to see you, Mrs. Folsby,"
I said. "I can imagine what you've been going
through. You have my sympathy, I assure you.
What a shock it must have been."

She stood aside to allow me to enter, then closed
the door.

"It *was* a shock," she said in a low voice. "I
found him, you know."

"So I heard. A horrifying experience."

She sighed deeply. "He had his faults," she said, "but don't we all? But he wasn't a mean man, and no one should have to die like that."

"No," I agreed, "no one should. Mrs. Folsby, I'd like to ask you a few questions. But first I want you to know I am not part of the police investigation, and it's entirely up to you whether or not you choose to answer."

She looked at me steadily. "Questions about the murder?"

"Yes," I said. "That and other things."

"Why do you want to ask?"

"Because your answers possibly, just possibly, might have some bearing on a private inquiry I am making: a credit check on a person Mr. Hawkin knew."

She considered a long time. "Very well," she said finally, "you ask your questions and then I'll decide whether or not to answer them."

"Excellent," I said. "Sergeant Rogoff, a friend of mine, told me you went to the studio after you phoned your employer and received no reply. Is that correct?"

She nodded. "The wife and daughter were out, and he hadn't come over for dinner. So I called to ask if he wanted me to bring him a plate. I did that sometimes when he was working late. He didn't answer, but I could see the studio lights were on, and I got concerned."

"Of course."

"So I went over to see if everything was all right. To tell you the truth, I thought maybe he had fallen asleep. Or passed out."

"Passed out? He was a heavy drinker?"

"He did his share," she said wryly. "Rum, mostly."

"Uh-huh. Tell me this if you will, Mrs. Folsby, when you entered the studio, did you see anything that might lead you to believe that he had been working? For instance, was there an unfinished painting on one of his easels?"

She thought a moment. "No," she said, "there was nothing on the big easel. That was the one he liked to use for his portraits. And nothing on the two smaller ones either."

I was disappointed. "So you saw absolutely no evidence that he had been working in the hours prior to his death?"

She closed her eyes briefly as if trying to recall details of that frightful scene. "Now that you mention it," she said hesitantly, "there was something odd. On the taboret next to the big easel was Mr. Hawkin's palette and the paints on it were still wet. I could see them glistening under the lights. Also, there was a long-handled brush alongside the palette, and that had wet paint, a kind of creamy crimson, on the bristles. That wasn't like him at all because he was very finicky about cleaning his brushes and palette when he wasn't working."

"But you saw no evidence of what he might have been working on?"

She shook her head.

"Curious," I said, "but I suppose there's a very obvious explanation for it." (I didn't suppose anything of the sort, of course.) "Another question,

Mrs. Folsby: When Mr. Hawkin was doing a portrait, did he ever allow anyone else in the studio other than the sitter?"

"Never," she said definitely. "He was very strict about that. He said the presence of an observer would distract the model and destroy his rapport with whomever he was painting."

"I expect most portrait artists feel that way. A final question, please. You know how people in Palm Beach love to gossip. I've heard rumors there was serious discord in the Hawkin family, an atmosphere of hostility in this house. Would you care to comment on that?"

"No," she said stonily.

I persisted. "You mean no discord or no, you don't wish to comment?"

"I don't wish to comment."

I admired her. There was loyalty up. I hoped there would be loyalty down.

"Perfectly understandable," I said, nodding, "and I wish to thank you for your patience and cooperation. You have been very helpful."

"I have?" she said, mildly surprised.

I bid her good-bye and left the house. Marcia Hawkin was coming up the walk carrying one of those miniature Tiffany's shopping bags. She saw me and stopped suddenly.

"What are you doing here?" she demanded.

"I stopped by for just a moment to express my sympathy to Mrs. Folsby on the death of your father."

She made a sound. I believe she intended it to be a sardonic laugh, but I thought it more a honk.

"My father was a goat," she said. "A *goat!*"

Then she strode into the house and slammed the door. The Villa Bile indeed.

I drove directly home, looking forward to an ocean swim that would slosh away, even temporarily, all the clotted human emotions I had dealt with that day. But it was not to be. I was just tugging on my new, shocking pink Speedo when my phone shrilled.

"What were you doing at the Hawkin place?" Sgt. Al Rogoff said in that gritty voice he uses when he's ready to chew nails.

I sighed. "Who squealed on me, Al? Mrs. Folsby? Marcia Hawkin?"

"Neither," he said. "That guard I parked outside the studio had orders to watch for visitors. He just reported seeing a guy wearing purple slacks and driving a maroon Miata. Who could that be but Monsieur Archibald McNally?"

"The slacks were lilac," I protested, "and the car is screaming red."

"What were you doing there?" he repeated. "Nosing around?"

"Of course," I said. "Any objections?"

"Not if you don't get in my way," he said. "Learn anything?"

"Al, is it trade-off time?"

"Run it by me first."

I related what Mrs. Folsby had told me: When she entered the scene of the crime she saw no painting on the easel but had noted wet pigments on Silas Hawkin's palette and brush.

Rogoff was silent a moment. "How do you figure it?" he asked finally.

"I don't," I said. "But it's intriguing, isn't it?"

"Your favorite word," he said grumpily. "You find things intriguing that I find a pain in the ass. If the guy was working on a painting before he was offed, where is it?"

"A puzzlement. Did you check Si's ledger? Is anything missing?"

He replied with a question of his own. "That guy you said you were doing a credit check on, Hector Johnson, is he related to Theodosia Johnson?"

"Her father."

"Uh-huh. Well, she's in the ledger. Hawkin did an oil portrait of her."

"I know, Al. I saw it at the Pristine Gallery. It may still be on display. Positively enchanting."

"Yeah? I'll have to go take a look. But the thing is—and I know you're going to find this intriguing—right after her portrait is listed in Hawkin's ledger another painting is noted. It's just called 'Untitled.'"

"That's odd."

"Not half so odd as the fact that we can't find it. All the other paintings in the studio have titles and are recorded in the ledger. The widow, the daughter, and the maid say they know nothing about 'Untitled,' don't know what it is, never heard Hawkin mention a word about it."

"And now you're guessing the same thing I'm guessing, aren't you, sergeant? That 'Untitled' was the painting Si was working on before he was murdered."

"Could be," Rogoff said. "And the killer walked off with it. Listen, Archy, are you still checking out this Hector Johnson?"

"Oh yes."

"And his daughter, too?"

"Definitely."

"Have you met them?"

"I've met her briefly, but I haven't met Hector."

"Keep on it, will you?" Al said. "Maybe Silas told them something about that untitled painting."

"I'll be happy to ask," I said. "It gives me an excuse to see her again."

"Oh-ho. A winner, is she?"

"Divine is an understatement," I assured him. "I think I'm in love."

"So what else is new?" he said.

I finally got him off the phone after promising to report on my meeting with Theodosia and Hector Johnson. It was then too late for a dip in the Atlantic. So I peeled off my snazzy Speedo, showered, and dressed in time to attend the family cocktail hour and dinner.

I then retired to my one-man dormitory to bring my journal au courant with the day's events. After reading over what I had scribbled, I was dismayed to see how my initial inquiry into the trustworthiness of Theo Johnson appeared to be interacting with the investigation into the murder of Silas Hawkin.

I simply refused to believe that the beautiful Madam X could possibly be involved in that heinous crime. But then Lucrezia Borgia was hardly a gorgon, and neither was Lizzie Borden. It was all enough to make one ponder the advantages of celibacy.

Which I did, and finally decided there were none.

5

A weekend intruded here, and a very welcome intrusion it was. For two sun-spangled days I was able to enact my favorite role of blade-about-town. On Saturday morning I played tennis with Binky Watrous on his private court—and lost. I treated Connie Garcia to lunch at the Pelican Club, challenged her to a game of darts—and lost. In the evening I played poker with a group of intemperate cronies—and lost.

I was more successful on Sunday. I spent most of the afternoon gamboling on the beach with Connie and a Frisbee, and demolishing a bottle of a chilled Soave I had never tried before. Tangy is the word. Then we picked up two slabs of ribs barbecued with a Cajun sauce and returned to Connie's digs with a cold six-pack of Heineken. A pleasant time was had by all. I was home and in bed by ten o'clock and asleep by 10:05, sunburned, slightly squiffed, exhausted, and oh so content.

I overslept on Monday morning, as usual, and found a deserted kitchen when I bounced downstairs. I fixed myself a mug of instant black, and built an interracial sandwich: ham on bagel.

I used the kitchen phone to call the office. I asked Mrs. Trelawney if the honcho could spare me a few moments that morning. She put me on hold, and I listened to wallpaper music a few minutes while she went to check. She returned to tell me His Majesty would grant me ten minutes at precisely eleven o'clock.

"Thank you, Mrs. T.," I said. "Tell me, have you ever cooked a goose—or vice versa?"

"Why, no," she said. "But I once took a tramp in the woods."

She hung up cackling, and I trotted out to my chariot, much refreshed by that silly exchange of ancient corn.

Twenty minutes later I was in my crypt at the McNally Building and lighted my first English Oval of the day, considering it a reward for having spent the entire weekend without a gasper. On my desk was a sheaf of faxed replies to my inquiries to national credit agencies regarding the financial status of Theodosia and Hector Johnson.

I read them all slowly and carefully, and, to put it succinctly, my flabber was gasted. It was not that they contained derogatory information about the Johnsons; they contained no information at all.

If those reports were to be believed, Theo and Hector had never had a credit card, never had a charge account, never bought anything on time, never made a loan or had a mortgage, never purchased anything from a mail order catalogue, never received a government check for whatever reason, had no insurance, owned no assets such as real estate, stocks, bonds, or other securities, and had never filed a tax return.

Improbable, would you say? Nay, dear reader. Utterly impossible! In our society even a toddler of three has already left a paper trail, carefully recorded on a computer somewhere. I refused to believe that two adults had no financial background whatsoever. Even if they scrupulously paid cash for all their purchases, what was the source of the cash and why was there no mention of bank accounts, checking and savings, and no record of having paid federal, state, and local taxes?

They had names and Social Security numbers. And that's all their dossiers revealed.

I tried to puzzle it out, resisting the urge to light another cigarette. The more I gnawed at it, the more ridiculous it seemed to me that the Johnsons could be totally without a financial history. There must be a logical explanation for it, but whatever it might be I could not imagine. I hoped my Palm Beach contacts would help solve the riddle.

It was then pushing eleven o'clock, and I rushed upstairs to my father's office, for if I was even one minute late he was quite capable of canceling the appointment.

Prescott McNally, Esq., was standing solidly planted before his antique rolltop desk, and in his three-button, double-breasted suit of nubby cheviot, looking somewhat of a relic himself. He cast a baleful glance at my awning-striped seersucker jacket and didn't invite me to be seated.

I recited a condensed account of my interview with Shirley Feebling in Fort Lauderdale and finished by suggesting the lady might be sincere in professing love for Chauncey Wilson Smythe-Hersforth.

"She seemed totally uninterested in a cash settlement, sir," I remarked.

"Nonsense," father said sharply. "Did you make a specific offer?"

"No, I did not."

"That was a mistake, Archy," he said. "The mention of dollars would have concentrated her mind wonderfully. I'm afraid the lady bamboozled you. Her protestations of love were merely a bargaining ploy. And even if she is smitten, as you seem to believe, how can she possibly profit from an unrequited love? She can't force that young fool to marry her, you know."

"No, sir, but she can carry out her threat to sell his letters to a tabloid."

"Don't be so certain of that," he admonished me. "I would have to research relevant law, but it might be claimed the letters are his property since he created them, and if so ruled, the sale and publication could be legally enjoined. But before we go to that trouble, I suggest you consult with Smythe-Hersforth. Obtain his approval of your

returning to Fort Lauderdale and making a definite offer to this woman. I believe the proposal of
an actual cash payment will persuade her to talk
business."

I was doubtful but made no demur. "How much
do you think we should offer?"

He went into his mulling trance, and I waited
patiently for his decision.

"I reckon a thousand dollars would be adequate," he finally said.

I was startled. "Isn't that rather mingy, sir?"

"Of course it is," he said testily, "and I expect
the woman will reject it immediately. But it will
serve as an opening move to begin bargaining.
It will require her to reveal what she believes
she should receive, and eventually, I trust, an
equitable compromise can be agreed upon. The
important thing is to shift negotiations away
from discussion of her alleged emotional injury
to the realm of a hard cash settlement. Do you
understand?"

"Yes, father, and I'll attempt to explain it to
CW, though he is not the swiftest man in the
world."

"When you speak to him you might also ascer-
tain how high he is willing to go. Five thousand?
Ten? Or more? The decision must be his. Now is
there anything else?"

"Just one more thing," I said hastily. "I had
occasion to speak to Mrs. Louise Hawkin prior to
the death of her husband. She said a friend was
seeking a divorce lawyer and asked if we might
recommend someone."

Father stared at me. "Do you really believe she was asking on behalf of a friend?"

"No, sir."

"Nor do I. And now that Mrs. Hawkin is a widow I doubt very much that she will inquire again about a divorce attorney. Your ten minutes are up."

I returned to my broom closet, slumped behind my steel desk, and silently groused. I was frustrated by that conversation with the senior. I thought he was totally mistaken about Ms. Shirley Feebling—but then I had met the lady and he had not. I really didn't believe she would accept a cash settlement, no matter how generous.

Still, I had no wish to flaunt my father's advice. His experience had been so much more extensive than mine, I simply had to defer to his judgment. But I am, as you may have guessed, an incurable romantic, and I mournfully reflected that if mein papa was correct and Shirley accepted money in lieu of love, I would be horribly disappointed and possibly take up the lute to express my weltschmerz in musical form.

Meanwhile, I had a job to do and when duty calls, yrs. truly can never be accused of shlumpery. I called Information and obtained the phone number of Hector Johnson. I had prepared a scam that, I felt, included sufficient truth to convince the most worldly-wise pigeon.

"The Johnson residence," a man's voice answered. Deep and resonant. A very slight accent. Midwestern, I guessed.

"Mr. Hector Johnson, please," I said.

"Speaking. Who is this calling?"

"Mr. Johnson, my name is Archibald McNally, and I am associated with McNally and Son, a law firm located on Royal Palm Way. I had the pleasure of meeting your lovely daughter during a recent art exhibit at the Pristine Gallery."

"Ah, yes," he said. "I'm afraid Theo is busy at the moment."

"No, no," I said. "It is you I'd like to talk to. Mr. Johnson, I am assigned to the real estate section of McNally and Son, and we have a number of very attractive properties for sale or lease in the Palm Beach area. Rather than deluge you with brochures and listings, I am taking the liberty of calling to ask if you have any interest in a Palm Beach estate, either as a residence or an investment."

"Not right now, thank you," he said. "But quite possibly at some time in the near future."

"In that case," I said, continuing to act the role of a pushy real estate hustler, "could I meet with you personally and perhaps get some idea of what you might be looking for? We have properties that range in asking price from a half-million to twelve, with financing readily available, I assure you. They are located on the beachfront, inland, and with Waterway frontages. Rather than try to sell you a particular offering, I'd much rather learn what you prefer, either now or, as you say, in the near future."

"That makes sense," he said. "You say your name is Archibald McNally?"

"That's correct, sir. Everyone calls me Archy."

He laughed. "Don't complain. Everyone calls me Heck. Who put you on to me, Archy?"

"Lady Cynthia Horowitz suggested I call," I said boldly. "She was quite impressed by your contribution to her latest effort at civic beautification."

I was hoping he would be impressed, and he was. "I was happy to help," he said. "And if you're a friend of Lady Horowitz I'll be glad to meet with you. When would you care to make it?"

"At your convenience, sir."

There was a brief pause. Then: "Well, I have an appointment with a business associate at three this afternoon, but if you could come by at, say, two o'clock, we should be able to get to know each other in an hour's time. How does that sound?"

"Splendid," I said. "I'm looking forward to it, and I promise you, no high-powered sales pitch."

"I'll hold you to that," he said, laughing again. "See you at two, Archy."

"Thank you, Heck," I said.

He gave me his address, and we hung up. I sat a moment staring at the dead phone and thinking of what a personable guy he was, how he projected warmth, confidence, good humor. Some people sound like duds when their voices come over the wire. Hector Johnson sounded like a political candidate who is absolutely certain he's going to win.

My second phone call was to CW's office. His secretary informed me that Mr. Smythe-Hersforth had departed that morning for a bankers' convention in New Orleans and was not expected back until Thursday morning. I thanked her, grateful that I could postpone for three days another go-around with a man silly enough to certify a proposal of marriage in writing.

I had time to buzz home and change into a costume more befitting a sober, industrious, and sincere real estate agent. I bounced down to the kitchen for a spot of lunch and found Ursi Olson preparing a Florida bouillabaisse that was to be our dinner that evening. But she paused long enough to make me an open sandwich of Norwegian brisling sardines with slices of beefsteak tomato and shavings of red onion on her home-baked sour rye. Life *can* be beautiful.

I found the Johnsons' condo to be on ground level and smallish. I figured if you stood on a chair and peered out the kitchen window to your left you might catch a glimpse of Lake Worth. But it was located in a decent neighborhood, the landscaping was well-groomed, and if the building didn't shout big bucks, there was really nothing to apologize for.

What suddenly made me think it a place of magical charm was that Theodosia Johnson opened the door when I rang, and my knees buckled. She gave me a smile as inflammatory as a nuclear meltdown, and I was immediately convinced that True Love did exist and I was its latest willing victim.

I saw her clothed in golden gossamer, though actually she was wearing white linen shorts and a man's rugby shirt the same color as her sky-blue eyes. Her long chestnut hair was bound up in a braid and piled atop her head. No queen ever wore a lovelier crown.

She addressed me as Archy, and I was so grateful I wanted to roll on my back on the floor and beg to have my stomach scratched. But instead I followed her through a short foyer to the living room, where she invited me to be seated and asked if I'd care for a drink.

My tongue seemed swollen to unmanageable proportions, and all I could do was shake my head. I simply could not stop staring at her. I know the room was decorated and contained furniture, but don't ask me to describe it; I only had eyes for Madam X, and the rest of the universe faded away.

"You heard about Si Hawkin?" she asked sorrowfully.

I nodded. "Dreadful," I said, not believing that croaky voice was mine.

"I wept for hours," she said. "He was *such* a good friend. And a major talent, don't you think?"

"Major," I repeated, wondering how I could stop my head from bobbing up and down like one of those crazy little birds that sips water perpetually from a glass.

"It must have been awful for his family," she went on.

She was trying her best to make conversation, poor dear, but I was so overwhelmed by her beauty that I could contribute nothing. I, Archy McNally, sometimes known to his confreres as Mighty Mouth, sat there like a perfect clod, and if my jaw was agape I wouldn't have been a bit surprised.

"Father will be along in a minute," Theo said, "and then I'll leave you two alone to talk business."

The possibility of her disappearing from view shocked me back to volubility. "Please don't do that," I beseeched. "I hope to speak to your father about your purchasing or leasing another property, and I'd be happy to hear your requirements as well as his. It's been my experience that women are much more knowledgeable than men in the planning or selection of a livable home."

"I do have some very definite ideas about what I'd like to have," she said. "For instance, daddy knows absolutely nothing about gardens."

I wasn't so stunned by her loveliness that I didn't pick up on that. I thought it exceedingly odd that a man who claimed to be an expert on orchids—according to my mother—would know absolutely nothing about gardens. Possible but highly unlikely.

Theo was speaking of her dream of someday having a home with a private gym when a beefy, thick-necked linebacker came striding energetically into the room.

"Heck Johnson," he shouted, thrusting out his hand.

"Archy McNally," I said, rising to my feet and shaking that big paw. His grip wasn't exactly a bone-crusher, but you knew it was there.

"What's this?" he demanded, looking about. "No drinks? Theo, you're neglecting your duties as a hostess."

"I did ask, dad, but Archy turned me down."
She smiled. She had one dimple. Left cheek. Oh,
lord! I was a goner.

"Nonsense," he said, and turned to me. "I'm
having a vodka gimlet. Theo gets it just right.
How about it?"

"Thank you, Heck, I will."

"Of course," he said. "Theo, be a darling and
mix two of your specials."

"Three," she said, and left the room.

He waved me back to my wicker armchair and
sat in the middle of a couch facing me. He crossed
his legs and carefully adjusted the crease in his
trousers.

I fancy myself something of a minor league
Beau Brummell, but Hector Johnson belonged in
the Hall of Fame. He was wearing a trig suit of
lightweight taupe wool, a shirt striped in pale
lavender with French cuffs, and a wide-spread
white collar closed with a knitted black silk cra-
vat tied in a Windsor knot. A fashion plate!

I guessed him to be about sixty, but his age was
difficult to estimate since it was obvious that he
was no stranger to facials, manicures, and mas-
sages. What was most impressive was his air of
assurance. This was a man, I decided, who never
had a doubt in the world. It was rather daunting to a goof like me whose theme song could be
"What's It All About, Archy?"

We chatted casually for a few minutes and,
without my asking, he remarked that he was
semi-retired and that he and his daughter were
so impressed by Palm Beach they were determined

to make it their permanent home.

"Y'see, Archy," he said, "we've lived all over the world. As a mining engineer I was forced to travel a great deal, and I think we're both ready to settle down."

I nodded understandingly, mentally adding mining engineer to his growing list of former occupations.

Our conversation was interrupted when Theo returned with our drinks. Hector had been exactly right; she *did* have a way with a gimlet: not too tart, not too heavy on the vodka, and with a delightful slice of fresh lime in each glass.

We toasted each other, sipped appreciatively and, again without my asking, he began to describe the type of dwelling he and his daughter would like to inhabit.

"On Ocean Boulevard," he said definitely, "or close to it. A view of the sea, if possible, or at least a short stroll to the beach. Three bedrooms at a minimum. Florida room, of course. A pool is not necessary, but I would like a nice piece of lawn, front and back. Wouldn't you say, Theo?"

"Room for a gazebo," she replied, almost dreamily. "A flower garden. Perhaps a small greenhouse. My private gym, of course. And an enormous kitchen."

Hector laughed. "Perfection is not for this world, sweet," he said, "but perhaps we can find a reasonable facsimile."

"I'm sure you can," I said. "Let me go through our listings, talk to colleagues, and bring you a very limited selection for your consideration."

"We're not ready to buy," he said. "I warned you about that."

"Of course," I said. "I understand completely. It sometimes takes a year, or even more, of viewing, evaluating, and finally making a decision. After all, you're choosing a home you'll probably live in for the rest of your lives, and you want it to be *right*. Believe me, I'm not going to pressure you. I have one client who's been debating a final choice for almost three years."

"You're a very patient man, Archy," Theo said.

"Yes," I agreed, "I am."

"Are you an attorney?" Heck asked suddenly.

"No, I am not," I said. "But my father is. His law firm represents some of the most reputable people in Palm Beach." (And a few disreputable, I was tempted to add.) "I do hope you'll ask friends and neighbors about McNally and Son. We're proud of our reputation."

They smiled at me encouragingly. They were seated close together on the couch, a rather hideous number covered with flowered cretonne. I could see little resemblance between father and daughter, and I wanted to ask about the missing Mrs. Johnson but naturally I didn't. Not quite comme il faut, y'know.

Our glasses were almost empty when I saw Hector peek at his watch. I would have expected it to be a gold Rolex, but from where I sat it appeared to be an old, clunky digital, which surprised me.

I finished my drink and rose. "I know you have another appointment, Heck," I said, "and I don't want to take up more of your time. Thank you for seeing me and for your kind hospitality. The gimlet was splendid!"

"Our pleasure, Archy," he said, standing. "When you have something special you think we should see, do give us a call."

"I'll certainly do that," I said. "And thank you again."

"I'll walk you to your car," Theo said, and I could have screamed with delight.

We went outside, she preceding me, and I saw how her tanned legs gleamed in the sunlight. As an experienced aesthetician I notice such things.

She laughed when she saw my red Miata. "What a little beauty!" she said.

"Isn't it?" I said, happy that she approved of my wheels. "They're producing new models in black and British racing green. I may trade it in."

"Don't you dare," she said, patting the hood. "This one is *you*. Where do you live, Archy?"

"Ocean Boulevard. The Atlantic is practically lapping at our doorstep."

"How wonderful," she said. "I'd love to see your home."

"Of course," I said, almost spluttering with pleasure. "Whenever you like." I handed her a business card. "Do give me a call."

"I shall," she said, looking at me thoughtfully. "Perhaps we could make an afternoon of it. There are so many places in the Palm Beach area I'd love to see and haven't had the chance."

"I'd be happy to serve as your cicerone," I said warmly. "Perhaps we might start with lunch."

"That *would* be fun," she said.

The thought then occurred to me that maybe the Chinless Wonder was bonkers in describing Theodosia as his soon-to-be fiancée. That might be his fantasy, but the way this Lorelei was coming on, it certainly didn't seem to be hers.

"Theo," I said, "there is something I'd like to ask and I do hope it won't upset you. I'm acquainted with Silas Hawkin's widow and daughter, and in his ledger they found a notation of a painting he had been working on at the time of his death. It's listed merely as 'Untitled.' They can't find the painting and have no idea what the subject matter might be. They requested I ask you if Si ever discussed it while he was doing your portrait."

She shook her head. "No, Si never mentioned anything else he was working on. I have no idea what 'Untitled' might be."

"I didn't think you would," I assured her, "but I promised to ask. Thank you so much for welcoming me to your home. I do appreciate it."

"I'm looking forward to that lunch," she said lightly.

She shook my hand, turned, and walked back to her condo. I watched her stroll away. An entrancing sight.

I sat a moment on the hot cushions of the Miata, trying to cool off and calm down. Madam X was fascinating, no doubt about it.

I had confused impressions of both the Johnsons. Despite his air of surety Hector struck me as the type of man who constantly has to reassure himself by exaggerating his wealth, accomplishments, and prospects. Not exactly bragging, you understand, but just keeping his illusions about himself intact.

As for Theo, I ruefully admitted I may have made an initial error by equating her beauty with sweetness, purity, modesty, innocence— all that swell stuff. Now I began to wonder if there might not be a darker side to her nature, including unbridled hedonism, willfulness, cold ambition, and other attitudes that added up to a self-centered young lady with an eye out for the main chance.

Maybe, just maybe, the suspicions of crabby Mrs. Gertrude Smythe-Hersforth were justified.

Musing on the complexities of human temperament I started up the Miata and headed slowly out of the parking area. As I did, another car entered. I glanced, drove on a few yards, stopped, and made a great show of lighting a cigarette while I watched in the rearview mirror.

The newcomer stopped in front of the Johnsons' town house. The driver alighted, rang the doorbell, and was immediately admitted. Apparently Hector's expected business associate.

The car he was driving was a gunmetal Cadillac de Ville. And he was a saturnine bloke with a profile like a cleaver. Undoubtedly the gink who had spoken so familiarly to Shirley Feebling in Fort Lauderdale.

I sat there, shaken, and looked up to the heavens for revelation.

Nothing.

I returned to the McNally Building and found on my desk a message requesting that I call Sgt. Rogoff immediately. I did, finding him at police headquarters, an edifice the sergeant called the Palace but which looks to me as if it should be in the hills overlooking the Cote d'Azur.

"What's cooking, Al?" I asked.

"Me," he replied. "Murphy's Law is in action. Whatever can go wrong *is* going wrong."

"Laddy," I said, "you do sound gloomy."

"I am gloomy," he said. "It's this Hawkin kill. You know if you don't break a homicide in the first forty-eight hours, the clearance rate drops like a stone. And I'm no closer to figuring it out than I was when the squeal came in. Listen, did you talk to the Johnsons?"

"About an hour ago. I didn't ask Hector, but Theodosia says she knows nothing about a Hawkin painting called 'Untitled.' "

He sighed. "Another long shot that ran out of the money. Archy, you've spoken to the widow and daughter a couple of times. Do you get the feeling there's hostility there?"

"You better believe it."

"Got any idea what it's all about?"

"Nope," I said. "I even asked Mrs. Folsby, the maid, but she's not talking."

"Yeah," he said, "I struck out with her, too. Well, it probably has nothing to do with Silas getting iced. Keep in touch, pal."

"Al, before you hang up," I said hastily, "did Hawkin have sex just before he died?"

"Why do you ask that?"

"Idle curiosity."

"As a matter of fact he did. Satisfied?"

"No," I said, "but I hope he was."

After the luscious bouillabaisse that evening, I scampered up to my cave to record the day's happenings in my journal. There was a lot to set down, but I found myself getting all bollixed up when it came to analyzing Theo Johnson's behavior and how it affected your humble servant.

Despite my revised opinion of her—I now believed her to be as much sinner as saint—she continued to quicken me, and probably for that very reason. Obviously she was not an ingenue but I could not begin to unravel her mysteries. Lolly Spindrift's title for her, Madam X, was perfect.

I had the impression that she thought me a lightweight. That was all right. I can be a bubblehead, sometimes naturally and sometimes deliberately when I mean to profit by it. I was content to have Theo consider me a twit. My reputation for deviousness is not totally undeserved.

All this brooding about Another Woman gave me a slight attack of the guilts, and so I phoned Connie Garcia. She sounded happy to hear from me.

"Connie," I said, "have you been trying to call me?"

"Why, no," she said, "I haven't."

"Well, my phone hasn't rung all evening, and I thought it might be you."

Silence.

Finally: "Archy," she said, "I think you need professional help."

We chatted casually of this and that, made a tentative dinner date for later in the week, and disconnected after mutual declarations of affection. My stirrings of culpability had been neatly assuaged.

Do you condemn me for infidelity? Might as well blame me because I lack wings and cannot fly. I mean it's all genetics, is it not? You examine any chap's DNA and it'll show that sooner or later he'll have athlete's foot and cheat on his mate. It's simply the nature of the beast.

6

I had several extremely important tasks scheduled for Tuesday morning: get a haircut, visit my friendly periodontist for my quarterly scraping, and drop by my favorite men's boutique on Worth Avenue to see if they had anything new in the way of headgear. I am a hat freak, and that morning I was delighted to find and purchase a woven straw trilby. Cocked over one eye it gave me a dashing appearance—something like a Palermo pimp.

I eventually found my way back to the McNally Building, slowed by the lassitude that affects all citizens of South Florida in midsummer. Denizens of the north are fond of remarking, "It's not the heat, it's the humidity." In our semi-tropical paradise we prefer, "It's the heat *and* the humidity."

So I welcomed the return to my itsy-bitsy office where the air-conditioning was going full blast and the ambient temperature approximated that of Queen Maud Land in Antarctica.

Since the affair of the Chinless Wonder vs. Ms. Shirley Feebling was on temporary hold, I was free to concentrate on the investigation into the background and financial probity of Theodosia Johnson and her father. I spent a half-hour phoning my contacts at local banks, following up on my initial inquiries.

I had hoped that what I would learn might solve the riddle of those anorexic dossiers I had received from national credit agencies. But what I heard only deepened the mystery. Apparently a year ago Hector Johnson had opened a checking account at a Royal Palm Way bank with a cashier's check drawn on a bank in Troy, Mich. The identification offered had been a Michigan driver's license. He had submitted the names of two Fort Lauderdale residents as references. He had made no additional deposits, and his current balance was slightly less than $50,000.

I thought about that for a while and realized that if the Johnsons were hardly nudging poverty they soon might be if their level of spending continued and no additional funds became available. Perhaps that was the reason for Hector's business meeting with the cold-faced gent who had accosted Shirley Feebling in the pizza joint.

Another puzzle was why, with limited resources, the Johnsons had commissioned Silas Hawkin to do a portrait of Theo. Si had told me he had not yet billed for the painting, but according to Lolly Spindrift the artist charged thirty grand and up for portraits. Quite a hefty bite, wouldn't you say, from a bank balance of less than fifty?

Sighing, I donned my jacket and my new lid and ventured out again into the sauna enveloping the Palm Beach area. Walking slowly and trying to keep in the shade, I made my way to the Pristine Gallery on Worth Avenue. The portrait of Theodosia Johnson was prominently displayed in the front window with a card chastely lettered: *The Last Painting by Silas Hawkin.* Rather a macabre touch, wouldn't you say?

The gallery appeared empty when I entered, but a bell jangled merrily as the door opened, and Ivan Duvalnik, the corpulent owner, appeared from an inner room. I had met him when I purchased a charming watercolor of begonias in bloom as a Christmas present for my mother. Momsy had been delighted with the gift, and the painting now hung over the mantel in our second-floor sitting room.

"Mr. McNally," he said, holding out a plump hand. "A pleasure to see you again, sir."

"It's good to see you, Mr. Duvalnik," I said, briefly pressing his damp flipper. "I'm dreadfully sorry about Si Hawkin."

"He was my shining star," Ivan said dramatically. "I shall not see his like again."

"I notice you're still showing the portrait of Theo Johnson."

His mouth twitched. "An irritation," he said. "The painting has not yet been paid for. As a matter of fact, Si asked me to hold off billing for it. So now the painting is part of his estate, and I suppose I shall have to represent his widow. It's a valuable work."

"That I can believe," I said. "I'm surprised the Johnsons haven't claimed it."

He was mildly astonished. "The Johnsons?" he said. "But it isn't their legal property. The portrait was commissioned by Chauncey Smythe-Hersforth. I thought everyone knew that. He certainly made no secret of it. He intended it to be his engagement gift to Theo."

"Of course," I said. "And speaking of gifts, I was hoping to ask Hawkin to do a small portrait of my mother as a birthday present for her. Although I doubt if I could have afforded him."

"He *was* pricey," Duvalnik admitted. "I wanted to charge a minimum of thirty thousand for the Johnson portrait but, as I say, I could never get a firm number from Si. I think perhaps he hated to see that painting go. It was his best work and he knew it. A few fine artists are like that; they do something special and they want to hang on to it. But I represent a number of other gifted portraitists if you're really interested in a present for your mother. First let me get you something to wet your whistle."

He brought me a glass of white wine. No Chilean chardonnay this time. It was dreadful plonk, but I smacked my lips gamely and told him how splendid it was. He showed me Polaroids and color slides of the works of several other artists, none of whom had Hawkin's talent. Prices ranged from twenty-five hundred to ten thousand.

"Let me think about it," I said. "If it's to be a surprise birthday gift I can hardly ask mother to sit for a portrait. I presume some of these people can do a painting from photographs."

"Naturally," he said. "No problem at all. Si Hawkin refused to work that way; he insisted on several sittings. He was a real pro."

"Was he working on anything new at the time of his death?" I asked casually.

"Not to my knowledge," the gallery owner said sadly. "Like the card in the window says, that portrait of Theo Johnson was Hawkin's final work."

"What a shame," I said. "Thank you for your help, Mr. Duvalnik. You'll be hearing from me."

And I tramped back to the McNally Building through parboiled streets, having picked up a few more tidbits of information that might prove valuable or might turn out to be the drossiest of dross. My investigations usually depend on the amassing of minor facts rather than major leaps of inspiration. When it comes to tortoise versus hare, I'm no cottontail.

It took a few minutes in my gloriously chilled office for my temperature, pulse, and respiratory rate to regain some semblance of normality. Then I phoned Lolly Spindrift at his newspaper, hoping to add a few truffles to my collection of bonbons.

"Hi, darling," Spindrift said in his high-pitched lilt. "Have you called to invite me to another lunch of champagne and caviar?"

"You mock," I said. "I haven't yet recovered from the last one."

"Wasn't that a kick?" he said. "We were talking about Silas Hawkin, and the next day the man is defunct. Let that be a lesson to you. Gather ye rosebuds while ye may, laddie."

"I fully intend to," I said. "Lol, I need some information."

"So do I," he replied. "Every day, constantly. My lifestyle depends on it. You've heard of quid pro quo, haven't you, darling? English translation: You scratch my back and I'll scratch yours. Not literally, of course, since we're of different religions. But if you've got nothing for me, I've got nothing for you."

"I have a little nosh that may interest you," I said. "You will, of course, refuse to reveal your source?"

"Don't I always?" he demanded. "Jail before dishonor. What have you got?"

"Si Hawkin had sex just before he was killed."

I heard Lol's swift intake of breath.

"Beautiful," he said. *"That* I can use. Can I depend on it?"

"Would I deceive you?" I asked. "With your authenticated file on the peccadilloes of Archy McNally?"

"Okay," he said, "I'll run with it. Now what do you want?"

"Have you heard any rumors that Silas Hawkin may have had, ah, intimate relations with any of the women whose portraits he painted?"

His laughter exploded. *"Any* of the women?" he said, gasping. "You mean *all* of the women! Darling, the man was a stallion, a veritable *stallion.*"

"Odd you should say that. I recently heard him described as a goat."

"More of a ram," Spindrift said. "Absotively, posilutely insatiable."

"Thank you, Lol," I said. "Keep fighting for the public's right to know."

"And up yours as well, dearie," he said before he hung up.

And that, I decided, was enough detecting for one morning. I reclaimed my horseless carriage in our underground garage and drove directly to the Pelican Club to replenish my energy. I might even have something to eat.

And so I did. I sat at the bar, ordered a Coors Light from Mr. Pettibone, and asked daughter Priscilla to bring me a double cheeseburger with home fries and a side order of coleslaw. She spread this harvest before me and shook her head wonderingly.

"On a diet, Archy?" she inquired.

"None of your sass," I said. "I have been engaged in debilitating physical labor and require nourishment."

She shrugged. "They're your arteries," she said.

As I made my way through all that yummy cholesterol I pondered the murder of Silas Hawkin and wondered if one of his clients with whom he had been cozy had slid that palette knife into his gullet. I could imagine several motives: jealousy, revenge, fury at being jilted for another woman.

If it was my case, and it wasn't, I would concentrate on the missing painting. Find "Untitled," I thought, and you'd probably find the killer. I had enough faith in Sgt. Al Rogoff's expertise to reckon he was on the same track.

But why would the murderer risk making off with the painting? It couldn't be sold, at least not locally, and if it was unfinished, as it apparently was, it would be of little value anywhere. The only logical conclusion was that the importance of "Untitled" lay in its subject matter. The killer didn't want it to be seen by anyone.

But if that was true, why wasn't the painting destroyed on the spot? After slaying the artist it would have taken the assassin only a few minutes to slash "Untitled" to ribbons, or even douse it with one of the inflammables in the studio and set it afire. But instead, "Untitled" was carried away.

Which led me to reflect on the size of the painting. The portrait of Theo Johnson, I estimated, was approximately 3 1/2 ft. tall by 2 1/2 wide. If "Untitled" had the same dimensions it was hardly something one could tuck under one's arm and then saunter away, particularly if the painting was still wet. A puzzlement.

I knew that art supply stores carried blank canvases already framed. But I also knew that most fine artists preferred to stretch their own canvas, buying the quality desired in bolts and cutting off the piece required for a planned endeavor. It would then be tacked to a wooden frame.

Still, it might be worthwhile to check the store where Silas bought his supplies. It was just barely possible he had recently purchased a stretched canvas that was to become "Untitled." And so, after I had consumed that cornucopia of calories in toto, I inserted myself behind the wheel of the Miata with some difficulty and set out for the Hawkin residence.

As I said, it was not my case, but it was of interest to me because of the peripheral involvement of Theo and Hector Johnson.

Also, I had nothing better to do on that sultry afternoon.

It had been my intention to ask the housekeeper for the information I sought, but when I rang the chimes at the main house the door was opened by Mrs. Louise Hawkin.

"Oh," I said, somewhat startled. "Good afternoon, Mrs. Hawkin. May I speak to Mrs. Folsby for a moment?"

"She is no longer with us," she said in a tone that didn't invite further inquiries.

But I persisted. "Sorry to hear it," I said. "Could you tell me where I might be able to contact her?"

"No," she said shortly. Then: "What did you want to talk to her about?"

"I just wanted to ask if your late husband used prepared canvases or if he stretched his own."

She stared at me. "Why on earth would you want to know that?"

I have a small talent for improv. "A young friend of mine is a wannabe artist," I told her. "He is a great admirer of Mr. Hawkin's technique and requested I ask."

She bought it. "My husband stretched his own canvas," she said. "A very good grade of linen. Good day, Mr. McNally."

And she shut the door. What I should have said was, "No more interest in a divorce lawyer, Mrs. Hawkin?" But I knew the answer to that.

I glanced toward the studio building. It seemed to be unguarded, and the crime scene tape drooped in the heat. I wandered over and tried the scarred oak and etched glass door, but it was locked. I turned away, then heard a "Psst!" that whirled me back. Marcia Hawkin was standing in the opened doorway, beckoning to me.

She drew me inside, then locked the door after us.

"What did she tell you?" she said fiercely.

Bewilderment time. "Who?" I asked.

"Her," she said, jerking a thumb in the direction of the main house. "Did she say anything about me?"

"Not a word," I assured her. "We had a very brief conversation about your father's work."

She clutched my arm and pulled me into the sitting area on the ground level. She leaned close and almost whispered. "She's a dreadful woman. Dreadful! Don't believe anything she says. Do you want a drink?"

"I think I better," I said, and she went into the kitchenette. I watched with horror as she poured me a tumbler of warm vodka.

"Miss Hawkin," I said, "if I drink that I'll be non compos mentis. Please let me do it."

I moved to the sink and mixed myself a mild vodka and water with plenty of ice. Meanwhile Marcia had thrown herself on the couch and lay sprawled, biting furiously at a fingernail. An Ophelia, I decided.

It would be difficult to describe her costume in detail without sounding indecent. I shall merely say that she wore an oversized white singlet, soiled and possibly belonging to her dead father, and denim shorts chopped off so radically that they hardly constituted a loincloth. But her lanky semi-nakedness made her seem more helpless than seductive. She was long and loose-jointed; a puppeteer had cut her strings.

"My stepmother is a bitch," she declared. "You know what that means, don't you?"

"I've heard the word," I acknowledged.

"What am I going to do?" she cried despairingly. "What *am* I going to do?"

Never let it be said that A. McNally failed to respond to a damsel in distress. But when the damsel in question appears to be a certifiable loony—well, it does give one pause, does it not?

"What seems to be the problem, Miss Hawkin?" I asked, speaking as slowly and softly as possible.

My soothing manner had the desired effect. She suddenly began talking rationally and with some good sense.

"Money," she said. "Isn't that always the problem?"

"Not always," I said, "but frequently. Surely your father left you well-provided for."

"I have a trust fund," she admitted, "but I can't touch it until I turn twenty-one."

That was a shocker. I had guessed her to be in the mid-twenties. "How old are you, Miss Hawkin?" I asked gently.

"Nineteen," she said. "I look older, don't I?"

"Not at all," I said gallantly.

"I know I do," she said defiantly. "But you don't know what my life has been like. When daddy was alive, money made no difference. He was very generous. Anything I wanted. But now I'm totally dependent on *her*. My food, the house, spending money—*everything*. It just kills me."

"Surely you have relatives or friends who'd be willing to help out."

She shook her head. "No one. I'm on my own, and I'm frightened, I admit it."

"Don't be frightened," I counseled her, "because then you won't be able to think clearly. You must keep your nerve and review your options calmly and logically as if you were called upon to advise someone else."

She looked at me queerly. "Yes," she said, "you're right. If I have the courage to act I can solve my own problems, can't I?"

"Of course. Courage and energy: That's what it takes."

She laughed. I didn't like that laugh. It came perilously close to being a hysterical giggle.

"Thank you, Archy," she said. "I may call you Archy, mayn't I?"

"I'd be delighted."

"And you must call me Squirrel," she said. "That's what daddy always called me."

"What an unusual nickname," I said, smiling.

"You think so?" she challenged, and abruptly she was back in her manic mood again. "I see nothing unusual about it. You just don't understand. No one can ever understand. I think you better go now."

My first impression had been correct: definitely an Ophelia.

I finished my drink hastily, bid her a polite farewell, and left her still sprawled, starting on another fingernail. I was thankful to be going. Those moments with her were too intense, too charged with things unsaid, furies suppressed and threatening to break loose.

I drove away without a backward glance. The master of that home might be deceased but it was still the Villa Bile.

When I arrived at the McNally digs, a *much* happier household, I found Jamie Olson in the garage hosing down my mother's antique wood-bodied Ford station wagon. He was smoking one of his ancient briars, the one with the cracked shank wrapped with a Band-Aid.

"Jamie," I said, "Mrs. Jane Folsby was the live-in at Silas Hawkin's residence, but she has suddenly left their employ. Do you think you can find out where she's gone?"

"Mebbe," he said.

"Try," I urged. "She's a nice lady, and I'd like to talk to her."

I had a pleasant ocean swim, the family cocktail hour that followed was just as enjoyable, and dinner that night capped my pleasure. Mother went upstairs for an evening of television in the sitting room, father retired to his study to continue his wrestle with Dickens, and I climbed to my suite to update my journal, sip a small marc, and listen to a tape of Hoagy Carmichael singing "Star Dust."

It was a normal evening at the McNally manse, all quiet, peaceful, content. But just when you start believing the drawbridge is up, the castle is inviolate, and the rude world can't possibly intrude, along comes leering fate to deliver a swift kick to your gluteus maximus.

On that particular evening the boot came at approximately 9:30 P.M. in the form of a phone call from Sgt. Al Rogoff. He spent no time on greetings.

"I'm beginning to wonder about you," he said.

"Are you?" I said, thinking he was joshing. "Wonder about what?"

"Do you know a guy named Chauncey Smythe-Hersforth? Lives in Palm Beach."

"Of course I know him," I said. "He and his mother are clients of McNally and Son."

"Uh-huh. And do you know a woman named Shirley Feebling? In Fort Lauderdale."

"I don't *know* her," I said warily, beginning to get antsy about this conversation. "I met her once for an hour. Why the third degree, Al?"

"Son," he said, "you're just too free with your business cards. About an hour ago I got a call from a dick I know who works out of Lauderdale Homicide. This afternoon they found Shirley Feebling in her condo shot through the back of her head. Much dead. They also found your business card and a batch of hot letters from this Smythe-Hersforth character."

I closed my eyes. Her T-shirt had been lettered PEACE. What a way to find it.

"Your father still awake?" Rogoff asked.

"Of course he's still awake. It's only nine-thirty."

"I think I better come over," he said. "Okay?"

"Don't tell me I'm a suspect," I said with a shaky laugh.

"Right now you and Smythe-Hersforth are the only leads that Lauderdale's got. I promised to check you out, both of you. Makes sense, doesn't it?"

"I guess," I said, sighing. "The second time my business card has landed me in the soup. You're correct, Al; I've got to stop handing them out. Sure, come on over."

"Be there in fifteen minutes," he said and hung up.

I sat there a few moments remembering that ingenuous and not too bright young woman with her firm belief in True Love and a sunny future. It didn't take long for sadness and regret to become anger and a seething desire for vengeance. The murder of Shirley Feebling affected me more keenly than the killing of Silas Hawkin. I could conceive that his actions might have led to his demise. But hers, I was convinced, was the death of an innocent.

I prepared to go downstairs and alert father to the arrival of Sgt. Rogoff. I glanced nervously at the darkness outside my window. Our snug home no longer seemed secure.

7

Al had the look of an exhausted beagle. He sat in front of my father's magisterial desk and in a toneless voice recited what little he knew of the murder of Shirley Feebling.

She did not show up for work at the topless car wash on Tuesday morning. The boss was not concerned; his employees were usually late and frequently absent for a day or two simply because they had better things to do than lave insect-spattered vehicles driven by the curious and/or lubricious.

But when there was no word from Shirl by noon, and her phone wasn't answered, a friend and co-worker with the unlikely name of Pinky Schatz became alarmed and stopped by her place after work. The door of Ms. Feebling's condo was unlocked, and inside Pinky discovered the sanguinary corpse. After a single scream, she dialed 911.

The homicide detective to whom Rogoff had spoken had revealed only that my business card and the letters of Chauncey Wilson Smythe-Hersforth had been found during the initial search. If any additional significant evidence was discovered, he just wasn't saying.

"And that's all I've got," the sergeant concluded. He turned to me. "What have *you* got?"

I glanced at mon père. He was the attorney; it was his responsibility to decide how much to reveal and how much to keep undisclosed in the name of client confidentiality. Al and I waited patiently while Prescott McNally went through his mulling routine, a process that endured long enough to calculate the square root of 2. Finally the guru spoke.

"Discretion?" he demanded, looking sternly at Rogoff.

"As usual," Al said.

Father then described the letters Smythe-Hersforth had written Shirley Feebling during a time the two apparently had been enjoying a steamy affair. Later the client had a change of heart, but the woman insisted he honor the proposal of marriage he had made in writing. If not, she vowed to sell his letters to any interested tabloid.

"Uh-huh," Rogoff said. "How much was she asking?"

"Archy?" papa said. "You take it from here."

"I went down to Lauderdale to see her," I told the sergeant. "I had just the single meeting and left my business card. She absolutely refused to discuss a cash settlement. She wanted to marry him and that was that."

"Where is the guy now—do you know?"

"His office says he left Monday morning for a bankers' convention in New Orleans and won't be back until Thursday."

Al had been making brief notes on all this in a fat little notebook he carried. Now he slapped the cover closed and bound it with a wide rubber band. He said casually, "Archy, you got any idea who might have clobbered the woman?"

I had learned to lie convincingly by age four. "Not a glimmer," I said.

"Sergeant," father said, "if inquiries by the Fort Lauderdale authorities prove—as I am certain they will—that Smythe-Hersforth was in New Orleans at the time of this unfortunate woman's death, I will deeply appreciate any assistance you may provide in retrieving our client's personal letters since they obviously will be of no further interest or import in the official investigation."

All that was said in one sentence. It's the way my old man talks.

"I'll see what I can do, sir," Rogoff said, rising, and the two men shook hands.

The sergeant was driving a police car that night, not his personal pickup truck, and I walked him outside. He paused to light a cigar and blow a plume of smoke toward the cloudless sky.

"Nice weather," he observed.

"You don't find it a trifle warm?"

"Nah," he said. "I like the heat. It keeps the juices flowing."

"And how are they flowing on the Hawkin homicide?"

"They ain't," he admitted. "We're going through the drill, talking to everyone. It's what I call an NKN case: nobody knows nothing."

"A double negative," I pointed out.

"The story of my life," he said. Then suddenly: "How about you? You got anything?"

"A crumb," I said. "Mrs. Jane Folsby has left the Hawkins' employ. For reasons the deponent knoweth not."

"Yeah?" he said. "Can't say I blame her for getting out of that nuthouse. Go to bed, sonny boy; I only wish I could. And remember what I said about your business cards. Will you, for God's sake, stop passing them out? Every time you do, someone gets whacked and I have to put in more overtime."

I watched him drive away, reflecting that his warning came too late. The last card I had distributed went to Theodosia Johnson. It was not a comforting thought. I went back inside. The door to father's study was shut, which meant he was deep in Dickens and port. So I trudged upstairs, finished scribbling in my journal, and prepared to crawl into the sack.

I cannot say my mood was melancholy, but neither was it chockablock with joie de vivre. I have never been a victim of presentiments, but that evening I must confess I had a sense of impending doom.

The only way I could calm my quaking spirits was to remind myself firmly that seriousness is a sin. I happen to believe that our Maker is the greatest farceur in the universe. And so sleep came only with the blessed remembrance of the sentiment: "Long live the sun! And down with the night!"

I thought it might be Pushkin. But then it might have been just Archy McNally. No matter. I slept.

And awoke on Wednesday morning revivified, alert, and wondering why I had been in such a funk the previous night. After all, I was alive, reasonably young, in full possession of my faculties (others might disagree), and inhabiting a world that offered such glories as lamb shanks braised in wine and tiramisu with zabaglione sauce. There was absolutely no reason to despair.

I knew exactly what I must do, but of course I had overslept and didn't arrive at my office in the McNally Building until a bit after ten o'clock. Oversleeping, I realized, was becoming a habit I seemed unable to break, and it occurred to me that I might have contracted trypanosomiasis. I have never been to Africa, but a chum of mine, Binky Watrous, had recently spent a weekend in Marrakech, and it was quite possible that, unknowingly of course, he had brought a tsetse fly home with him. It was troubling.

The moment I was behind my ugly desk I phoned Jack DuBois, my pal at the Royal Palm Way bank handling Hector Johnson's checking account.

"Jack," I said, "you told me that when Johnson made his initial deposit with a cashier's check from

Troy, Michigan, he presented a driver's license as ID and supplied the names of two Fort Lauderdale residents as references."

"That's right."

"Could I have the names and addresses of the references, please?"

He groaned. "Archy, it seems to me I'm doing all your work for you."

"Jack, there's no such thing as a free lunch."

"Lunch?" he cried indignantly. "You promised me a dinner."

"I was speaking metaphorically," I soothed him. "You shall have your dinner complete with appetizer, soup, entrée, dessert, and whatever else your ravenous hunger and thirst demand. Now let's have the names of Johnson's references."

"Wait a sec while I call them up on my screen," he said. "We've got new software and it's a doozy. When are you going to get a computer, Archy?"

"Give me a break," I pleaded. "I can't even operate a battery-powered swizzle stick."

Eventually I received the information requested. Hector Johnson's two references were J.P. Lordsley and Reuben Hagler. I studied their addresses and reckoned that if I left immediately, I could manage a relaxed drive to Fort Lauderdale, enjoy a leisurely snack, check out both individuals, and be back in time for my daily dunk in the sea.

But it did not happen. My phone jangled ere I could depart, and a feminine voice inquired, "Archy McNally?"

I recognized that coo, and my heart leaped like an inflamed gazelle. "Theo!" I said. "How nice to hear from you."

"I do hope I'm not interrupting," she said. "I know how busy you must be."

"Work—" I said. "It's a four-letter word and I try to avoid it."

"Let me help," she said, her voice positively burbling. "You did offer to show me your home, you know, and it's such a lovely day I was hoping to persuade you to take a few hours off."

"Splendid idea!" I practically shouted. "And as I recall, lunch was also mentioned. Still on?"

"Of course. Daddy is using our car this afternoon, so could you pick me up?"

"Delighted," I said. "Half an hour? How does that sound?"

"I'll be waiting for you, Archy," she said softly and hung up, leaving me to interpret her final words in several ways, not all of them honorable.

I was happy I had worn dove gray slacks and my navy blue blazer adorned with the Pelican Club patch: a pelican rampant on a field of dead mullet. I also sported tasseled cordovan loafers (no socks) and a mauve cashmere polo shirt, the cost of which had made a severe dent in my net worth.

Thankfully the heat and humidity of the previous day had dissipated and it was a brilliant noontime with a cerulean sky brushed with horsetail clouds, and a sweet ocean breeze moving the palm fronds. I should have been elated by the anticipation of spending a few enchanting hours with Madam X, but I must admit two questions dampened my euphoria.

One: If the Chinless Wonder was correct in stating that he was to become the fiancé of Theodosia Johnson—and commissioning her portrait certainly proved the sincerity of his intent—why did she seem so eager to enjoy a luncheon with yrs. truly? She had to be aware that Chauncey was out of town, and her cozying up to another man in his absence was a mite off-putting.

I was not accusing her of blatant infidelity, mind you, and I had no desire to make a moral judgment. Not me, who believes "connubial bliss" is an oxymoron. But her conduct *was* a puzzle. I concluded she had a motive I could not ken.

The second question was where in the world was I going to take Madam X to lunch. You must understand that Connie Garcia, partly due to her position as social secretary to Lady Horowitz, maintains a network of spies, snitches, close friends, and catty enemies who like nothing better than to relate the behavior of Archy McNally, particularly when I am observed in activities sure to ignite Connie's Latin temper. If I was seen lunching with the nubile Ms. Johnson, it would undoubtedly be reported to the lady with whom I was intimate, and I didn't wish to imagine what her reaction would be. Incendiary, I was certain, and possibly damaging to the McNally corpus.

But all my uncertainties and hesitancies vanished when I rang the bell of the Johnsons' condo and the door was opened by Theo. A vision! Physical beauty, the eggheads tell us, is ephemeral, of no lasting value, and we must admire only the inner virtues. I much prefer a swan-like neck.

She was wearing a slip dress of tangerine silk. With her apricot-tanned shoulders and peachy complexion she was a veritable fruit salad of delight. Once again her beauty had the effect of answering all my questions and banishing all my doubts. Suspect this woman of chicanery? Nonsense! Might as well accuse the Venus de Milo of being a pickpocket.

"Archy!" she said, clasping my hand. "You look smashing. What is that crest on your jacket?"

"The Pelican Club. A private dining and drinking establishment."

"Wonderful. Are we going there for lunch?"

"No, no," I said hastily. "It's a comfortable spot, but regretfully the cuisine is something less than haute. We'll find a place with a more enticing menu. But first let me show you the McNally home."

What a pleasure it was to have that paragon seated alongside me in the Miata as we zipped over to Ocean Boulevard and gazed on the glimmering sea.

Theo was wide-eyed as she glimpsed the mansions fronting the Atlantic. "The money!" she said.

"Playpen of the idle rich," I admitted blithely. "But not all of us. The McNallys, for instance. We work, we're hardly multis, and our spread is relatively modest. My father had the great good sense to buy years and years ago before real estate prices rocketed into the wild blue yonder."

I parked on the graveled turnaround at our three-car garage and led my guest on a stroll through our smallish estate.

"We employ a live-in couple who have their own apartment over the garage," I said. "The greenhouse is my mother's domain. No pool, you'll notice. What's the point with the ocean a short trot away? The doghouse belonged to Max, our golden retriever, but he's gone to the great kennel in the sky. Let's see if mother is at work."

We found her in the potting shed. She stripped off a rubber glove to shake hands with our visitor.

"How nice to meet you, Miss Johnson," she said brightly. "I've already met your father at our garden club. What a charming man he is."

"Thank you, Mrs. McNally. Your home is lovely."

"But you haven't seen the inside yet," I protested. "It's nothing but bare walls and a few hammocks."

"Don't believe a word he says," mum advised.

"I don't," Theo said with more conviction than I liked.

"Archy, will you and Miss Johnson be staying for lunch?"

"Not today, darling," I told her. "We want to see some of the local scenery."

"Well, do come back," she urged Theo. "Perhaps you and your father might visit some evening."

"I'd love that, Mrs. McNally. Thank you so much."

We walked toward the house. "She's beautiful," Theo said. "And so—so *motherly.*"

"Isn't she," I agreed. "I just adore sitting on her lap."

"You're a nut," she said, laughing.

"And now for the fifty-cent tour," I said. "Let's make it fast because the pangs of hunger are beginning to gnaw."

I showed her everything: kitchen, father's study, living and dining rooms, second-floor sitting room, master and guest bedrooms, and my own little suite on the third floor. All the furnishings were of good quality but obviously mellowed. The interior looked as if everything had been inherited, which was exactly the ambience my father had striven to create when he moved up from Miami.

"It's all so handsome," Theo said, suitably impressed. "So solid and warm and comfy."

I didn't tell her the truth, that everything in the place had been purchased in the past thirty years from decorators, galleries, and antique shops. Our home was a stage set. But it was convincing.

We reboarded the Miata, and I had what I fancied was a minor stroke of genius.

"You know," I said thoughtfully, "there are many fine restaurants in Palm Beach, but it's such a scrumptious day, why don't we take a drive down to Boca Raton along A1A. I know a marvelous place in Boca where we can lunch alfresco."

"Sounds divine," Theo said.

So having reduced the possibility of being spotted by one of Connie Garcia's spies to an absolute minimum, I turned southward. We followed the corniche, and my companion never stopped exclaiming at the glory of the vistas and the wealth displayed by the private mansions and luxury condominiums along the way.

I drove directly to Mizner Park, my favorite mini-mall in South Florida. There we entrusted the Miata to a valet and secured an umbrella table at the Bistro L'Europe. Outdoor dining at Mizner is a charming way to enjoy anything from a boutique pizza to a five-course banquet. But, of course, the main attraction is people-watching.

I cannot recall the exact details of our lunch. I have a vague recollection of sharing an enormous Caesar salad with Theo after we had demolished a duck terrine. I do remember very well that everything I consumed was ambrosial. That may have been due to the full bottle of Beaujolais we finished, but I prefer to believe my pleasure was heightened by being in the company of such a ravishing dining partner.

"Archy," she said, nibbling on a garlic crouton, "why have you never married?"

I had an oft-repeated response to that. "I am very prone to allergies," I told her. "Research has shown that more than half of all divorces are caused by one spouse becoming allergic to the other. I just can't take the chance."

That sinfully entrancing dimple appeared and she shook her head hopelessly. "You're a devil," she said.

"That wounds," I said. "All I wish to be is your guardian angel. Where are you from, Theo?"

"Michigan," she said promptly. "Isn't everyone?"

"During the tourist season one might think so. I understand Michiganders refer to Florida as the Lower Peninsula. Tell me, if a man is a Michigander, is a woman a Michigoose?"

She ignored that antiquated wheeze—and rightly so. "Where are *you* from?" she asked.

"Right here. One of the few residents actually born in Florida."

"You don't sound like a native Floridian."

"I went to prep school up north and then later to Yale."

I told her the story of why I was booted out of Yale Law and she was mightily amused. "You *are* a devil," she said, "and I really shouldn't be associating with you."

"Perhaps you shouldn't," I said boldly. "I understand you're soon to be affianced."

She lifted her chin and looked at me coolly. "Maybe," she said, "and maybe not. I haven't yet decided. Do you know Chauncey Smythe-Hersforth?"

"Yes."

"And his mother?"

"I am acquainted with the lady."

"Then surely you know why I am postponing a decision."

I said nothing.

"Meanwhile," she went on, "I am living the way I want to live. I'm an independent cuss. Does my behavior shock you?"

"No, it does not. But it puzzles me."

"You feel I should leap at the chance of marrying Chauncey?"

"You could do much worse. Me, for instance."

"Let me be the judge of that," she said.

"May I ask how old you are, Theo?"

"You may ask but I shan't answer. Older than you think, I'm sure."

"Another personal question you may or may not wish to answer: Is your mother living?"

"Yes. My parents are divorced. My mother has remarried and is presently living in San Diego. And now I have a personal question for you: Do you have a ladyfriend?"

"I do."

"But you're not faithful to her."

"Is that a question or a statement?"

She laughed. "A statement. I do believe you're as selfish as I am."

"Quite possibly," I acknowledged. "Theo, would you care for dessert?"

"Yes," she said decisively, staring at me. "You."

I sought to quell a slight tremor.

She discussed the logistics of our assignation as calmly as if she were making an appointment for a pedicure. Daddy had driven down to Fort Lauderdale that morning. It was a business trip and daddy would be gone all day. And daddy had promised to phone before he started back to Palm Beach so they could make dinner plans.

In addition, both condos adjoining the Johnsons' were unoccupied, the owners having gone north for the summer.

"So you see," Theo concluded, "we'll have all the privacy we could possibly want."

"Yes," I said, tempted to add, "But God will be watching." I didn't, of course, since it verged on blasphemy.

We didn't converse on our return trip to Palm Beach although there were a few occasions when I suspected she was humming. I was simply amazed at her insouciance. She sat upright, smiling straight ahead, shining hair whipping back in the breeze. She looked as if she owned the world, or at least that part of it she coveted.

We arrived at the Johnsons' condo, and I suggested that since the blood-red Miata was such a noticeable vehicle, it might be more discreet if I parked some distance away. But Theo would have none of that, insisted I park at her doorstep, and led the way inside. And instead of inviting me into a bedroom, she rushed to that hideous cretonne-covered couch in the living room and beckoned. I scurried to her side.

She undressed with frantic and unseemly haste, and all I could think of was a cannibal preparing for a feast of a succulent missionary.

I shall not attempt to describe the rapture of that afternoon. It is not that I lack the vocabulary—you know me better than that—but it is because some events in one's life are so private that it is painful to disclose them, even if they are pleasurable.

I can only permit myself to record that Theodosia Johnson was all women. Not all woman but all women. She reduced the plural to the singular, multiplicity to one. After knowing her, there seemed no need for another. She was the Eternal Female, capitalized, and at the moment I was bewitched. Not bothered and bewildered— just bewitched.

There was one intimate detail I am forced to reveal because it has a bearing on what was to follow. Theo had a small tattoo of a blue butterfly on the left of her tanned abdomen, almost in the crease of her thigh. It was, to the best of my recollection, the first time I had ever kissed a butterfly.

I returned home too late for my ocean swim— a mercy since I hadn't the strength—but in time to shower and dress for the family cocktail hour and dinner. My thoughts, needless to say, were awhirl, but I believe I hid my perturbation from my parents. The only discomposing moment came during our preprandial martinis when I eagerly asked my mother, "What did you think of Theo Johnson?"

The mater gave me her sweet smile. "She's not for you, Archy," she said.

It was cataclysm time. "Why on earth not?" I demanded.

Her shrug was tiny. "Just a feeling," she said.

I was subdued at dinner and retired to my quarters as soon as decently possible. I wanted to note the day's adventures in my journal but was unable. I merely sat rigidly, counting the walls (there were four), and tried to solve the riddle of Madam X.

I was still in this semi-catatonic state when Connie Garcia phoned. Her first words—"Hi, honey!"—were an enormous relief since they signified she had not yet learned of my hegira to Mizner Park with Theo Johnson.

"Listen," she went on, "seems to me you gabbled about a dinner date this week. When? Put up or shut up."

"Let me consult my social calendar," I said. "My presence has been requested at so many—"

"Cut the bs," she interrupted. "It's on for tomorrow night at the Pelican Club. I called and Leroy is planning to roast a whole suckling pig. How does that sound?"

"Gruesome," I said. "I *am* a suckling pig."

"As well I know," Connie said. "Around eight o'clock—okay?"

"Fine," I said. "I'll even change my socks."

I realized, after hanging up, that perhaps an evening with the open, forthright, and completely honest Ms. Garcia was exactly what I needed. After an afternoon spent with the disquieting and inexplicable Ms. Johnson, it would be like popping a tranquilizer. Of course after dinner Connie would expect me to expend some energy in her Lake Worth condo, but that prospect didn't daunt me. I hustled to the medicine cabinet in my bathroom and slid two B-12 sublingual tablets under my tongue.

Wasn't it John Barrymore who said, "So many women, so little time"? If he didn't say it, he should have.

8

Chauncey Wilson Smythe-Hersforth returned from New Orleans on Thursday morning, and at eleven o'clock he and his mother had a conference with my father. I was not invited to attend. But after it ended the Chinless Wonder came down to my office wearing a grin so smarmy I wanted to kick his shins.

"This is your *office?*" he said, glancing around. "My walk-in closet at home is bigger than this."

"Most of my work is done on the outside," I said frostily. "Like going down to Fort Lauderdale to interview Shirley Feebling on your behalf."

He immediately composed his features into a theatrical expression of sorrow. "That was a terrible thing," he said, shaking his fat head. "Just terrible. She was a nice girl, Archy. I really liked her."

I made no response.

"What's the world coming to?" he demanded rhetorically. "Violence everywhere. Silas Hawkin murdered and now this. A decent citizen isn't safe on the street anymore."

I had enough of his profundities. "What's happening with your letters?" I asked.

The smarmy grin returned. "Your father is going to pull every string he can to get them back from the Lauderdale police. They're of no use to them, are they? I mean I have a perfect alibi; a hundred people saw me at the convention. Listen, Archy, how much money did Shirley want?"

"She didn't want any. She just wanted to marry you."

"She should have known that was impossible," he blustered, running a finger between collar and neck. "The difference in our class and all that . . . "

"Uh-huh," I said. "And what was your mother's reaction to your proposing marriage to Shirley?"

That deflated him. "Well, uh, in your father's office she just said, 'Boys will be boys.' But when I get home tonight I expect she'll have more to say on the subject."

"Yes, I expect she will," I said with some satisfaction. "Tell me, CW, did Shirl ever say anything about someone threatening her or following her or annoying her?"

"No, she never mentioned anything like that. I think it was a druggie who broke in to rob her. She caught him at it and he killed her."

"Could be," I said, waiting for him to say, "She was just in the wrong place at the wrong time."

"She was just in the wrong place at the wrong time," he said, keeping his reputation for fatuousness intact. "Well, it was an awful thing, but in

all honesty it's a load off my mind to have that
business about the letters cleared up."

Which I thought was somewhat akin to the classic question: "But other than that, Mrs. Lincoln,
how did you enjoy the show?"

"I can't wait to tell Theo Johnson," he went on.
"She'll be so relieved."

I was as aghast at hearing that as I'm sure you
are in reading it. "Good lord, CW," I said, "don't
tell me you informed your intended fiancée about
Shirley Feebling?"

"Of course I did," he said, stroking that ridiculous pushbroom mustache. "Theo and I promised
to be completely frank and honest. No secrets. We
tell each other absolutely everything."

If that were true, I reflected, I better leave for
Hong Kong immediately.

I finally got rid of him with a keener apprecia-
tion of why Ms. Johnson was postponing her decision to become affianced. The man was a pom-
pous ass, and Theo had the wit to recognize it.

It was then noonish and time to saddle up if
I expected to make that delayed trip to Fort
Lauderdale. So I grabbed my notes on Hector
Johnson's bank references and went down to our
underground garage to embark. It was probably
a fool's errand, I glumly reckoned, and if so I was
just the man for the job.

The Miata was cranky on that drive and I realized my darling was badly in need of a tune-up
and perhaps a new set of tires. So I didn't pretend
I was competing in the Daytona 500 but took it
easy and arrived in Lauderdale a bit after two

o'clock. I stopped at a Tex-Mex joint for a bowl of
chili hot enough to scorch my uvula and a chilled
bottle of Corona. Then I headed for the address
of the first reference.

It was easy to find. J.P. Lordsley was a men's
clothier on Federal Highway south of Oakland
Park Boulevard. It seemed to be a hip-elegant
shop where Hector might have purchased his fancy duds. I admired his chutzpah in supplying the
name of a clothing store as a bank reference. I
didn't even bother going in the place.

The second required a little more time to locate.
The address of Reuben Hagler was on Copans
Road and I drove past twice before I realized
it was a hole-in-the-wall tucked into a rather
decrepit strip mall half-hidden by dusty palms and
tattered billboards. I parked and found a narrow
door bearing a sign: REUBEN HAGLER, INVESTMENT
ADVISER. It was squeezed between the office of a
chiropodist and a store selling raunchy T-shirts.

I didn't enter. Because sitting out front was a
gunmetal Cadillac De Ville, and I was certain
Mr. Hagler would have a profile like a cleaver.
The Caddie had Michigan plates, and I remembered the number long enough to jot it down on a
matchbook cover with my gold Mont Blanc when
I returned to the Miata.

I drove even more sedately on the trip back
to Palm Beach. I had a lot to ponder. And the
result of all my intense ratiocination? Zilch. I
needed help.

I had hoped to keep Sgt. Al Rogoff out of this
nonsense. After all, I was engaged in nothing

more than a credit investigation, and it was really none of his business. But conviction was growing that possibly, just possibly, Hector Johnson might be involved in the Shirley Feebling homicide.

I drove directly home, garaged the Miata, and went looking for my mother. I found her in the greenhouse, sprinkling can in hand, murmuring to her plants.

"See here, Mrs. McN.," I said, "last night you said Theo Johnson wasn't for me and ascribed that opinion to a vague feeling. Couldn't you be a bit more specific?"

She paused and stared at me thoughtfully. "Archy, I just thought her a little too determined, a little too aggressive."

"Certainly nothing she said."

"Oh no. She was quite polite. It was her manner, the way she carried herself. I suppose you think I'm being foolish."

I swooped to kiss her cheek. "Not at all," I said valiantly. "I think you're a very wise lady."

"She's after you, Archy," mother said, nodding, and that's all she'd say.

Ordinarily, after hearing that a woman was "after me," I might preen. But as I left the greenhouse a cobweb drifted across my forehead, and as I wiped it away I thought of those female spiders who, after the ecstasy of the bedchamber, devoured their mates. I imagine the poor chaps might seek their fate with a curious mixture of passion and helplessness. Just like me.

I went into the main house and was heading

upstairs when Jamie Olson stopped me in the hallway.

"That Mrs. Jane Folsby," he said. "Used to be the Hawkins' live-in."

I nodded.

He handed me a grimy slip of paper. "Got her phone number," he said. "No address, but I hear she's staying with her sister in West Palm Beach."

"Thank you, Jamie," I said gratefully and slipped him a sawbuck. Then I continued up to my nest, stripped off my travel-wrinkled jacket, and phoned Al Rogoff at headquarters.

"Can you give me an hour?" I asked him.

"Five minutes," he said.

"Then I'll talk fast," I promised. "I've got two names and one license plate. I'd like you to check them out with the gendarmes of Troy, Michigan."

"And why should I do that?"

"I would prefer not to say."

"Then I would prefer to reject your request," he said puckishly.

Silence.

"Tell you what," he said finally, "I'm going to make you an offer you can't refuse. I'll do your digging for you, but if and when I get the skinny I won't turn it over until you tell me why you want it. Okay?"

"You drive a hard bargain."

"No, I don't," he said. "I drive a sensible bargain."

"You have a point," I agreed. "Very well, it's a deal."

I gave him the two names, Hector Johnson and Reuben Hagler, and the latter's license tag.

"Johnson?" the sergeant repeated, and I could hear interest quickening in his voice. "Isn't he the guy you're running a credit trace on?"

"That's correct."

"And his daughter was the model for Hawkin's last painting?"

"Yes," I said. "Except for 'Untitled.' "

"Uh-huh," Al said. "All right, I'll see what I can do. Don't expect a report tomorrow, Archy. These things take time. But eventually I'll get back to you."

"A consummation devoutly to be wished," I said.

"When are you going to learn to talk like a human being?" he demanded and hung up.

I showered and dressed informally for my dinner at the Pelican Club with Connie Garcia that evening. I thought I looked rather posh in a jacket of carmine houndstooth check and slacks in what I considered a muted olive plaid. But during the cocktail hour the guv commented that I looked like a sideshow barker, which I thought unnecessarily cruel. But then the old man considers an ascot an affectation so his sartorial opinions really can't be taken seriously.

I arrived early at the Club and put Mr. Pettibone to the test by ordering an Emerald Isle. Again I failed to stump him. He just nodded and said, "Gin, green crème de menthe, bitters," and set to work. The result was quite tasty but packed such a wallop I thought it best to switch to

Labatt's Ale, and I was sipping that when Connie
arrived.

She looked delicious, as usual, but that woman would be ravishing in a cast-iron muumuu.
Fortunately she was wearing a silk jacket and
shorts in a sea foam shade that complemented
her suntan perfectly. Her long black hair was
up in a chignon, and she was the cynosure of all
eyes—including mine. We moved immediately to
the dining room before Leroy's whole suckling pig
was reduced to a glistening skeleton.

Glancing around at the crowd of famished din-
ers I was happy to see that Americans were finally getting off their pernicious health kick. I mean
there was a time when, scared silly by nutrition-
ists, everyone seemed to believe that if they limited their diet to oats, turnips, and other goopy
stuff, they'd live forever. Rubbish! Man does not
live by tofu alone. Go for it, America!

We had roasted pork chops and sweet-and-sour
sauce, minted noodles, and a salad of arugula and
endive with blue cheese dressing. Crusty pum-
pernickel baguettes. Dessert was a passion fruit
tart served with fresh pineapple ice cream. If all
that doesn't put your gastric juices in full flood,
go back to your yogurt and see if I care.

Connie was in a bright, chatty mood that evening. As we gourmandized and steadily emptied
our bottle of cab, she prattled on about Lady
Cynthia Horowitz's activities and the latest Palm
Beach scandals, real and alleged. It was during
dessert that she asked, "Want to hear the latest
rumor?"

"Of course," I said. "Gossip is mother's milk to me."

"Remember your asking me about Hector Johnson? Well, the talk is that he's taking a close interest in Silas Hawkin's widow. In fact, from what I hear, the two of them are what used to be called an item."

"No kidding?" I said, feigning a mild but not excessive interest. "He's pitching her, is he?"

"Apparently," Connie went on. "It started the day after Silas was killed. Now Johnson is at her house almost every day, and they've been seen together all over the place."

"Comforting the bereaved, no doubt."

"Oh sure," she scoffed. "Louise Hawkin also happens to be a well-put-together lady and probably stands to inherit a bundle. Johnson just moved faster than the other middle-aged bachelors in Palm Beach."

"I wonder what the daughter thinks of it."

"Marcia? Oh, she's a ding-a-ling; everyone knows that. About a year ago she was picked up at midnight wandering stark naked down Ocean Boulevard."

"I never heard that one," I said. "Drunk? Or stoned?"

"I don't think so," Connie said. "Just a crazy, mixed-up kid."

"Aren't we all?" I said lightly. "You know what I'd like at the bar?"

"A stomach pump?" she suggested.

"Slivovitz," I said. "To settle the old tumtum."

"Oh God," she said. "I hope you won't start

howling at the moon again."

"I've never done that," I protested. "Have I?"

"Yes," Connie said.

She had recently purchased a new car, a white Ford Escort. Not enough pizzazz for my taste, but Connie loved it. She led the way back to her place and I followed in the Miata.

Connie lives in a high-rise condo on the east shore of Lake Worth. Her one-bedroom apartment is small but trig, and the view from her little balcony is tremendous. It's not really my home-away-from-home, but I had been there many, many times and knew where she kept the Absolut (in the freezer) and that you had to jiggle the handle of the toilet to stop it flushing.

We sprawled on her rattan couch, shoes off, and just relaxed awhile after that humongous meal. We were so comfortable with each other that we weren't bothered by long silences. Connie put on a Spanish tape and we listened to a great chantootsie sobbing. I think her songs were all about love betrayed but my Spanish isn't all that good.

The tape ended and Connie didn't flip it, for which I was thankful. She rose and held out her hand. I clasped it and trailed after her into the bedroom. It was a very feminine boudoir with lace ruffles on the bedspread and French dolls propped on the pillows. Over the bed was a framed poster of the movie *Casablanca*. Connie has a thing for Bogart.

We undressed as slowly and unconcernedly as an old married couple while we wondered if that

passion fruit tart might not have been better with
pistachio ice cream. Very domestic. Then we slid
into bed, and those B-12s didn't let me down.

Connie was a languid lover that night, and it
surprised me; she's usually quite kinetic. But I
was grateful; I was more in the mood for violins
than electric guitars. So it was sweet to hear
murmurs rather than yelps and to embrace softly
rather than jounce.

Then I think we both may have drowsed a bit
because when I glanced at her illuminated bedside clock it was close to two A.M.

"I think I better hit the road," I said in a low
voice.

Connie opened her eyes. "Yes," she said. "Super
evening, Archy. Thank you."

"Thank *you*," I said. "And happy dreams."

She watched me dress. "Who is she, Archy?"
she asked quietly.

I paused with one leg in my slacks and one leg
out, an awkward posture as any guilty lad will
tell you. "Who is whom?" I inquired, expecting the
worst and getting it.

"That woman you had lunch with at Mizner
Park yesterday."

I resumed getting into my trousers. "I suppose
it would be fruitless to deny it," I said.

"Yes," she said steadily, "it would."

"What if I told you she was my cousin?" I said
hopefully.

"Then by actual count she would be the seven-
teenth female cousin you've claimed."

I decided to be absolutely honest—a dreadful mistake. "The lady in question," I said, "is Theodosia Johnson, daughter of Hector. Chauncey Wilson Smythe-Hersforth hopes she will become his fiancée. McNally and Son have been requested by Chauncey's mother to investigate Theodosia's credentials and make certain she is worthy of becoming a member of the Smythe-Hersforth clan."

"And part of your investigation included taking her to lunch in Boca Raton?"

"There is no adequate substitute for a personal interview," I said piously.

Connie turned her head away from me and stared at the wall. "Son," she said, "it's coming out your ears."

I finished dressing and got my pale pink shirttail caught in the zipper of my slacks. I tried to free it to no avail. The tail hanging out looked like—well, you know what it looked like. Connie turned back to watch my struggle. She began to giggle.

"I hope you have to go home like that," she said. "Serves you right."

"Listen," I said furiously, "my luncheon with Miss Johnson was strictly in the line of business. We went to Mizner Park because she had heard of it and wanted to see it. It was a simple business luncheon, and that's all it was. I don't expect you to believe that, but I'd like to remind you that some time ago you and I vowed to have an open relationship. Both of us could see and consort with whomever we wished. Isn't that correct?"

Unexpectedly she amiably agreed. "You're right, Archy. My first reaction, after Mercedes Blair told me of seeing you at the Bistro L'Europe—she was having a pizza at Baci—was to hire a hit man and have you blown away. But that, I decided, was a childish reaction. Archy, I have made up my mind. From now on you are completely free to share lunch or dinner or anything else with whomever you please. And I promise not to be jealous or to attack you physically in retaliation."

"Well put," I said enthusiastically.

"And in return, I expect the same consideration from you."

"Granted," I said. "And gladly."

"Good," she said. "Because tomorrow night I'm having dinner at the Ocean Grand with Binky Watrous."

Outrage detonated. "Binky Watrous!" I cried. "But he's a close friend of mine!"

"I know," Connie said calmly. "And I do believe he hopes to become a close friend of *mine.*"

"I should warn you," I said darkly, "his table manners are not of the most delicate. He's been known to suck his teeth while slurping a beef ragout."

"I think I can endure it," she said, "after seeing you manhandle a stuffed avocado. And on Saturday night I have a movie date with Ferdy Attenborough."

"Ferdy?" I almost shouted. "Another old buddy! Connie, how can you possibly be seen in public with that man? He has an Adam's apple that looks like he swallowed an elbow."

"I think he's charming," she said. "In any event, the choice is mine, is it not?"

"Yes, yes," I said irascibly, finally getting my shirttail freed from the zipper. "But I question your choice. I fear you are doomed to grievous disappointment."

"No problem," she said cheerfully. "There are plenty of others waiting in the wings. Surely you have no objections, do you?"

"Of course not," I said, stiff-upperlipping it.

"As Shakespeare said, all's fair in love and war."

"It was Smedley," I said, "but you're quite right. I hope you have a merry time."

"I intend to," she said evenly.

I did not kiss her a fond good-night.

I drove home in a tumultuous mood. Binky Watrous! Ferdy Attenborough! And perhaps scores of unnamed others waiting in the wings. I was shocked, *shocked*. Naturally I wished Consuela Garcia all the happiness in the world, but the thought of her sharing her felicity with other johnnies was a tad discombobulating. More than a tad if you must know the truth.

I entered my home through the kitchen, making certain to relock the back door. I paused a moment in the kitchen to pick up a cold bottle of St. Pauli Girl from the fridge. I toted it upstairs, moving as quietly as I could on our creaky staircase. Then I was alone in my own chambers—no French dolls on the pillows—but in no mood for sleep. I believe I mentioned previously that I was bewitched by Theo Johnson's conduct. Connie's revelations completed the triumvirate; I was now also bothered and bewildered.

Binky and Ferdy? Good pals, of course, but birdbrains! I found Ms. Garcia's declaration of her intentions totally incomprehensible. I mean we had enjoyed so many jolly times together that I saw no reason for her to seek male companionship elsewhere. How could she possibly find another chap who can match my repertoire of ribald limericks?

I opened my bottle of beer and sat behind my desk. I was still fully clothed and still broody. It just seemed so unfair of Connie, so unjust, so un-everything. Oh, I may have a few minor faults; I admit I am not a perfect swain—but then what man is?

But after a few swigs of brew I began to regain that cool detachment I have always proudly considered an integral part of my character. I frankly acknowledged I was suffering a twinge, a *wee* twinge, of jealousy, which I had heretofore believed myself incapable of feeling.

Even worse, I realized, I was guilty of an unconscionable possessiveness. I expected fidelity from Connie, with no desire to provide faithfulness in return. A rank injustice, obviously, and moreover a distressing breach of civilized behavior. I should be ashamed.

But I wasn't. Because I recognized too clearly my limitations. I mean I could not soar like a condor, could I? Nor play "Turkey in the Straw" on a zither. Nor remain loyal to one woman. In other words, without the vilest form of hypocrisy, I could not be what I was not. It was a quandary.

Amidst all this muzzy meditation I slid a cassette of Cole Porter tunes into my player, clamping earphones to my noggin so as not to disturb my parents whose bedroom was directly below. And as I listened to all that evocative music I tried to distinguish between True Love, romantic love, and affection. Precise definitions escaped me.

And so the night dwindled down as I sat alone, sipping beer, and brooding about love and women and my own incapacity to make a permanent commitment. After a time I realized the poignant songs I was hearing impinged on my perplexities.

How about "Just One of Those Things"?

Or "From This Moment On"?

But the one that summed up my private philosophy most accurately, I mournfully concluded, was "Anything Goes."

9

I awoke late on Friday morning, as you may have surmised, and after a comforting breakfast of kippers and scrambled eggs I arrived at the office a little before noon. I resolutely shelved my personal problems for the nonce. When duty calls, McNally is not one to cup his ear and mutter, "Eh?"

I called the phone number of Mrs. Jane Folsby, provided by Jamie Olson, and waited for seven rings. I was about to hang up when a woman said, somewhat breathlessly, "Hello, hello, hello?"

It was a rich voice, totally unlike Mrs. Folsby's chirp, and I guessed it might be her sister.

"Could I speak to Mrs. Jane Folsby, please?" I said.

"May I ask who's calling?"

When I hear that I'm always tempted to say, "Yes, you may," and then wait. But it didn't seem a ripe time for fraternity house humor, so I merely said, "Archy McNally," and hoped for the best.

"Just a minute," she said.

It was more than a minute but I used the time profitably to light my first English Oval of the day, and what a treat it was. Finally the chirper came on the line.

"Mr. McNally!" she said. "How nice to hear from you. How on earth did you find me?"

"My spies are everywhere," I said. "How are you, Mrs. Folsby?"

"Couldn't be better."

"Glad to hear it. I was sorry to learn you had left the Hawkins."

"Sorry?" she said. "No need for that because I'm not. After Mr. Hawkin passed I knew it was time for me to go."

I waited for more but she didn't seem inclined to offer any additional information.

"Mrs. Folsby," I said, "I have a question I hope you may be able to answer. Do you happen to know where Silas Hawkin purchased his art supplies?"

"Why, certainly," she answered. "He bought all his canvas and paints and things from Grabow's right here in West Palm Beach."

"Grabow's," I repeated. "That's a big help. Thank you so much." I hesitated a moment, wondering if I dared push her. I decided to take the chance. "Tell me, Mrs. Folsby," I said as sympathetically as I could, "what was your reason for leaving the Hawkins? I hope there was no unpleasantness."

"Mr. McNally," she said sharply, "there are certain things a lady doesn't talk about."

I could not, for the life of me, imagine what those things might possibly be. But then I consoled myself with the thought that perhaps I had been associating with an abnormal breed of ladies.

"I understand completely," I said, although I didn't. "Thank you again for your assistance and I wish you the best of good fortune in the future."

"Thank you," she said faintly.

I hung up and finished my cigarette, still mired in the stygian as to what happened at the Hawkin ménage that a lady couldn't or wouldn't talk about. Mrs. Folsby was no mossback, and if she refused to utter a word or even drop a teeny hint it had to be something truly horrendous. To say my curiosity was piqued is putting it mildly.

I looked up Grabow's Art Supplies in the Yellow Pages and made a note of the address, telephone number, and proprietor's name, Luther Grabow. I grabbed up the white linen golf cap I was sporting that day and went downstairs to the Miata, with absolutely no idea why I was jaunting to West Palm to talk to Mr. Grabow. I could claim it was "gut instinct"—that favorite cliché of authors of detective novels. Actually, I had nothing better to do.

I found Grabow's Art Supplies in a freestanding building off Dixie Highway. It looked as big as a warehouse and the interior gave the same impression: row after row of steel racks holding an incredible assortment of everything from Crayolas to jointed six-ft. mannequins of polished wood that could be adjusted to any possible position including, I presumed, obscene.

The man behind the sales counter was seated on a high stool. He was reading a paperback, and I was bemused to note it was a Western. It seemed an odd choice for a clerk in an art supply emporium. He looked up when I approached.

"Could I speak to Mr. Luther Grabow, please," I said.

He inspected me. "I'm Luther Grabow," he said, "but I'm not buying."

"And I'm not selling," I said. "Mr. Grabow, I understand the late Silas Hawkin was a customer of yours."

He continued to stare. "Who told you that?" he demanded.

"His widow," I said, lying without hesitation.

He softened. "Yeah," he said, "he was a customer. That was a helluva thing, him getting knocked off like that. I don't say it just because he was a regular customer but because I admired the guy. He was a real professional and knew exactly what he wanted. Never settled for anything but the best. And a good painter. Not great, mind you, but one of the best around."

"Mrs. Hawkin told me he stretched his own canvases."

"That's right. The most expensive linen I carry."

"Did you sell him the wooden frames?"

"Assembled? Nah. He bought what we call sticks, the wood sides, top and bottom. Dovetail joints. You put together the size and shape you want. Hey, what's your interest in all this?"

He was a wizened little fellow, almost emaciated, with a Vandyke so jetty it looked dyed, and no larger than a merkin. The eyes behind wire-rimmed specs were alert and suspicious.

I handed him a business card and after he had examined it I plucked it away, remembering Sgt. Rogoff's warning. "My firm is settling Mr. Hawkin's estate," I glibly explained. "We have made a very careful inventory of his unsold works, using his own ledger. The one item we've been unable to locate is a painting he was apparently working on at the time of his death. It is carried in his ledger simply as 'Untitled,' but there is no indication of its size or subject matter. We were hoping you might be able to help."

His stare was owlish. "He was working on it when he was killed?"

"The police believe so."

"And it's missing?"

"That's correct."

"Do the cops think the killer took it?"

"A possibility."

He was silent for such a long time I had almost given up hope of gleaning any additional information when he suddenly sighed and began to speak.

"I guess there's no reason I shouldn't tell you," he said, "as long as you keep my name out of it. I don't want to get involved. Okay?"

"Certainly," I said.

"About a month ago Hawkin came in and told me he wanted to try acrylic on wood. It was a technique he had learned in Europe years ago, but then he decided to concentrate on watercolors and oil on canvas. Anyway, he wanted a whole palette of acrylics and a nice piece of wood. I had the primer and colors in stock, but I had to special order the panel from a guy in Boston."

"That's interesting," I said. "What kind of wood was it?"

"Seasoned oak. A beautiful plank. Just perfect. Hawkin was happy."

"Do you recall the dimensions?"

"Sure. Half-inch thick. Eighteen inches by twenty-four inches."

"That's not very large," I commented. "Most of his oil paintings were much larger."

"That's right," he agreed. "But where are you going to get a huge plank of oak that hasn't got a flaw? Not to mention what the damned thing would weigh."

"Yes," I said, "that would be a consideration. So the size Hawkin bought could easily be carried?"

He nodded. "No problem."

"Did Hawkin say anything at all about what he intended to do with it? The subject matter of the painting?"

Owl eyes flickered. "Why, no," he said finally. "He never mentioned a word about it, and I never asked."

I knew he was lying, but there wasn't a thing I could do about it. I thanked him for his kind cooperation and walked out. I was not too displeased with the interview. If Hawkin had painted "Untitled" on that wood panel, his killer could easily have tucked it under one arm and strolled away. I knew Al Rogoff would be interested in what I had learned but decided not to inform him pro tem, figuring I might need it in the future for a bargaining chip. Such are the ways of the world.

I drove back to the McNally Building, and my train of thought (really a trolley car) was curious. It may have been due to seeing all those artists' supplies, but I suddenly recalled Sargent's portrait of Madam X. Totally unlike Theodosia Johnson, of course, but I could visualize her in that black velvet gown with the marvelous décolletage.

Do you think I need professional help?

I am attempting to make this account as honest as possible so I must confess that after I returned to my office I had contemplated taking a short nap. But it was not to be, for propped against my stained coffee mug (POVERTY SUCKS) was a message stating that Mrs. Louise Hawkin had phoned and desired I return her call, which I did.

"Mr. McNally," she said briskly, "Hector Johnson, a good friend, tells me you are a real estate agent."

"Not a licensed broker," I said hastily, "but I do work closely with our Real Estate Department." That was true enough; I went to all their parties and frequently participated in their office pools.

"Since Si died," she went on, "I have decided to put our property here on the market, and I'd like to discuss it with you."

"Of course," I said, having little doubt I could sustain my impersonation of a realtor. "What time would be convenient for you?"

"Why, right now if you can make it," she said. "I intend to be in all afternoon."

"Excellent," I said. "Be there within the hour. Thank you for calling, Mrs. Hawkin."

Ordinarily the Real Estate Department of McNally & Son does not handle residential properties but is limited to recommending to our clients the purchase or sale of commercial parcels and raw land. But occasionally they were called upon to broker the sale of the homes of Palm Beach residents who had gone to the great Gold Coast in the sky, and so they had all the printed forms required for listing.

I picked up a file of the necessary bumf and headed southward in the Miata, ruminating on Mrs. Hawkin's mention of Hector Johnson as "a good friend." That certainly gave credence to what Connie Garcia had told me about Louise and Hector being an "item." The pot was beginning to boil, I reflected, and the bubbling delighted me. I enjoy the mess *other* people make of their lives, don't you?

And when I pealed the chimes at the Hawkin home, who should open the door but Hector Johnson himself. Surprise! He looked as elegantly jaunty as he had the first time we met and his hearty assurance hadn't deserted him.

"Archy!" he shouted, grasping my hand and pulling me into the house. "Glad you could make it! Good to see you again!"

In contrast to that enthusiasm, my response must have sounded like a mumble but, in any event, I don't believe he was listening. He led me into the Florida room where Louise Hawkin was half-reclining on a white wicker couch. She was wearing lounging pajamas in a garish flowered pattern, and since she was gripping a tall drink I didn't offer to shake hands.

"Mrs. Hawkin," I said, "I'm happy we meet again. I hope you're well, ma'am."

She gave me a glazed smile. "Tip-top," she said.

Not completely smashed, I reckoned, but about halfway there. I mean she spoke intelligently but slowly and carefully as if fearful of slurring. And her movements were also slow, careful, and seemingly planned beforehand as if she might suddenly spill her drink or knock over a lamp.

"Darling," Hector Johnson said, and I chalked that up, "you and I are indulging. Surely we can offer our guest the same opportunity. Archy, we're working on gin and tonics. How does that sound?"

"Just right," I said.

"Shall I mix it?" Hector asked the hostess.

"I'll get it," she said thickly, set her glass aside, and lurched to her feet. "Besides," she added, "I have to make wee-wee."

Johnson laughed uproariously. I managed a strained smile. She walked from the room in slow motion, and Hector and I sat facing each other in matching armchairs. Then he launched into one of the strangest conversational gambits I had ever heard.

"What do you think about luck?" he demanded.

I blinked, then stared at him, wondering if he

might be attempting an elaborate joke. But he was quite serious. "Nice to have," I said lamely.

"When you need it," he continued, *"desperately* need it, it's gone. When you don't give a damn—win or lose, who cares?—there it is. Funny thing, huh?"

"Yes," I said, thinking, what's *with* this man?

"Real estate agents get six percent from the seller," he said, looking at me thoughtfully. "Am I correct?"

"Generally," I said. "But on commercial properties and undeveloped land it's usually ten percent."

"Uh-huh," he said, still looking at me. "I was the one who told Louise to give you a call."

There was no mistaking his meaning, but I wasn't going to help him. Let him spell it out.

"You ever pay a finder's fee?" he asked casually.

"It's not unheard-of," I said.

"Didn't think it was," he said with a wolfish grin, then concluded swiftly with, "Keep it in mind," as Louise Hawkin came back into the room carrying my drink.

I sampled it cautiously. Heavy on the gin, light on the tonic. If she had been drinking those bombs all afternoon it was no wonder her smile was glazed.

"Mrs. Hawkin," I said, "I presume the property will not be legally yours until your late husband's will is settled."

"No," she said, "it's mine now. The title is in my name."

"Louise is a lady of property," Johnson put in. "But that doesn't pay for the liverwurst, does it, darling? Land-poor is what it's called."

No matter how impeccably he was dressed, it was a louche thing to say, was it not? I mean his words and tone seemed calculated to belittle the widow, reduce her to the role of a hapless mendicant.

"Did you have a specific asking price in mind?" I asked her.

She glanced at Hector Johnson.

"Two million five," he said promptly. "For everything."

"Suppose I send out a professional appraiser," I suggested. "No cost to you. He or she will know the value of comparable parcels in the neighborhood and will be able to make an informed estimate of how your property should be priced to sell quickly."

"Two million five," Johnson repeated. "Asking, of course. Louise will be willing to negotiate. Won't you, sweetie?"

"What?" she said. "Oh, sure. Negotiate."

"Suppose I leave these listing applications," I said, placing my folder on an end table. "Have your attorney review them before you sign. They're standard boilerplate by which you grant McNally and Son the right to represent you in the sale of your home for a specified period of time at a specified percentage of the selling price."

"Honey," Louise Hawkin said anxiously, "what do you think?"

"Sounds legit," he told her. "I'll take a look at the contract."

"Mrs. Hawkin," I said, "if your home is sold, do you intend to remain in the Palm Beach area?"

"Of course she's going to stay," Hector answered. "Get rid of this white elephant, use part of the proceeds to buy or lease a smaller place, maybe on the beach, and have enough left over to invest in something that'll provide her with a guaranteed income. Doesn't that make sense?"

The moment he used the phrase "guaranteed income," my opinion of his financial acumen plunged to subzero. Dear old dad had taught me years ago that there is no such thing as a guaranteed income. As pop said, "Who guarantees the guarantor?" Scary, huh?

"Whatever Mrs. Hawkin wishes," I said. "It's her future happiness that's at stake, and she must decide how it best may be achieved."

"Dear Hector," she said, gazing at him blearily, "I don't know what I'd do without your advice."

He rose, porky face glowing, and seated himself on the couch next to her. He picked up her hand and kissed the knuckles. "Just like Archy said, baby," he crooned, "your happiness is all that counts."

I must tell you I felt acutely uncomfortable. I was invited, but I had the impression of having barged into an intimate and probably semi-drunken tête-à-tête. I was certain that after I departed they would dance the horizontal hula-hula.

That was hardly my business or my concern. What did trouble me was the role of Svengali that Hector Johnson seemed to have assumed.

It was hard to believe that in the short period since her husband's murder Louise Hawkin
had succumbed to the man's forceful charm and
blandishments.

Unless, of course, their affair had started
before Silas Hawkin's death. That could be easily
explained. Hector's daughter had posed for the artist. It would not be extraordinary if he had met and
become friendly with the Hawkin family. Perhaps
what I had just witnessed was a relationship that
had existed not for days but for months. One never
knows, do one?

By then I'd had just about enough of the Hawkin
and Johnson families for one day, thank you, and
was looking forward to a quiet evening at home. I
intended to retire to my digs after dinner and play
my favorite Al Jolson cassette while bringing my
journal up to date. I might even have a small marc
to help me forget that as I labored, Connie Garcia
and Binky Watrous were dining together. I hoped
their raspberry soufflé would collapse. A savage
desire, I admit, but surely understandable.

Unfortunately I was no sooner ensconced behind
my desk, marc in fist and Jolson singing "Swanee,"
than my phone buzzed. When it's an outside call it
rings; when it's an interior call it buzzes. Don't ask
me why. The caller was Jamie Olson downstairs
in the kitchen.

"Woman parked outside," he reported. "Wants
to talk to you."

"What woman?"

"Won't say."

"Did you ask her to come in?"

"Won't come in."

"What's she driving?" I asked, dreaming it might be Connie's white Ford Escort and that she had had a squabble with Binky and had sought me out for comforting. I would, I decided, provide it generously.

"A black Jeep Cherokee," Jamie Olson said.

I sighed. "I'll be right down."

It was parked on the graveled turnaround in front of our garage. The door on the passenger side was opened as I approached. I peered within. Marcia Hawkin. She was wearing a soiled cotton trench coat buttoned up to the neck. I wondered what she wore underneath—if anything. Right about then, I figured, Jolson was singing "I'm Sitting on Top of the World." I wasn't.

"Marcia," I said. "How nice. Won't you come in?"

"No," she said and beckoned.

I slid in but left the door ajar a few inches in case I had to make a hasty exit. If she was as dotty as Connie had implied, a fast retreat might become necessary. I know there are times when my father is convinced he spawned a dunderhead, but there are also times when I have the wit to calculate possible dangers and take the proper precautions.

She didn't turn to look at me but stared straight ahead through the windshield. "She's selling our home," she announced. "The studio. Everything. Even my bed. Can she do that?"

I thought it best to feign ignorance, hoping she was not aware of my visit that afternoon.

"Your mother?" I asked.

"Stepmother," she corrected me angrily. "Can she sell the house?"

"Is the title in her name?"

"Yes."

"Then she can dispose of it any way she wishes."

"Shit!" she said furiously. "I love that place. Where am I going to live?"

"Surely she'll buy or lease another dwelling. Perhaps smaller but just as attractive and comfortable."

"I don't want another," she said. "I'm not going to live with her anymore. Never, never, never!"

She seemed so distraught I hesitated to say anything but felt I had to express sympathy for her plight. "Do you have family or friends you could stay with?" I asked.

"I told you I have no one. It's all his fault."

"Whose fault?"

"Hector Johnson. That bitch's father."

The word didn't shock me so much as her tone. Pure venom.

"Marcia," I said quietly, "sometimes things happen we feel are outrageous. The best thing to do is accept with resignation and as much grace as we can muster."

Finally she turned to look at me. "That's bullshit," she said. "I'm not going to meekly accept what's happening. I've done that all my life—accept. But I'm not going to do it anymore. Believe me, I know what's going on."

"What's going on?" I asked her.

"That's for me to know and you to find out," she answered, a response so childish I felt like weeping. "You know that saying: Don't get mad, get even? That's what I'm going to do—get even."

"I hope you won't do anything foolish," I ventured.

Her laugh was a cackle. "They're the fools," she said. "Not me. They'd like to put me away—did you know that?"

I was overwhelmed by her mysteries. "Who wants to put you away? For what? And where?"

"I'm as normal as you are," she said hotly, which I thought was an artless comparison. "You're sure she can sell the house?"

"She can," I repeated, "if the title is in her name."

"That's all I wanted to know," she said. "You can go now."

This abrupt, impolite dismissal was a minor affront from an obviously disturbed young woman, and I was happy to make my escape. I started to climb out of the Jeep when she suddenly yanked me back and kissed me on the lips, her tongue darting.

"There!" she cried. "See?"

I got out and before I could turn and close the door she had started up and pulled away with engine roar and a spurt of gravel. I stood there and watched the Cherokee make a wild turn onto Ocean Boulevard and speed away.

I went back upstairs to finish my marc and hear Jolson singing "Baby Face." I worked steadily on my journal until eleven-thirty. Then I closed up shop and, feeling brain dead, prepared for bed. But the aggravations of that wretched day had not yet ended.

My phone rang. Not buzzed but rang.

"Hi, luv," Connie Garcia said cheerily. "I'm home safe and sound. All locked up, bolted, and chained. I knew you'd want to know."

"Yes," I said.

"I hate to tell you this, Archy, but I had a wonderful time tonight."

"Why should you hate to tell me?" I said, gritting the old bicuspids. "I'm happy you enjoyed yourself."

"And Binky," she said, giggling. "I also enjoyed him."

It was too much.

"He's such good company," she prattled on. "Why didn't you tell me he can do birdcalls."

"Oh yes," I said. "His imitation of a loon is especially realistic."

"And tomorrow night it's Ferdy Attenborough," she went on blithely. "We're going to La Vieille Maison in Boca."

"How nice," I said stiffly. "Do try the quail with grapes."

"I intend to," she said. "It'll be a welcome change from cheeseburgers at the Pelican Club. Actually, I called to tell you that you were exactly right. You and I should become more socially active. Separately. I mean we should both date other people. Our relationship was becoming much too restrictive. Don't you agree?"

It was impossible to disagree since I had been

warbling that tune for years. "As long as you're happy," I said.

"Oh, I am," she said. "Deliriously. I hope you don't mind, Archy."

"Mind?" I said loftily. "Of course not. Why on earth should I mind?"

"I'm glad to hear you say that. On Monday Wes Trumbaugh is taking me to a dinner-dance at his club."

"Wes Trumbaugh?" I screamed. "Connie, that man is the biggest lecher in Palm Beach!"

"Oooo," she said, "that does sound fascinating. Good-night, Archy, and sleep well."

She hung up. Sleep well? Hah! I fiercely punched my pillows twice, once for Binky, once for Ferdy. Then I added a third for Wes Trumbaugh.

10

I would prefer not to write about that weekend. I would prefer it never happened. I would prefer the world went directly from Friday night to Monday morning.

But unfortunately it did occur: two ghastly days during which I made a complete ass of myself and am still apologizing for my abominable conduct.

I shall not detail all my disgraceful actions during those forty-eight hours. Suffice to say that I ate too much, drank too much, smoked too much, laughed too loudly, and told pointless jokes. My most shameful memory is standing on a table at the Pelican Club at two A.M. trying to recite "When Lilacs Last in the Dooryard Bloom'd" to a jeering audience as hammered as I.

I awoke on Monday wondering if it might be possible to commit hara-kiri with my Swiss Army knife. An ax-murderer, having dispatched wife,

158

children, in-laws, and the family dog, always
tells the police, "The devil made me do it." I
would have liked to make that defense but my
pride would not allow it. No, my beastly behavior
was completely the fault of yrs. truly, Archibald
McNally.

I usually scrape my jowls with a conventional
single-edged razor but that morning, being somewhat unsteady, I opted for an electric shaver,
fearing I might nick the old jugular. It was only
after drinking a quart of cold water and a pint of
hot coffee that I started to regain a slight semblance of normality.

I arrived at the office before noon, determined that henceforth I would forswear ciga-
rettes, strong drink, and ham hocks. I sat at my
desk, absentmindedly lighted an English Oval,
and jumpstarted my groggy cerebrum. The result
of my lucubrations? The murder of Silas Hawkin
was really none of my business. The murder of
Shirley Feebling was really none of my business.
My job was merely to investigate the bona fides
of Theodosia Johnson.

Yet I could not ignore a conviction that the
two homicides and my assignment were inextri-
cably mixed. One loose end that might lead to
untangling this snarl was Reuben Hagler, the
self-styled investment adviser of Fort Lauderdale.
Another was Marcia Hawkin's fury and implied
threats. A third was the don't-give-a-damn attitude of Madam X. And the fourth was her
father's patent attempt to cozy up to the Widow
Hawkin.

This logical recap included all of my questions but provided none of the answers. So I decided to forgo logic, do a bit of improv riffing and see what happened. Hey, if you can't get a little fun from your job, seek employment elsewhere. Thus spaketh A. McNally.

Pinky Schatz. Do you remember the name?

She was the confidante of Shirley Feebling and had the misfortune of finding that poor woman's corpse. I was sure Pinky had been interrogated by the Fort Lauderdale police, but sometimes a material witness doesn't tell the cops everything he or she knows, not in an effort to impede the investigation but because of a personal motive. Or the witness doesn't fully comprehend what observations and/or knowledge are germane. In any event, I reckoned it might help my own inquiry if I met Ms. Schatz and heard her story personally.

She was not listed in the Fort Lauderdale or Pompano Beach telephone directories. She and Shirl had been co-workers so I called the topless car wash. The man who answered had a growly voice, and I guessed him to be Jake, the woolly mammoth.

"Yeah?" he said.

"Could I speak to Pinky Schatz, please."

"She don't work here no more."

"Do you have her present home address?" I asked. "This is the McNally Insurance Company. We have a check for her in payment for damages her car suffered in a recent collision, but our letter was returned to us marked 'Not at this address.' I imagine she's moved and neglected to inform us."

"I don't know where she's living," he said. "Try the Leopard Club on Federal. She's dancing there."

He hung up before I could thank him.

I had heard of the Leopard Club. It was said to be an upscale and pricey nude dancing establishment where the performers mingled freely with the patrons, most of whom were suits carrying calfskin attaché cases. I had never been tempted to visit since the idea of sipping an overpriced aperitif while a naked young woman gyrated on my table seemed to me a betrayal of Western Civilization.

However, I resolutely conquered my squeamishness and set out to find Pinky Schatz. But first I drove the Miata to my garage in West Palm Beach where I left it for a tune-up, eschewing new tires until my checking account was off life-support and breathing normally. I was given a loaner, a black three-year-old Buick LeSabre. It was rather sedate for my taste but certainly less noticeable and less likely to be remembered than my jazzy little chariot.

Two hours later I entered the Leopard Club, after passing a tenner to the muscular sentry at the door. A score of men, mostly middle-aged and solemn of mien, sat at small tables and watched nude dancers on a brightly lighted stage oscillating more or less in rhythm to music from overhead loudspeakers.

There were a half-dozen dancers, each au

naturel except for a single garter about one thigh. Tucked into the elastic strip were folded bills: ones, fives, tens, a few twenties: tips from appreciative customers. When the music ended, the dancers left the stage and came down to cajole patrons into paying an added fee for a solo dance atop their table. Meanwhile the music started again, and a new set of dancers pranced onto the stage and began to demonstrate their flexibility.

I had been approached by a surly waitress, fully clothed, who took my order for a bottle of Heineken. She brought it almost immediately along with a tab for ten dollars I was apparently expected to pay instanter. But before I did, I asked if Pinky Schatz was present.

"Yeah," the waitress said, "the fatso redhead on the stage. You want I should send her over when the set ends?"

"Please," I said, paid for the beer, gave her a five-dollar tip, and glanced sorrowfully at my rapidly shrinking wallet.

The music paused briefly, the dancers left the stage, a new squad took over. The "fatso redhead" came sashaying toward my table. She had the loveliest silicone I've ever seen.

"Hi, honey," she said, beaming. "You asked for me?"

"If you're Pinky Schatz."

She nodded. "That's right, and I bet you want a table dance. It's my specialty."

"No, no," I said hastily. "Just a little conversation."

"Oh-ho," she said. "Well, that's okay, too. You can tell me how your wife doesn't understand you. Can I have a drink?"

"Of course. Whatever you want."

"Hey, Mabel," she called to the waitress. "My usual." Then she leaned to me. "They'll charge you for booze," she whispered, "but it's just iced tea."

I liked her. She was a large, vital woman with a ready smile and a hearty laugh. Marvelous skin tone. Also, she had a tattoo of an American flag on her left bicep, and that reminded me of you know who.

Her drink was served and we lifted our glasses to each other.

"You're a tall one," she said. "I like that. How come you asked for me?"

"You were a close friend of Shirley Feebling, weren't you?"

Her face hardened and she started to rise. I put out a hand to stop her.

"Please don't leave," I begged. "I'm not a cop, and this is very important to me."

She sat down slowly. It was odd conversing at a minuscule table with a rosy, naked woman, but I swear to you I wasn't distracted. Charmed, as a matter of fact, but not unduly aroused.

"Who are you?" she demanded.

I had devised a scam on the drive down from Palm Beach. It was a cruel deception but I could think of no alternative.

"My name is Chauncey Smythe-Hersforth," I said. "Did Shirl ever mention me?"

Her big eyes grew even bigger. "Oh gawd," she said. "You're the guy who wanted to marry her."

I nodded.

Her hand fell softly on my arm. "I'm sorry, Chauncey," she said. "Really sorry."

"Thank you," I said. "Listen, I need your help. The police seem to be getting nowhere on this, and I want the guy who did it found and sent to the chair. You can understand that, can't you?"

"Sure," she said. "Me, too. Shirl was my best friend, and a sweeter girl never lived."

"Did she ever say anything about someone following her or annoying her or making threatening phone calls? Anything like that?"

"I told the cops. She said that for the last few days—this was before she was killed—she kept seeing this Cadillac. It was around all the time while she was at work and at home and when she went shopping."

"A Cadillac? Did she describe the model and color?"

"Not the model. She said it was a funny color, like bronzy."

"Did she get a look at the driver?"

"Not a good clear look. She said he had a hatchet face. She said she thought she had seen him before in the pizza joint near the car wash."

"Pinky, have you any idea who she was talking about? Did you ever meet a hatchet-faced man who drives a car like that?"

She looked at me steadily, her stare unwavering, unblinking. It shocked me because when people are about to lie, they put on a look like that.

It is not true that liars are shifty-eyed, blink frequently, or turn their gaze away. Experienced liars hope to prove their honesty by a steady, wide-eyed look expressing complete probity.

"Why, no," Pinky Schatz said. "I never met a man like that. I have no idea who he could be. That's what I told the cops."

I thanked her, slipped her fifty dollars, and left the Leopard Club. I was depressed. Not so much by the sadness of that joint—lonely, longing men and bored, contemptuous women—but by what I considered the blatant falsehoods of Pinky Schatz. It wasn't difficult to imagine the motive for her lies. It was fear.

It was latish when I arrived back in Palm Beach and it seemed silly to return to my office and stare at the walls. So I went for a swim, removed the ocean's residue with a hot shower and loofah glove, and dressed for what I devoutly hoped would be an uneventful evening.

And it was until about nine-thirty. I had gone up to my lair after dinner and was recording in my journal the mise-en-scène at the Leopard Club when my phone did what phones are supposed to do. I wasn't sure I wanted to pick it up, fearing it might be Connie calling to tell me what a frabjous evening she was having with Wes Trumbaugh.

But I answered. It wasn't Connie. It was Theodosia Johnson.

"Hey, Archy," she said, "how would you like to buy a girl a drink?"

"Love to," I said. "Do you have any particular girl in mind?"

"Yes," she said, laughing, "this girl. Daddy is using the car tonight so you'll have to come get me."

I hesitated. It was a rather dicey situation. After all, she was practically betrothed to the Smythe-Hersforth scion and he *was* a client of McNally & Son. I decided to express my fears.

"What about Chauncey?" I asked her. "Mightn't he object?"

"He doesn't *own* me," she said coldly. "Besides he just dropped me off after dinner and is on his way home to mommy."

"Be there in a half-hour," I said. "Will casual rags be acceptable?"

"Pj's will be acceptable," she said.

What a sterling woman!

I pulled on a silvery Ultrasuede sport jacket over a pinkish Izod and flannel bags, thrust my bare feet into black penny mocs, and paused long enough to swab the phiz with Obsession. Then I dashed.

I pulled up outside the Johnsons' condo and Theo exited immediately, pausing just long enough to double-lock her door. Then she came bouncing down to the LeSabre.

"Archy," she said, "how many cars do you own?"

"Just one. But the Miata's in the garage for an enema. Theo, you look smashing!"

It was the truth. She was dressed to the tens in honey-colored silk jacket and pantaloons. Her only jewelry was a choker of braided gold, and if the Chinless Wonder had donated that he had more taste than I had given him credit for.

"Thank you, dear," she said and leaned forward to kiss my cheek. "Yummy," she said. "Obsession?"

"Correct, supernose," I said. "You know everything, and it's scary. We're going to the Pelican Club. Nothing fancy, but the drinks are huge and if you want to sing 'Mother Machree' no one will call the cops."

"Great," she said. "My kind of joint."

That phrase she used—"My kind of joint"—jangled the old neurons. It sounded like something Pinky Schatz might say. But from the soon-to-be fiancée of Chauncey Wilson Smythe-Hersforth?

I mean we all make critical judgments, usually immediate, of people we meet, based on their appearance, speech, behavior. We instantly decide: He's a nudnick. She's a cipher. And so forth. Sometimes these initial impressions are modified or even totally revised after closer acquaintance, but it's amazing how often first reactions prove to be accurate.

I had thought Theo Johnson to be a well-bred young lady, independent, emancipated, and rather freewheeling in the morality department. But her saying "My kind of joint" made me wonder if there was a coarser side to her nature I had not heretofore recognized. Does that make me a snob? I thought you had already determined that.

In any event, my confusion grew. I simply could not categorize this woman; she was truly Madam X. Her taste in clothes and makeup, her table manners and social graces seemed faultless. And, of course, her physical beauty was nonpareil. I think perhaps what I found most inexplicable was her tattoo. It was like finding a hickey on the neck of the Mona Lisa.

"Where did you and Chauncey dine?" I asked as we sped westward.

"Cafe L'Europe."

"Excellent. I hope you had the veal."

"I did," she said. "Archy, I think you and I enjoy the same things. Don't you agree?"

"Oh yes!" I said. "Yes, yes, yes!" And she laughed.

Jolly Pandemonium was the leitmotiv of the Pelican Club that night. It was at its noisiest and smokiest. Dart players were darting, table-hoppers were hopping, and everyone was guzzling happily and laughing up a typhoon.

"Uh-huh," Theo said, glancing around, "I belong here. Is Chauncey a member?"

" 'Fraid not."

"Didn't think so," she said with a wry-crisp smile. "Not his scene. He's such a fuddy-duddy. I mean he still reads newspapers. Can you believe it?"

I made no comment but led her into the dining area. Lights were dimmed, dinner was no longer being served, but there were a few couples lingering, holding hands across tables and looking into each other's eyes for promise. I claimed my favorite corner spot, and we were no sooner seated than Priscilla came sauntering over.

"You know the reputation of this man?" she asked Theo.

Madam X actually giggled. "I can imagine," she said.

"No, you can't," Pris said. "Whenever there's a full moon he gets long hair on the backs of his hands."

"Love it," Theo said, tilted her head back and bayed a long "Wooooo!" at the ceiling.

"Just what I need," Priscilla said. "A couple of loonies."

"Enough of your sass," I said. "We may be loonies but we're thirsty loonies. Theo?"

"Wine," she said promptly.

"Pinot Grigio?"

"Just right."

"A bottle, please," I said to Pris. "And try not to crumble the cork."

"Keep it up, buster," she said, "and I'll crumble *your* cork."

She strolled into the bar area, and Theo laughed. "You've known her a long time, Archy?"

"Years. Her family runs the place. Brother Leroy is our chef. Daddy Simon is bartender-manager. And her mom Jasmine is our housekeeper and den-mother. The Pettibones made the Pelican Club a winner. We were going down the drain before they took over."

"I hope you'll ask me here again."

I didn't quite know how to reply to that, but I was saved by Priscilla serving our wine. Chilled just right and with a slight flowery aroma.

Theo sipped. "Loverly," she said. "Thank you for coming to my rescue. I was in the doldrums."

"I've visited the doldrums," I said. "Miserable

place. It's near the pits, isn't it?"

"Too near," she said, not smiling.

We drank our wine slowly, comfortable with each other. What a selfish delight it was to be in the company of such a beautiful woman. I tried not to stare at her but it was difficult to resist. "Feasting your eyes" is the cliché, and mine were famished.

"I know so little about you," I mentioned casually, trying not to sound like a Nosy Parker. "Tell me."

"Not a lot to tell," she said just as casually. "Besides, I hate to look back, don't you? The past is such a drag. The future is much more exciting."

She had neatly finessed me, and I feared that if I asked specific questions she'd think me a goof.

"All right," I said, "let's talk about your future. Have you decided to become Chauncey's one-and-only?"

She gave me a mocking half-smile. "Let's talk about it later," she said. "Right now I'm with you."

"For which I give thanks to Aphrodite," I said. "A.k.a. Venus. The goddess of love and beauty."

"It's skin-deep," she said.

"Beauty?" I asked. "Or love?"

"Both."

That seemed to me a rather harsh judgment, but I had no desire to argue.

"And what about your lady?" she asked me.

"We have an open relationship. Tonight she's at a dinner-dance with another chap."

"And you're jealous?"

"Of course not."

"Liar, liar, pants on fire!" she said with a boomy laugh. "Tell me, Archy, what do you do when you're not real-estating."

"Eat, drink, smoke, swim in the ocean, play tennis, golf, and poker, watch polo, read trash, listen to pop singers, occasionally attend the theatre, opera, ballet, charity bashes, and private shindigs, buy clothes and trinkets, write to old friends, party with new friends, and sleep. I think that about covers it."

"Not quite," she said. "You didn't mention sex."

"I didn't want to offend your sensibilities."

"What makes you think I have any?" And before I could come up with a saucy rejoinder, she said, "You know what I'd like to do after we finish this bottle of wine?"

"Have another?"

"No," she said, "take a walk on the beach. Could we do that?"

"Of course," I said. "Sorry I can't provide a full moon to prove my hands don't grow hair. There's just a sliver."

"It'll be enough. Can I take off my sandals, roll up my pants, and wade in the surf?"

"Whatever turns you on."

She looked at me with a crooked smile. "I asked Chauncey the same thing earlier this evening. He said the water might be too cold, I might cut my bare feet on shells, and the Beach Patrol might pick us up for loitering."

"Well, yes," I said. "All those things could happen."

"But you don't care, do you, Archy?"

"Not much."

She reached across the table to clasp my hand. "I told you how alike we are," she said. "I wish you were the marrying kind."

"What kind is that?"

"Chauncey," she said, almost bitterly. "Let's finish this divine wine and go."

And so we did. When I signed the tab, Priscilla looked about to make sure Theo was out of earshot and then whispered, "You're asking for trouble, son."

"What do you mean by that?" I demanded.

"I just *know*," she said and moved swiftly away.

I drove back to the shore and parked the Buick in the McNally driveway. Hand in hand, Theo and I trotted across Ocean Boulevard and stepped down the rickety wooden stairway to the sea. That splinter of moon was obscured by clouds, and an easterly breeze was warm and clammy. We didn't care. It was the wine, I suppose, and the joy of being alone on the beach at midnight.

Theo kicked off her sandals, rolled the cuffs of her pantaloons above her knees, and strode into the milky surf, kicking her way through. I stood on dry land, bemused, and watched her cavort. She seemed suddenly released, laughing, bending to scrub her face with cupped handfuls of saltwater. I wouldn't have been a bit surprised if she stripped starkers and plunged in. But she didn't.

I walked back to the wall, sat on the sand, lighted a cigarette. I had finished it before she came gamboling out, flicking glittery droplets from her fingertips and caroling, "Super, super, super!" She plumped down beside me and asked for my handkerchief to dry sodden strands of her chestnut hair. There wasn't much moonglow, but I could see her face was shining.

"Was that what you wanted?" I asked.

"It was what I needed," she said, and then gestured toward the dark, rolling sea. "What's out there, Archy?"

"Water. Lots of it."

"No, I mean eventually."

"Eventually? Africa. Around Morocco, I'd guess."

"Let's go."

"Tonight?"

"Whenever."

Her voice was light but I felt she was serious. Certainly half-serious.

She turned, took my face between her cool palms, kissed me, drew away. She leaned forward, hugged her knees. "Do I scare you?" she said.

"Of course not," I lied valiantly, because to tell you the truth she did. A little. There was a wildness in her, a willfulness that was daunting.

"Do you think I'm pretty?" she asked suddenly.

"More than pretty," I said. "Lovely. Beautiful."

"Yes," she said, nodding, "I know. And I thought it would bring me happiness but it hasn't. Like an actress who knows, just *knows* she has a special talent. But she can't get an acting job so it doesn't do her a damned bit of good. Just goes to waste. Do you understand what I'm saying, Archy?"

"Yes."

"I've got the looks and the body," she went on. "It's not conceit; I just know. But things didn't work out the way I thought they would. Bad luck, I guess."

"Your father spoke to me about luck," I told her. "He said, in effect, that when you need it desperately, it doesn't appear. But when you don't give a damn you have all the luck in the world."

"Did daddy say that? Well, he should know. Take off your clothes."

"What?"

"Take off your clothes," she repeated, unbuttoning her jacket.

"All right," I said.

I must inform you that anyone who attempts to make love on a sandy beach soon learns the meaning of true grit. But we managed, and we were so enthusiastic, so joyously *vocal* that I suspect both of us were tempted to wonder "Was it as good for me as it was for you?"

I shall not fully describe the scene—dying moon, scudding clouds, sultry wind—because I've always felt love scenes are best played on bare stages. There may be scenery artfully arranged but it becomes invisible when the butterfly flutters—as it did that night.

And then, triumphant, we both laughed. At our own madness, I imagine. It was a sweet moment, but brief. Because as we nakedly embraced, Theo murmured, "Tonight at dinner I told Chauncey I'd marry him. That's why he hurried home, to tell mommy the news."

"Oh," I said, which I admit was not a very cogent reaction. But I was stunned.

"Do you blame me?" she asked softly.

"Blame?" I said. "Of course not. What right do I have to blame you? It's your life and you must live it in whatever fashion you decide. Believe me, darling, I wish you all the happiness in the world."

She made no reply but rolled away from me and slowly began to dress. I did the same, and we made ourselves presentable in silence. Finally I stood shakily and helped her to her feet. We hugged tightly a moment. I was affected, thinking it a final farewell.

"Thank you for tonight," I said huskily. "The only word for it is memorable. I know we shan't be seeing much of each other from now on."

She drew away far enough to tap my cheek lightly with her fingertips. "Silly boy," she said.

I don't believe we exchanged a dozen words during the drive back to her condo. When we arrived I saw a white Lincoln Town Car parked outside, next to a gunmetal Cadillac De Ville.

"Daddy's home," Theo announced. "The Lincoln is ours. The Caddie belongs to a friend."

"Oh?" I said. "He's got Michigan plates. Down for a visit?"

"No, he moved here recently. Just hasn't switched to a Florida license yet."

I didn't push it.

She gave me a parting kiss. "Thank you, Archy," she said. "Fabulous night." She whisked out of the car. I waited until she was safely inside, then I

headed homeward. I was not as fatigued as you
might expect. I wasn't eager to dance a polka, but
I was more replete than exhausted.

It was too late to shower since the gurgling of
the drain would disturb my parents. I did my best
with a washcloth to capture the vagrant grains
of sand that remained on my carcass. Then I
brushed the old choppers and donned a pair of
silk pajama shorts emblazoned with multicolored
crowns and scepters. Fitting, for I felt like royalty
that night. Don't ask me why.

I waited patiently for sleep to come, knowing it
would not take long. Meanwhile I did some heavy
brooding on The Case of Madam X. I was not so
concerned with the murders of Silas Hawkin and
Shirley Feebling as I was with the unaccountable
personality of the lady herself. I simply could not
solve her.

Did I know any more about her than I did when
our evening began? Yes, I did, but what I had
learned was disquieting. Her character seemed
so complex, with nooks and crannies I had not
yet glimpsed, let alone explored.

Surely you've seen matryoska. (I think that's
the correct spelling.) They're Russian nesting
dolls. Remove the top half of the largest wooden
doll and within is a smaller. Remove the top of
that one and an even smaller doll is within. This
continues for five or six dolls. You finally come to
the last, which is solid wood and no larger than
an unshelled peanut.

That's how I thought of Theodosia Johnson. She
was a series of nesting women, and I had hardly

begun to get down to the solid core. I was slowly unlayering her, and the awful thought occurred to me that when I finally uncovered the penultimate woman, there might be nothing within.

I could not forget her final comment on the beach after I had suggested our just completed coupling would be the last. "Silly boy," she said, an obvious implication that her affiancing to Chauncey Wilson Smythe-Hersforth, or even her marriage to that bubblehead, need not bring our fun and games to a screeching halt. A very amoral attitude, and it disturbed me.

I mean I am not a holier-than-thou johnny. Far from it. But her insouciance was startling. I have always been a hopeful romantic, but it was still something of an epiphany to learn that a woman of ethereal beauty could have earthy desires.

Or if not earthy, at least sandy. As well I knew.

11

I awoke on Tuesday morning in time to breakfast with my parents in the dining room. Ursi served paper-thin latkes with little pork sausages and apple sauce, and a big wedge of casaba with a crisp winy flavor.

The boss wanted to know if I required a lift to the office, his not-so-subtle way of telling me it would be nice if I got to work on time for a change. I explained I had to return the Buick and pick up my rejuvenated Miata. He accepted that without comment and took off alone in his black Lexus 400.

I drove over to West Palm Beach and reclaimed my little beauty, sparkling after a bath and wax job. Then I returned to the McNally Building around ten-thirty to find on my desk two telephone messages, both asking me to call. The name Hector Johnson was familiar, of course, but I stared at the other, Luther Grabow, and at first it meant nothing.

Then a lightbulb flashed above my head just as it does in comic strips. Luther Grabow. Ah-ha. The owner of the store where Silas Hawkin bought his art supplies. Intrigued, I phoned immediately and identified myself.

"Oh yeah," he said. "Listen, your firm is settling Si Hawkin's estate—am I right?"

"That's correct, Mr. Grabow." The experienced liar always remembers his falsehoods.

"And you told me one painting is gone. Is it still missing?"

"It is. It's listed in his ledger as 'Untitled,' but we haven't been able to locate it."

"The paintings you did find—were they on canvas?"

"All of them."

"So the chances are good that the missing work is the one he did on that wood panel I told you about. You agree with me?"

"Completely," I said. "There were no paintings on woods in Mr. Hawkin's inventory."

Long pause. Then he sighed. "I've been thinking about it," he said, "and I decided there's no reason I shouldn't tell you. The reason I didn't before was that I thought it might make the widow unhappy. You know? But when you sell off his stuff, she's going to get all the proceeds—am I right?"

"Oh yes," I said, padding my deception. "Mrs. Hawkin is the sole beneficiary."

"Then I might as well tell you. When Hawkin ordered the oak panel and said he was going to try acrylics, I asked him what he had in mind and he said he was planning to do a nude."

I may have gulped. "A nude?"

"That's what he said. He told me he had done some nudes when he was young, but then he found out there was more money to be made doing portraits."

"Did he tell you who the model would be?"

"Nah. He just said it was going to be a nude."

"Thank you very much for your cooperation, Mr. Grabow," I said. "I appreciate it and will make certain you are adequately recompensed for your professional assistance."

"That would be nice," he said.

I hung up, lighted a cigarette, and stared at the ceiling. A nude? I wondered if Silas Hawkin had met Pinky Schatz. Ridiculous. Or was it?

My second call, to Hector Johnson, was just as puzzling.

"Hiya, Arch," he said breezily. "How're you doing?"

I don't object to the diminutive Archy for Archibald, but I have an intense aversion to being called Arch. Too much like an adjective.

"Fine," I said. "And you?"

"Couldn't be better. I want to buy you lunch today. How about it?"

"Sounds great," I said.

It didn't. To be candid, Hector Johnson and men like him dismay me. They know all about professional football, they understand baccarat, and they can cure an arthritic septic tank. I mean they're so *practical*. I know little about such things. But then, on the other hand, if you're seeking an apt quotation from Publius Vergilius Maro, I'm your man.

"Do you like tongue?" Hector asked. I could think of a dozen snappy retorts to that query, some of them printable, but he plunged ahead before I could reply. "Nothing like a tongue sandwich on rye with hot mustard and a cold beer. You know Toojay's Deli on U.S. One, up near Jupiter?"

"Yes, I know it," I said, wondering why he was picking such a distant spot. Tongue sandwiches were available closer to home. His home, for instance.

"Meet you at twelve-thirty," he said briskly. "Okay?"

"I'll be there."

"My treat," he said, and hung up.

Toojay's is an excellent deli, no doubt about it, but hardly the place for a quiet, intimate luncheon even in midsummer when the tourists are absent. I could only conclude that Hector didn't want to be seen conferring with me in more familiar Palm Beach haunts. But what his reasons might be I could not fathom.

I arrived at Toojay's fashionably late, and it was as crowded and clamorous as I expected. I looked around for Hector and spotted him sitting at a table for four. With him was a gent with a profile like a cleaver and the body of a very tall jockey. I had absolutely no doubt that he drove a gunmetal Cadillac De Ville and his name was Reuben Hagler.

I made my way to their table, dodging the
scurrying waitresses. By the time I arrived I had
what I hoped was an unctuous smile pasted on
my puss. Johnson rose to greet me, but the other
man remained seated.

"Heck," I said, shaking his hand, "good to see
you again."

"Likewise," he said. "Arch, I want you to meet
Reuben Hagler, an old buddy of mine. Rube, this
is Archy McNally, the dude I told you about."

The old buddy didn't rise or offer his hand, but
he did grant me a glacial nod. I gave him one in
return and sat down next to Hector, across from
Hagler. The two men had glasses of beer but no
food. Johnson snapped his fingers at a passing
waitress, a habit I detest.

"How about it?" our host asked. "Tongue sandwiches all around with fries and slaw? And a beer
for you, Arch?"

There were no objections, and that's what he
ordered. Hector glanced at his wristwatch but it
wasn't the old digital he had been wearing the
first time we met. Now it was a gold Rolex, and I
wondered if it might have been a gift from Louise
Hawkin.

"Don't want to rush you, Arch," he said, "but
Rube and I have an important business meeting in about an hour so we'll have to eat and
run."

"No problem," I said and looked at the man
sitting opposite. "What business are you in, Mr.
Hagler?"

"Investments," he said. "Interested?"

"Sorry," I said. "At the moment I'm teetering on the edge of abject poverty."

Hector laughed but not Reuben. He didn't strike me as the kind of man who laughed often, if at all.

"If you change your mind," he said, "look me up. I'm in Lauderdale. I can promise you a twenty percent return with no risk."

When pigs fly, I thought, but didn't say it.

Our luncheons were served. They were enormous sandwiches with what I estimated was a half-pound of tongue between two slabs of sour rye. We set to work, but gluttonizing didn't bring our conversation to a halt.

"Arch," Hector said, "I got something to ask you, but first I want you to know you can talk in front of Reuben here. We've been friends a long time, and we got no secrets from each other. Right, Rube?"

"Right," the other man said.

"And he knows how to keep his mouth shut," Johnson added.

"I don't blab," Hagler agreed.

"Now tell me," Hector went on, "you work in the real estate department of your daddy's law firm. Is that correct?"

"Usually," I said cautiously, "but not all the time. Occasionally my father gives me other assignments. Things that require special handling."

"Well, I'm glad to hear that," he said, "because it's been bothering me. I couldn't figure out how you got involved if all you did was real estate."

"I don't understand," I said, understanding very well. "Involved in what?"

"That's what I like," Hector said, addressing the other man. "A closemouthed guy. Archy don't blab either. Well, a few days ago this Chauncey Smythe-whatever, a fellow my daughter has been dating, comes to me and says he wants to marry Theo and he wants my approval. Can you top that? In this day and age he wants the father's permission before he pops the question. Is that nutsy or what?"

He looked at me to gauge my astonishment.

"Amazing," I said.

"Yeah," he said. "This Chauncey—hey, Arch, what in hell kind of a name is Chauncey?"

"I believe it's of French derivation."

"No kidding? Well, this Chauncey works in a bank and I guess he's got mucho dinero. You know anything about that?"

He was, I decided, one brash lad. "I don't believe the Smythe-Hersforth family is hurting," I said carefully.

"Uh-huh," he said, shoveling in more coleslaw, "that's what I thought. Well, that's all to the good; every father wants to see his little girl well-provided for. But from what he said I figure his mama holds the purse strings. Am I right? Hey, let's have another round of beers."

And without waiting for our acquiescence he did his finger-snapping shtick again. I was glad he did because it gave me time to frame a discreet answer to the question about who controlled the Smythe-Hersforth millions. But I needn't have bothered; Hector didn't pause for a reply.

"The reason I figured that," he continued, "is because this guy who wants to be my son-in-law told me his mother asked her lawyers to investigate my daughter. Is that right, Arch?"

If the Chinless Wonder had been there at that moment I could have cheerfully throttled the numskull, possibly by force-feeding him a dozen of those colossal tongue sandwiches.

I realized I had no choice but to tell the truth, even though it is foreign to my nature. "That's correct, Heck," I said. "I have been assigned the job of gathering information about your daughter."

Unexpectedly he accepted it quite good-naturedly. "I can understand that," he said. "Can't you, Rube? The old lady's got a lot of loot and she doesn't want her sonny boy falling into the hands of a gold digger. Isn't that about it?"

"Something like that," I agreed, taking a deep swallow of my beer.

"Sure," Reuben Hagler put in. "If I was the old lady, I'd be doing the same time. Smart—know what I mean?"

"Absolutely," Johnson said. "She's protecting her own, and who can blame her for that? So I went to Theo and asked her if she really liked this guy. And she—"

"Wait a minute," I interrupted, suddenly horrified. "You didn't tell Theo I was investigating her, did you?"

"Hell, no!" Hector said, drowning his remaining fries in catsup. "Positively not! Because that girl's got a lot of pride, and if she knew she was being tracked she'd have dumped that Chauncey so fast he wouldn't know what hit him. No, I didn't tell her, Arch; I just asked if she wanted to marry Chauncey, and she said she did. So I phoned him and gave him the go-ahead."

Both men looked at me, and I wondered what they were expecting me to say. All I could manage was a weak, "You gave him permission to propose to Theo?"

"That's right," Hector went on. "He seems like an okay guy. Maybe not too swift, if you know what I mean, but solid. You agree, Arch?"

"Oh yes," I said, wanting to add "especially between the ears," but didn't.

"So now," Hector said, "the only thing standing in the way of these two swell kids getting hitched, as far as I can see, is the report you deliver to Chauncey's mommy. When I first told Rube about all this, he said I should offer you, you know, like a nice tip. But that's how Rube thinks—always dollars and cents."

"It's my way," Hagler said tonelessly.

"But I told him if I did that you'd be insulted. Was I right?"

I couldn't believe this totally inane conversation was taking place. Larry, Moe, and Curly were gobbling tongue sandwiches and discussing the fate of a lovely young woman. Where were Abbott and Costello when they were so sorely needed? And who's on first?

"You were quite right," I told Hector. "I would have been insulted."

"Sure you would. Because you're a straight arrow; I knew that from the start. You haven't heard anything bad about Theo, have you?"

"Not a word," I said. "No gossip. Not a hint of scandal. Nothing."

"And you won't find anything," he assured me. "That girl is true-blue, believe me. So that's what you'll tell old lady Smythe-whatshername?"

"If I had to report today," I said, "that's what I'd tell her."

If he caught my tergiversation he gave no sign of it. "That's great!" he enthused. "Listen, Rube and I have got to run. But I want to thank you from the bottom of my heart for having a nosh so we could clear the air. I'm happy to know you're on our side."

We finished our beers and rose to depart. I noticed that not Hector Johnson but Reuben Hagler paid for lunch, and with a hundred-dollar bill. We walked outside into the afternoon sunshine. We all shook hands. Hagler's grip was cool and surprisingly boneless. I thanked them for lunch and we all agreed to do it again real soon.

I paused to light a cigarette. I watched them get into Johnson's white Lincoln and jazz away. Those two, I reflected, were definitely not gentlemen. But then, on occasion, neither am I.

I drove back to Palm Beach in a fractious mood. I was furious with the Chinless Wonder for telling his prospective father-in-law that the bride-to-be was being investigated. How dense can you get? But then I sighed and acknowledged the man was what he was—a brainless twit—and there was no point in getting angry at what God hath wrought. As Groucho Marx said, "Why wax wroth; let Roth wax you for a change."

Still reviewing that crazy luncheon, I concluded it was a clear case of attempted manipulation. If I was naive, which I trust I am not, I would have said Hector Johnson was simply a concerned father who wanted only the best for his "little girl" and would do whatever he could to insure her happiness.

But I could not believe his motives were as innocent as that. For instance, his mentioning that Reuben Hagler had suggested I be offered a "tip" for a favorable opinion on Theo was surely a trial balloon to test my mendacity. If I had expressed even a mild interest, I'm sure our conversation would immediately have degenerated into vulgar haggling. To wit: How much did I want to turn in an A-plus report card on his daughter?

The whole thing was a jeroboam of annelids. What had begun as a simple investigation of the character of a young woman had become as complex as an inquiry into the causes of the Seven Years' War. And I was certain more surprises awaited me.

Sure enough, one was awaiting when I drove into the underground garage of the McNally Building. The moment I dismounted from the Miata, Herb, our porcine security guard, came bustling over, his huge revolver in its dogleg holster slapping against his thigh.

"You got a visitor, Mr. McNally," he said. "Been waiting a long time."

"Oh?" I said. "Where? In my office? The reception room?"

"Nah," he said, jerking a thumb. "Over there."

I turned to look. A black Jeep Cherokee. Marcia Hawkin. "Oh lordy," I said aloud and stared about wildly for an escape route. But I was doomed. The Cherokee door swung open, a white arm beckoned. I shuffled over, dreading another go-around with that young lady. And her greeting did nothing to relieve my angst.

"Where have you been?" she demanded angrily.

I wished I had my father's gift of raising one eyebrow. "Luncheon," I said. "People do have them, you know."

"Get in," she commanded imperiously.

I got in, wondering how I could possibly connive to drop off this spacey child at the nearest day-care center.

And she looked like a child, wearing a navy middy piped with white and a pleated skirt of creamy silk. Her face was scrubbed, and she seemed young enough to roll a hoop or engage in an exciting game of jacks. But she was smoking a joint; that muddied the picture.

"How are you, Squirrel?" I asked.

That pleased her. "You remembered my name!"

"Of course."

"You're my very best friend," she said. "Really."

I was as much saddened as startled. I had met her—what? Twice? Thrice? And now I was her very best friend. I was aware of her hostility toward her stepmother and reckoned she had adopted me as a confidant since the death of her daddy. I had never before served as a father figure and it made me a mite uneasy.

"I know how much you miss him," I murmured.

"My father?" she said. "He was the most wonderful and the most horriblest person in the world."

I looked at her. "Horriblest? Marcia, I'm not sure there is such a word."

"Well, you know what I mean. A devil. He was a devil." She offered me the roach. "Would you like a toke?" she asked.

"No, thank you."

She pinched it out carefully, wrapped the stub in a facial tissue, and tucked it into her purse. It was an ugly thing: red plastic with a tarnished chain handle. It looked like something from a garage sale.

"Listen, Archy," she said, "I want you to do me a favor."

I was immediately wary. If she asked me to assassinate her stepmother or blow up Fort Knox I wouldn't be a bit surprised.

"If I can," I said cautiously.

She took a white envelope from that awful purse and handed it to me. "Keep this," she said. "But you must promise not to open it unless something happens to me."

I inspected the envelope, sealed and with no writing on the outside. "Marcia, what do you think is going to happen to you?"

"I don't know," she said. "But if something does, then you can open the letter. It explains everything."

I sighed. "You're being very mysterious," I told her.

"Screw that," the child said. "All I want you to do is promise not to open the envelope unless something happens to me. If nothing happens, then you give the letter back to me."

"Nope," I said, "I won't do it. You're too vague. What if you decide to go to the Bahamas for a week. Do I open the envelope? What if you get appendicitis and they pop you in a hospital. Do I open the envelope? What if you're busted on a shoplifting charge. Do I open the envelope? What I'm trying to tell you, Squirrel, is that you've got to be more specific. Just saying 'If something happens to me' doesn't cut the mustard."

She thought about that, gnawing on the lower lip with her upper incisors. "All right," she said finally, "I'll be more specific. You must promise not to open the envelope and read the letter unless I die. Okay?"

"You're not going to die," I said.

She flipped out. "Stop arguing!" she screamed at me. "Stop treating me like a stupid kid! Just do what I asked you! Promise me this instant!"

I put a hand on her arm. "Take it easy," I said as softly as I could. "Of course I promise to do what you ask. I'll keep the envelope and won't open it until you die. And you can have it back, unopened, whenever you like. Is that satisfactory?"

"Yeah," she said, beginning to sniffle, "that's fine." She took another tissue and wiped her nose. "I'm sorry I blasted you, Archy, but people have been pushing me around and I can't take it anymore. But everything's going to get better. You'll see. My money worries will be over and I'll be able to live my life the way I want to."

"Glad to hear it," I said, suspecting she was handing me a lot of hooey.

"Oh yes," she said and smiled for the first time. "Things are going to change. I'm in the driver's seat now and certain people are going to do things my way if they know what's good for them. They think they're so smart but I'm smarter."

I hadn't the slightest idea of what she was talking about, of course, but her words sounded to me like a threat against a person or persons unknown, and that worried me.

"Marcia," I said, "I don't wish to pry. I know nothing about your personal affairs and have no desire to know. But if you're in a sticky situation and would like advice, assistance, or just encouragement, I'd be happy to help."

"I don't need help," she said disdainfully. "From you or anyone else. Daddy is dead and can't tell me what to do. No one can tell me what to do. I'm in control of my own life now. For the first time. And I know how to do it."

I was convinced she didn't. She wasn't a child, she was an infant, an impetuous, disturbed, and possibly violent infant. I saw no way to aid her without becoming immersed in the same madness that was obviously engulfing her. So I did nothing. Save yourself. It's a hard and sometimes cruel dictum. But it's the first law of survival.

"I wish you the best, Squirrel," I said. "I hope all your plans succeed." I opened the door of the Cherokee, holding that damned white envelope. "Please let me know how you make out."

"Sure," she said with an elfin grin that broke my heart.

I stood there and watched her gun up the ramp and out of the garage. I was in no mood to return to my claustrophobic office, so I remounted the Miata and headed for home. I needed a long, slow ocean swim, the family cocktail hour, and a merry dinner with my parents to reassure me that God was in his heaven and all was right with the world.

And it worked—for a while. I arose from the table feeling content and full of beans (actually they were haricots verts with slivered almonds), but then my father summoned me to his study. I followed him with the premonition that my serene mood was soon to evaporate.

"Glass of port, Archy?" he inquired.

That cinched it. When the patriarch invites me to have a postprandial libation it usually means he's going to give me a world-class migraine in the form of an unwelcome assignment. The proffered drink is his a priori apology.

He did the pouring, from one of his crystal decanters into Waterford goblets. He seated himself behind his massive desk and I took the nearest leather club chair. We sipped our wine. I thought it rather musty but I didn't tell him that.

"Anything new on Chauncey Smythe-Hersforth's young lady?" he asked.

"No, sir," I replied. "Nothing definite."

"His mother came in today. Apparently her son has proposed and the woman in question has accepted. Were you aware of that, Archy?"

"Yes, sir."

"I wish you had informed me."

"I learned of it only last night, father."

He accepted that. "Mrs. Smythe-Hersforth was quite upset. Perhaps indignant would be more accurate."

"I can imagine."

"However, I think she is reconciled to the fact that her son is determined to marry. Unless, of course, your investigation should prove the lady to be completely unsuitable."

"I've uncovered nothing to date that would disqualify her, sir." Naturally I said nothing of uncovering the lady herself.

"But you're continuing your investigation?"

"Yes, father, I am."

"Good. But our client has raised another objection. Before she gives her final blessing to the match she is determined to retrieve her son's letters to that unfortunate woman in Fort Lauderdale—what was her name?"

"Shirley Feebling."

"Yes. Mrs. Smythe-Hersforth fears that if she gives her approval, it's possible that before, during, or shortly after the marriage those embarrassing letters might surface as a cover story in one of our more lurid tabloids."

"She has a point."

"Indeed she does, Archy. I told her of the efforts I have made, with the assistance of Sergeant Rogoff, to seek the return of the letters from the Lauderdale police, to no avail. Their position is that they can release no evidence, particularly that found at the murder scene, until the case is cleared."

"That's understandable, father."

"Of course it is," he said crossly. "They're entirely in the right, even though Chauncey is not a suspect. So apparently his letters will remain in their possession until the homicide of Miss Feebling is solved."

He looked at me intently, knuckling his Brillo mustache. I knew what he wanted me to say and I said it.

"Let me look into it, father."

"Yes, Archy," he said gratefully, "you do that. Nothing illegal, of course. Do not, in any way, shape, or form, interfere with the official investigation. But though I admire your ingenuity, I must tell you I doubt you will succeed where, to date, the police have failed. However, I want to be able to assure our client that McNally and Son has done its best to accede to her wishes." He paused a moment and gave me a wry smile. "Also," he added, "your investigation should result in a large number of billable hours."

I laughed. "I expect it will, father," I said.

He finished his glass of wine and stood up. It was my dismissal. The moment I left he would pack and light one of his James Upshall pipes,

pour another port, and get back to Dickens. I
wondered if he had started *The Mystery of Edwin
Drood.*

"Kindly keep me informed of the progress of your
investigation," he said. Very patrician. I admired
him. He had the intonation just right.

I nodded, left his study, and started upstairs.
I paused at the second-floor sitting room, where
mother was watching a rerun of "The Honey-
mooners." I kissed her good-night and she patted
my cheek while laughing delightedly at Ralph
Kramden. I continued up to my own cloister.

It had been a long, arduous day, and instead of
a shower I opted for a bath. I frothed the water
with a mildly scented oil and launched a squad-
ron of rubber duckies Connie had given me as a
gag. Then I slid in with a moan of contentment.

An hour later I was dried and had donned one of
my favorite kimonos, the one printed with images
of Elmer Fudd at play. I sat at my desk and worked
hard at my journal, recording everything that had
happened since the last entry. I do work hard, you
know, though I suspect you may think I'm just
another pretty face.

I remembered to jot notes on what Luther
Grabow had told me of Silas Hawkin's intention
to paint a nude on wood; the insane luncheon with
Hector Johnson and Reuben Hagler; and the even
madder conversation with Marcia Hawkin in an
underground garage.

That last item reminded me to take the white
envelope from my jacket pocket and slip it into
the top desk drawer. But before I did that, I held

it up to the strong light of my student lamp. Unfortunately it appeared to be a security envelope—one of those with an overall pattern printed on the inside—and I could decipher nothing of what Squirrel might have written on the letter within. Frustrating, but I swear I was not tempted to steam it open. Subsequent events made me wish to hell I had.

Finished with my scribbling, I reviewed everything I had written since my initial interview with Mrs. Gertrude Smythe-Hersforth. Even more frustrating, for it seemed to me I had compiled a compendium of disparate facts and fancies. If there was a pattern, a design no matter how bizarre, I simply could not see it. Mishmash would be an apt description.

And now there was another spud in the stew: my father's request that I investigate the murder of Shirley Feebling. I could understand his doubts that I would succeed where, so far, the Lauderdale homicide detectives had failed. But neither the squire nor the police, as far as I knew, were aware of the existence of Reuben Hagler, the "old buddy" of Hector Johnson, father of the woman I had been assigned to dissect.

There were connections, I was convinced, but they were so tenuous as to be ungraspable. (There is such a word; you can look it up.) After a long bout of jumbled pondering I decided I had no choice but to engineer another meeting with Pinky Schatz, close friend of the slain Shirl Feebling. I could not forget my impression that the bouncy Ms. Schatz had lied to me because of fear. But fear of whom

I could not imagine. Unless he drove a gunmetal Cadillac.

All this Sturm und Drang was so depressing. I really don't know how psychiatrists do it. I mean they listen to woeful confessions of ridden people every day. All they hear is weeping, wailing, and the gnashing of teeth: stories of hate, abuse, greed, lust, violence, and other swell stuff. Who could blame the shrinks if they went home at night and, to survive, read fairy tales—or anything that ends "And they lived happily ever after."

I suppose I was in that mood when I determined to call Connie Garcia. I needed a dose of normality. It was close to midnight, and I let her phone ring and ring. But she did not answer.

I went to bed. I was not gruntled.

12

I might have slept forever on Wednesday morning but I was gradually nudged awake by the persistent ringing of my bedside phone. I opened one eye wide enough to see the clock dimly. It was either 9:05 A.M. or a quarter to one P.M. But since a low sun was striking through my bedroom window I judged a new day had just begun.

"H'lo?" I said in the middle of a jaw-cracking yawn.

"Don't you ever get to your office on time?" Sgt. Al Rogoff complained.

"That's why you called?" I said sleepily. "To comment on my working habits?"

"Wake up," he said sternly, "and try to listen. Have you seen Marcia Hawkin lately?"

I woke up. I saw no reason to prevaricate. "Yesterday afternoon," I told him. "At the McNally Building. We had a talk."

"About what?"

"Pure craziness. She was off the wall."

199

"That I can believe," Al said. "We've got a sheet on that young lady. Picked up for strolling naked on Ocean Boulevard at midnight. Picked up for throwing rocks at seagulls. Picked up for setting off illegal fireworks. Nothing serious. No charges. But the girl is a total fruitcake. What was she wearing when you talked to her?"

I tried to recall. "Uh, blue middy blouse with white piping, pleated silk skirt, scuffed running shoes."

"Uh-huh," Rogoff said. "That tallies. She have wheels?"

"Black Jeep Cherokee. Al, what's this all about?"

"Her mother called this morning. The kid didn't come home last night. She's gone and so is the Cherokee. We usually wait forty-eight hours on things like this. People stay overnight at a friend's house or pull off the road to grab some sleep. But since the Silas Hawkin homicide is still open, I got interested and decided to give you a call. Did she say anything about leaving home?"

"No."

"Meeting someone?"

"No."

"Going somewhere in particular?"

"No."

"Thank you for your kind assistance," the sergeant said with his heavy irony. "Would you care to make a wild guess as to where this loony might be?"

"Haven't the slightest," I said. "Al, did you hear anything from Michigan on those two names I gave you?"

"*Nada.* I told you these things take time. When I do hear, you'll be the first to know—after you tell me why you want the skinny. Archy, if you hear from Marcia Hawkin give me a shout."

"Sure I will," I said.

I hung up and crawled out of bed. It was just what I needed—a moral dilemma first thing in the morning. Should I open that cursed envelope or shouldn't I? Recalling my promise to Marcia, I decided not to. Only if she died, not if she was merely missing. I told myself she was sure to show up. Told but not convinced.

There was no one in the kitchen when I clattered downstairs, so I fixed my own breakfast: a large GJ, instant black coffee, and two toasted English muffin sandwiches with fillings of brisling sardines in olive oil. Look, you eat what you want for breakfast; don't give me a hard time.

I should have enjoyed that mini-meal but I didn't. Because the tickling of guilt continued. Had I been as sympathetic with Squirrel as I could have been? Might I have expressed more forcibly my willingness to help her? In other words, had I failed another human being in trouble? But then I am neither Dr. Schweitzer nor Mother Teresa. Looking for a saint, are you? Ta-ta.

I futzed about the house till noontime. I prepared my laundry and dry cleaning for the weekly pickup. I scanned several personal letters I had received which I had intended to answer but now were so dated there was no point. I tore them up. I clipped my fingernails. I examined my tongue in the bathroom mirror. Yuck.

Actually, as I well knew, I was delaying what I had to do: drive to Fort Lauderdale and confront Pinky Schatz. I didn't relish another visit to the Leopard Club; all those juicy dancers and desiccated spectators seemed unbearably dreary. I mean when it comes to nudity, public revelation is in reverse ratio to private stimulation. Or something like that.

But when duty's bugle blares, yrs. truly is ready to lead the charge. Also, I consoled myself with the opportunities the trip offered to jigger my expense account. And so I set off whistling a merry tune and reflecting that if one strove to maintain a positive attitude, life could be a bowl of *pasta con fagioli.*

There had been reports of potential hurricanes heading our way, departing the coast of Africa and boiling westward. You'd never know it from that day's sky. Pellucid is the word. About the same shade of blue, I decided, as the wings on Theo Johnson's butterfly tattoo. But I digress.

I parked outside the Leopard Club and approached the guarded portal. The sentinel on duty was not the same chappie I had previously encountered. This one had the head of a bald eagle and the body of an insurance salesman.

"Is Pinky Schatz dancing today?" I inquired politely.

"Nah," he said. "She called in sick."

"Sick?" I cried. "Good heavens, I must bring the poor girl some chicken soup or calf's-foot jelly. Do you happen to know where she lives?"

The griffin looked at me. "Yeah," he said, "I know. But you don't."

"True enough," I said, taking out my wallet. "A Jackson?"

"A Grant," he said firmly.

Sighing, I handed over a fifty. He consulted a tattered notebook he extracted from his hip pocket. He gave me Pinky's address, and I was startled. I knew the building: an elegant high-rise condo on the Galt Ocean Mile.

"Fancy," I commented.

"What else?" he said. "If you got it, flaunt it. And Pinky's got it."

"How true, how true," I agreed.

It took another twenty minutes to drive down to the Galt Ocean Mile. On that stretch of beach a row of huge high-rise condos forms a concrete wall that effectively prevents the peasants from viewing the seascape. Life is unfair; even tykes know that.

I found Pinky's building and pulled into the Guest Parking area. I neglected to eyeball the other cars. That was an error because when I started to open the lobby door Reuben Hagler was about to exit. We both halted, shocked, and exchanged stares.

"Hey, Mr. Hagler," I said, my voice ripe with false joviality, "imagine meeting you here."

"Yeah," he said. "Small world."

"A friend is coming down from New York," I explained, "and wants to rent for a year. I understand they have some attractive rentals in this building."

"I'd guess so," he said. "One of my investors lives here, and he's got a lush pad. Have a nice day."

"You, too," I said, and we traded puny smiles.

I paused to light a cigarette slowly, long enough to observe him get into that gunmetal De Ville I should have spotted. He drove away and I discovered I was suffering a mild attack of the heebie-jeebies. Did you ever catch Bela Lugosi in *Dracula?* That was Reuben Hagler. He looked as if he had just yawned, stretched, and climbed out of his coffin.

Of course Hagler could have been telling the truth and had just visited a male client rather than Pinky Schatz. And if you believe that, I told myself, leave an extracted molar under your pillow and expect the Truth Fairy to arrive.

I sauntered over to the security desk, where a uniformed stalwart (armed) was on duty.

"To see Miss Pinky Schatz, please," I said.

"Name?" he demanded.

I remembered who I was just in time. "Chauncey Wilson Smythe-Hersforth," I told him.

"What was that?" he said.

"Just announce me as Chauncey," I advised.

He looked up her number in a ledger, stabbed his phone, and murmured. "Okay," he said to me. "Apartment Nineteen-ten. First elevator on your right."

"Thank you," I said. "Attractive building. Do you have any security problems here?"

"Do dogs have fleas?" he asked, reasonably enough.

I rode a silent, Formica-paneled elevator to the nineteenth floor. The corridor was ceramic tile. Impressive, but the color was off-putting: a sort of pasty pink. I remembered how my tongue had looked that morning.

Ms. Schatz opened the door wearing a diaphanous peignoir. I was aware of it but all I could see was her face. Ah, bejaysus, but she was sporting a fine mouse under her left eye. It was of recent vintage and I knew that within an hour it would be rainbowed. Raw steak or leeches wouldn't help. Pancake makeup might.

"Good lord," I said, "what happened to you?"

"An accident," she said dully. "Come on in."

It was a one-bedroom condo decorated in a style I call Florida Glitz. That includes veined mirrors, patterned tiles, silver foil wallpaper, a glass cocktail table on a base of driftwood and, of course, the requisite six-ft. ficus tree made of silk. I mean the place shrieked. But the glitter was dimmed by an overall scruffiness; everything needed an industrial-strength douche.

"I wasn't going to let you in," she said. "I don't feel so hot."

"Would you like me to go?" I asked.

"Nah," she said, "you can stay. I was about to have a wallop. Would you like one, Chauncey?"

"A wallop of what?"

"All I got is gin. I like to mix it with diet cream soda. How about it?"

"I think not," I said hastily. "But a splash of gin on the rocks would be nice."

I watched her mince into the kitchen. She

may have been injured but she still jiggled. She
returned a few moments later with our drinks.
She had given me more than a splash of gin but
that was all right; I needed it; deceit makes me
thirsty.

She lolled on an enormous couch covered with
greasy cerise velvet. I sat in an overstuffed armchair big enough to accommodate King Kong. I
looked at her but she didn't look at me. She was
busy feeling that discoloration under her eye.

"Hurt?" I said.

"I've been hurt before," she said defiantly. "The
story of my life. How did you find out where I live,
Chauncey?"

"Fifty bucks."

Her smile was sour. "That Ernie," she said.
"He'd sell his sister if anyone wanted to buy, which
no one does. How come you looked me up?"

"I just want to find the man who killed Shirley
Feebling."

"Yeah?" she said, and gave me a cruel, knowing
glance. "You sure you're not looking for a replace-
ment? Like me?"

Sad, sad, sad.

"Pinky," I said, "can we stop playing games?
Please. I'm certain you know more about Shirl's
murder than you've told the police."

She said nothing, just sipped her noxious drink
and kept touching her bruise.

"I thought she was your best friend," I continued.

"I got a lot of best friends," she said. "Women
and men both."

"I can promise you protection," I told her.

"No, you can't," she said. "Not total. I don't mind getting hurt occasionally; that comes with the territory. But I don't want to end up like Shirl, with my brains splattered."

"You won't. If you're willing to tell what you know, the cops will pick him up and shove him behind bars. You have nothing to fear."

"What are you talking about?" she said. "Who is *him?*"

I decided I might as well go for broke. "Reuben Hagler," I said. "The man who just gave you that black eye. Drives a Cadillac with Michigan plates. You knew he was tailing Shirley. And you know or suspect he was the one who put her down."

"You're nuts," she said, affectedly bored.

"How did he get to you?" I went on. "Threats of what might happen if you talked? Or a payoff?"

She suddenly stood up. "You get out of here," she screamed at me. "Right now!"

"But then again," I said thoughtfully, "maybe you weren't just an innocent witness. Maybe you were in on it from the start, an accomplice who helped that creep knock off your best friend."

She collapsed back onto the couch. The glass fell from her hand and shattered on the tile floor. Gin and diet cream soda made an ugly pool, the color of old blood. She began wailing, her face muffled in the cushions.

"Leave me alone," I heard her say. "Just leave me alone. I can't take anymore. Please, just leave me alone."

I rose, finished my gin, and departed. I left

her sobbing on the couch. It was not one of my proudest moments. But you comprehend the reason for my cruelty, do you not? I reckoned she would report my visit to Reuben Hagler. And he would be forced to react. If he was guiltless, he would seek me out and denounce me for vile slander. And if he was involved in the murder of Shirley Feebling, he would seek me out and . . . I didn't want to envision what he might do.

I don't wish to imply that I was acting heroically, offering myself as a sacrificial lamb in order to snag an assassin. But Shirl's death continued to haunt me, and my personal safety seemed of minor import compared to finding and bringing her murderer to justice. Lofty, huh? Well, I do have a moral code. A bit skewed, I admit, but it's *mine*.

Look, at that point all I had was a suspicion that Reuben Hagler had stalked her. I had no proof and couldn't conceive what his motive might have been. So I had no choice but to force events. I thought of my actions as a lighted fuse. If I was correct, there would be a stupendous KA-BOOM! If I was mistaken, there would be a mild sizzle as the fuse burned out.

I was engaged in this mental nattering on the drive back to Palm Beach. I believe I was just leaving Boca Raton on A1A when my cellular phone sounded. It was lying on the passenger seat and its harsh ring startled me because I rarely get calls when I'm on the road. I suspected it would be a wrong number but it wasn't; Sgt. Al Rogoff was calling.

"Where are you now, Archy?" he asked in that sepulchral voice he uses when he's about to announce the world is coming to an end in fourteen minutes.

"North of Boca," I reported. "Heading home. What's up, doc?"

"Did you tell me Marcia Hawkin was driving a black Jeep Cherokee when you saw her yesterday?"

"That's right."

"Uh-huh," he said. "Well, right now there's a black Cherokee in the lake. It's upside down and the divers say there's a woman inside."

I was silent.

"You there?" he said.

"I'm here. Where is it, Al?"

"Off Banyan Road. You know it?"

"Yes."

"We're trying to get a cable on the car to haul it out. You want to stop by?"

I didn't. "Yes," I said, "I'll stop by."

By the time I arrived there was a crowd of spectators, perhaps twenty or thirty, many in bathing suits. Two gendarmes were herding them back from the scene of operations.

There was a short wooden pier extending out into Lake Worth. It looked relatively new and mounted on one side was a steel gantry with canvas slings for lifting small boats out of the water. The police tow truck had backed up alongside the pier, the cable from its winch stretched taut into the lake.

I joined the rubbernecks, spotted Rogoff, and

yelled to him. He waved and came over to escort me past the guards. He was wearing khaki slacks and scuffed loafers. His shield was clipped to the shoulder of his white T-shirt.

"I was on a forty-eight," he explained. "Then they called me to come in to honcho this mess."

"Who found the car?"

"Some kid who was snorkeling. Just chance. It could have laid there for days, weeks, or months without being spotted. We got a hook on it, but like I told you, it's upside down and it's a tough haul."

We walked down to the shoreline. The winch was whining and the cable was retracting very, very slowly. We stood silently and watched the Jeep come skidding out of the lake. The winch stopped when the car was in the shallows. Then four huskies, two uniformed cops, and two wet-suited divers began turning it over. It was a muscle job, and it took five tries before they got the Cherokee onto its wheels.

"Rather them than me," Al said. "Instant hernia."

The winch started up again, not straining now, and the car was pulled up onto the beach. Water streamed from it and strands of seaweed were clinging to the windshield. We moved forward for a closer look. The door on the driver's side was open and the window was shattered.

"Take a look," Rogoff said.

I peered within. Marcia Hawkin was lying face up in the back. Her eyes were wide. She stared at nothing. She was still wearing the middy blouse and silk skirt but one shoe was off. That single bare foot—small, pale, limp—affected me most.

"Squirrel," I said softly.

"What?" Al said.

"Squirrel," I repeated. "Her nickname. Her father called her that."

"Then he knew," Al said roughly. "She was a real wacko."

Thomas Bunion, the Assistant ME, was there and directed the removal of the body after photographs and a video had been taken of the car's interior.

"What's that?" I asked Rogoff, pointing through a back window.

He shielded his eyes from the rays of the lowering sun. "Looks like a sheet," he said. "All wadded up. Stained. Could be blood. Or maybe stuff in the water. I'll leave it to the wonks."

"Al," I said, "did you drive your pickup here?"

"Sure," he said. "It's parked up near the road. Why?"

"Want to follow me back to my place?"

He looked at me. "Now why should I do that?"

"Because," I said, "I have something I think you better see."

And I told him how Marcia Hawkin had given me a letter to be opened only in the event of her death. The sergeant listened intently.

"You haven't opened it, Archy?" he asked when I had finished.

"Of course not. I promised her."

"I wish you had told me this morning when we talked about her."

"Why should I have done that, Al? She had just been reported missing. And you told me yourself that the Department would take no action for forty-eight hours."

"Yeah, but if I had known she left you a letter it might have changed things."

"How so?"

"Because it meant she figured she could die—and soon. Most young kids think they're going to live forever. Where is the letter now?"

"In my desk at home."

"Let's go," he said.

We were at the Chez McNally in less than an hour. I stopped in the kitchen to pluck a bottle of Sterling vodka from the freezer and fill a plastic bowl with cubes from the ice tray. Then we tramped upstairs to my barrack.

Al likes to claim he's inured to the sight of violent death. He's lying, of course, because he's a sensitive man. I don't even try to pretend. That bare foot of the dead Marcia Hawkin had spooked me. The sergeant made no objection when I poured us heavy vodka-rocks. We both gulped and sighed.

I sat behind my desk, took out Squirrel's white envelope, and held it out to him.

"Don't you want to open it, Archy?" Rogoff said. "After all, the girl gave the letter to *you*."

I shook my head. "It's totally irrational," I admitted, "but I just can't. You do it."

I handed him my opener, which looks like a miniature Persian dagger. He slit the flap of the envelope carefully and shook out the contents, a single sheet of white notepaper, and unfolded it with the tip of the dagger. He bent over my desk to read.

"Well?" I said impatiently. "What does it say?"

He chuffed a dry laugh. "Written in ink, addressed 'To Whom It May Concern.' How does that grab you? And it's signed Marcia Hawkin."

"All right, all right!" I cried. "But what does it *say?*"

He looked up at me with a queer expression. "One sentence," he said. "It says 'I murdered my father.'"

13

That evening, during the cocktail hour, I informed my parents of the death of Marcia Hawkin. They were as much bewildered as shocked, for the sudden and brutal loss of two lives in one family seemed totally inexplicable. Mother, I believe, was ready to ascribe it to a cruel vagary of fate. But father, I knew, suspected dark mischief was afoot. He is instinctively suspicious of linked events others might term a coincidence.

"Was the young woman a suicide, Archy?" he inquired.

"I really don't know, sir," I answered. "Sergeant Rogoff promised to tell me what he can after the cause of death has been established."

"She was a friend of yours?" he asked, busying himself with the martini pitcher.

"She thought so," I said defensively, "although I had spoken to her only three or four times. She seemed quite disturbed."

"How awful," the mater said. "Perhaps her

father's murder was the reason. I must send Louise a letter of condolence."

"No need, mother," I said, "I intend to call on her tomorrow, and I'll express our sympathy."

"Oh yes, Archy," she said, "that would be nice. And be sure to ask if there is anything we can do to help."

And we left it at that. I mentioned nothing of the final letter Marcia had entrusted to my care. Rogoff and I had decided to keep that dreadful message from public knowledge until its authenticity could be determined. As Al said, she was such a scatty kid she might have imagined the patricide.

"Or protecting someone else," I suggested. "The actual killer."

"Yeah," the sergeant said. "That, too."

Dinner that evening was baked salmon with a heavenly crust of dill. I knew it was a magnificent dish, but it was one of the rare occasions in my life when my appetite faltered, and I refused a third helping. As soon as decently possible, I excused myself and retired to my aerie.

There I poured myself a marc and opened a fresh packet of English Ovals. Wasn't it Mark Twain who said, "It's easy to stop smoking; I've done it a dozen times." If it wasn't Mr. Clemens, it might have been Fred Allen. No matter; I had no intention that evening of even trying. I lighted up, sipped my brandy, and thought of Marcia Hawkin. Squirrel.

I tried to recall everything she had said during our final conversation. Then I consulted my journal, which offered some assistance but no actual quotations. She had spoken of taking control of her own life, of solving her money worries, of outsmarting persons unknown who were apparently treating her with contempt.

I did remember exactly one thing she had said, and in light of what I had witnessed that afternoon it was so poignant I drained my drink and poured another. She had said, "I'm in the driver's seat now." But the last time I saw her, she wasn't in the driver's seat at all, was she? She was crumpled in the rear of a sodden car, one pale, dead foot dangling.

I endured that aching memory as long as I could, and then I phoned Consuela Garcia. I had to talk to a young woman who was still alive. After what had happened to Shirley Feebling and Marcia Hawkin I was beginning to fear I had become a Jonah and all the ladies of my acquaintance were doomed.

"Hiya, Archy," Connie said warmly. "I'm glad you called. Did you hear what happened to Marcia Hawkin? It was on TV."

"Yes," I said, "I heard."

"Sounds like suicide to me," she said. "The poor kid. Maybe her father's murder pushed her over the edge."

"Maybe. What have you been up to, Connie?"

"Oh, this and that. Lady Horowitz is running me ragged. Right now we're planning a buffet dinner for fifty. The McNallys are on the A-list. Isn't that nice?"

"Splendiferous," I said, delighted she wasn't

going to give me a blow-by-blow account of her date with Wes Trumbaugh. "What are you serving the serfs?"

"Cold seafood. Lobster, shrimp, crabmeat, scallops, oysters, periwinkles, calamari, and lots of other swell stuff."

My appetite returned with a jolt. "I'll starve myself for two days to prepare for that feast," I promised. "Plenty of flinty white wine?"

"Of course."

"Wonderful. When can I see you again, Connie?"

"Soon," she said. "Give me a buzz on Friday, Archy. Okay?"

"Will do," I said happily. "Get a good night's sleep."

"I'm already in bed."

"Under that poster of Bogart? 'Here's looking at you, kid.' "

She giggled and hung up.

I went in for my shower, but my mopes had already been sluiced away. I had a prof at Yale who was something of a misogynist and was fond of paraphrasing Thoreau by remarking, "Most women lead lives of noisy desperation."

Not Connie Garcia. She is a bubbler and always inflates my spirits except, of course, when she is dumping a bowl of linguine on my head as punishment for a real or fancied infidelity. But other than her occasional physical assaults, she really is a 24-karat woman.

Lacking only a blue butterfly tattoo.

That was my last lubricious thought before Morpheus and I embraced. Away we went. I

awoke on Thursday morning ready to slay dra-
gons. I donned a somber costume, for I had decided
that my first port of call would be the Hawkin
home, an obligatory visit of condolence I hoped
to make as brief as possible.

It was a 3-H day in South Florida: hot, humid,
hazy. I wondered, not for the first time, if
I wouldn't have been wiser to opt for roofed
transportation rather than a convertible. But
surrendering my dashing Miata would destroy
my self-image of a damn-the-torpedoes buckler
of swashes. I wasn't quite ready to do that. Sometimes egoism demands sacrifices.

When I turned into the Hawkins' driveway I
saw, parked at the front door, the white Lincoln
Town Car belonging to Hector Johnson. My first
reaction was to turn and flee, but then I thought
why should I. His presence might even be an assist
in my expressing the McNally family's sympathies
as quickly as possible, and then leaving him to
provide additional solace to the twice-bereaved
Louise.

But it was Theodosia Johnson who opened the
door. Madam X was wearing a longish dress of
aubergine silk, and she seemed preternaturally
pale, features composed but drawn. It was the face
of a woman who had suffered a sleepless night—
completely understandable if the Hawkins and
Johnsons had been as intimate as I imagined.

"Archy," she said, clasping my hand and draw-
ing me inside, "it's good of you to come."

"How is Mrs. Hawkin?" I asked.

"Surviving," she said. "But just barely."

She led me into the Florida room. Louise and Hector were seated close together on the couch. He was holding her hand, gazing at her with an expression of sorrowful concern. On the cocktail table before them was a silver coffee service, three cups and saucers, and a bottle of California brandy. Johnson glanced up as I entered, and Mrs. Hawkin gave me a befuddled stare as if not quite certain of my identity.

"Ma'am," I said, beginning to recite my rehearsed speech, "I'd like to extend the condolences of myself and my parents. It is a terrible tragedy. If there is any way we can help, please let us know."

"Thank you," she said in the wispiest of voices.

"Hey, Arch, how about a cuppa jamoke?" Hector asked in his brutish way. "With a slug of the old nasty to put lead in your pencil."

"Oh, father," Theo said in a tone of disgust that expressed my own.

"Thank you, no," I said. "I just stopped by for a moment to offer the sympathy of the McNally family. Mrs. Hawkin, is there anything at all we can do to assist you?"

She looked at Johnson. "Nah," he said to me. "It's damned decent of you, but Theo and I are going to take care of our Louise. And she's going to be just fine. Aren't you, hon?"

She nodded and reached for a coffee cup with a trembling hand. But before she could lift it to her lips he slopped in a dollop of brandy.

"Father," Theo said sharply, "that's enough."

"Not yet," he said. "She's got a lot of grief to

forget and this is the best medicine."

His daughter sat down abruptly in a rattan armchair, crossed her legs, and immediately one foot began to jerk up and down in vexation. I remained standing, knowing I should depart but enthralled by this unpleasant scene that was threatening to become a high-octane confrontation.

"Louise," Theo said, "wouldn't you like to lie down for a while? Take a pill and get some rest."

"She doesn't need a pill," Hector said. "Those things are poison. Just leave her alone; she'll get through it."

"The woman needs sleep," Theo said angrily. "Can't you see that?"

I was bemused by the way they spoke, as if Mrs. Hawkin was not present. But I don't believe the poor woman was even aware of the contention swirling around her. She sipped her brandy-laced coffee and stared vacantly into space.

"Just mind your own business, kid," Hector said. "I know what I'm doing."

"Since when?" Theo said. "She just lost her husband and stepdaughter. Give her a break."

He looked at her coldly. "Keep it up and you'll get a break," he said.

There was no mistaking the menace in his voice, and I suddenly realized this was more than a family squabble. Their conflict was fascinating, but I had no desire to be a witness to violence. Chivalrous heroism comes rather far down on my list of virtues.

"Theo," I said, "I wonder if I might have a glass of water."

She glared at me, furious that I was interrupting the wrangle. But then she softened, her taut body relaxed; she recognized my effort to end an unseemly shindy in a house of sorrow.

"Sure, Archy," she said, rising. "Come with me."

She led the way without hesitation as if it was her home and there was no need to ask permission from the owner. But once we were in the tiled kitchen her wrath returned.

"That crude son of a bitch," she said, leaning close so I could hear her low voice. "Couth? He never heard the word. He just bulls his way through life, all fists and elbows. He'll get his one of these days. Do you really want a drink of water?"

"Yes, please."

She took it from the tap on the refrigerator door, and I drained the glass gratefully.

She reached to stroke my hair. "You look very handsome this morning, Archy," she said. "Dressed so formally. But I prefer you in something more casual. Or nothing at all."

Her brazenness shocked me and she must have seen it in my face because she laughed delightedly and pressed her body against mine. "Don't worry, darling," she said, "I'm not going to be a problem. I'm going to marry Chauncey and become a nice little hausfrau."

"You may find you enjoy it," I told her.

"Do you really believe that?" she asked.

"No," I said, and she kissed me.

I drew regretfully away. Her flesh felt glossy

under that silk, and she was wearing a scent I could not identify, although I suspected canthari- des might have been one of the ingredients.

We moved back to the Florida room, and I made a respectful farewell, which Louise Hawkin and Hector Johnson barely acknowledged. Madam X gave me a wave and a devilish smile, and I left the Villa Bile. My original label for that house now seemed more apt than ever.

I exited to find Sgt. Al Rogoff leaning against the fender of his parked pickup. He was wearing civvies—a suit of khaki poplin, white shirt, black knitted tie—and puffing one of his fat cigars.

"I thought you were on a forty-eight," I said to him.

"Still am," he said. "And still working my tail to the bone. Who's inside besides Mrs. Hawkin?"

"Theodosia and Hector Johnson."

"I'll wait till they leave. I'd like to talk to the widow alone."

"You may have to wait until Hades has a cold snap," I informed him. "The Johnsons have taken over."

"Oh-ho," he said. "It's like that, is it?"

"Apparently."

He gestured toward the white Lincoln. "Is that his?"

"Yep."

"Nice," Rogoff said. "Do you know what he did before he moved down here?"

"You name it, Al, and he's done it. I've heard a dozen different versions of his former occupa- tion."

"Yeah?" the sergeant said, grinning. "I know what it was."

I stared at him for a few beats before I caught it. "You swine!" I cried. "You heard from Michigan."

"That's right," he said. "I was going to give you a call. Want to come to my place tonight? We can talk about it then."

"Can't you tell me now?"

"No. I want to go inside and brace Mrs. Hawkin."

"Forget it," I advised. "The lady is half in the bag. Hector has been invigorating her morning coffee with California brandy."

"All to the good. *In vino veritas.* Come over to my wagon around nine o'clock. Okay?"

"I'll be there," I promised. "Is the scoop on Johnson and Hagler interesting?"

"Very," he said. He tossed away the stub of his cigar, straightened his jacket, began striding up to the door.

"Al," I called, and he turned back. "About Marcia Hawkin," I said. "Was it suicide?"

He smiled grimly. "Not unless she managed to wring her own neck."

What a curtain line that was! I drove back to the McNally Building with my thoughts awhirl. The Miata had just had a tune-up and I wished my brain could get the same. I mean I simply could not make sense of what was happening: three homicides and the seemingly irrational behavior of the people involved.

Oh, I could concoct several scenarios but all were too bizarre to convince even a fantasist

like me. I kept trying to rein in my super-
charged imagination and remind myself that
usually the most complex evils are the result of
the most prosaic of motives: greed and revenge,
for instance. But even concentrating on the
basics of crime detection yielded no hint as
to the connection between the murders of Silas
Hawkin, Shirley Feebling, and Marcia Hawkin.
If there was a solution to that conundrum, it
eluded me.

Only temporarily, of course. I assure you I shall
not end this account by confessing failure. You'd
never speak to me again.

I had hoped to spend the remainder of that
morning sitting quietly in my office composing
my expense account. Quiet was necessary since
my monthly swindle sheet demands intense crea-
tivity. I will not claim it is *totally* factual but it is
based on fact. The theme is exaggeration rather
than prevarication. To quote an historic American epigram, "I am not a crook."

But peace was not to be mine. I found on my
desk a message from our receptionist stating that
Mrs. Jane Folsby had phoned and requested I
return her call. I immediately did so and let the
phone ring seven times but received no reply. I
put the message aside and began assembling the
bills, memos, vouchers, and receipts that were to
provide evidence, however flimsy, for my claimed
reimbursement.

I had hardly started when my phone rang and
I hoped it might be Mrs. Folsby. No such luck. I
recognized that whiny voice at once.

"Archy?" he said.

"Chauncey," I said, "how are you?"

"All right," he said. "I guess."

"I understand congratulations are in order."

"What? Oh, you mean me and Theodosia. Well, sure, thanks."

"You must be a very happy man."

"Uh, not completely. Archy, I have a problem. I'd like to talk to you about it. Get your input."

"CW," I said, "if it's legal input you require, I suggest you consult my father. I'm just a rank amateur."

"Well, uh, it's not really legal input," he whined. "At least not at this stage. It's more friendly input I need."

By this time the input madness was sending me right up the wall. But I was determined not to be the first to surrender. "Well, I can provide that," I told the Chinless Wonder. "I presume you're speaking of personal input."

"That's right," he said eagerly. "Intimate input."

"Confidential input?"

"Correct! Top secret input."

Then I knew I was never going to win the Great Input War. "Chauncey," I said, sighing, "what exactly is it you want?"

"Can you come over to my office?"

"At the bank? Now?"

He had the decency to say, "Please."

"You wouldn't care to chat over lunch? At Bice perhaps?"

"Oh no," he said hastily. "No, no, no. Someone might overhear. My office would be best."

"Better than my garage," I said, alluding to our previous meeting. "Very well, CW, I'll come at once."

"Thank you," he said, and the whine had an overtone of piteousness.

I walked to his bank, only a short distance on Royal Palm Way. The building was definitely *not* Florida. It looked like a Vermont relic of the 1920s: heavy granite exterior, towering pillars, a marbled, high-ceilinged interior, brass-barred cages for the tellers. And a funereal silence. Even the antiquated clients spoke in whispers.

And the private office of Vice-president Chauncey Wilson Smythe-Hersforth was more of the same. It was huge, oak desk unlittered, furnishings in grave good taste. No file cabinets, no computer terminals, no indication that any business at all was conducted in that somber chamber. And it probably wasn't. CW's sinecure was due to mommy's wealth being invested with the private banking division. If she ever pulled her bucks, the Chinless Wonder might find himself flipping burgers at McDonalds.

"What's this all about?" I asked after he got me planted in a leather wing chair alongside his desk.

Before he replied he made certain his door was firmly closed and locked. Then he returned to the calfskin throne behind his desk.

"It's confidential, Archy," he said portentously. "I trust that's understood."

I looked at him. I was about to make an impudent remark, but then I saw the poor dolt was truly disturbed. As he had cause to be, having been cuckolded before he was married. And I was the lad who had put the horns on him. Levity on my part would have been rather pitiless, wouldn't you say?

"Of course," I said solemnly. "What seems to be the problem?"

He drew a deep breath. "Well, uh, Theo Johnson has agreed to marry me. I first asked her father for permission, of course."

"Of course," I said, wondering if he had fallen to one knee while making his proposal to Madam X.

"And mother has given her conditional approval to our union," he added.

Yes, he actually said "our union."

"Then things seem to be going swimmingly," I commented.

"Uh, not quite," he said, not looking at me. "Theo wants me to sign a paper."

I must admit the lower mandible dropped a bit. "Oh?" I said. "What kind of a paper, CW?"

"A sort of a contract," he confessed, fiddling with a letter opener on his desk.

"Are you talking about a prenuptial agreement?" I asked. "A contract that spells out the property rights of both spouses—and their children, if any—in the event of separation, divorce, or death?"

"I guess that's what it is," he said miserably.

"Uh-huh," I said. "And how much is the lady asking?"

He looked up at the ceiling—anywhere but at me. "Five million," he said.

I am proud to say I did not whistle or emit any other rude noise. "Rather hefty," I observed.

"Oh, it's not the sum that bothers me," he said. "Because, of course, Theo and I would never separate or divorce, and we're both in good health. In any event, I'd leave her well-provided for in case I should die. No, the money isn't an issue. The problem is that if I inform mother of this—what did you call it?"

"Prenuptial agreement."

"Yes. Well, uh, if I tell mom about it, she might change her mind about Theo. You understand? In fact, she might become so furious that she'd rewrite her will. And then where would I be?"

"You're her only child, are you not? And the closest family member. I doubt very much if she could disinherit you completely."

"Maybe not," he said worriedly, "but she could cut me down to the bare minimum, couldn't she? And then would I have enough to promise Theo the five million she wants?"

"Ah," I said, "you do have a problem. I presume your mother has been introduced to your fiancée."

"Yes, they've met. Once."

"And how did they get along?"

"Well, uh, they didn't exactly become instant pals."

I nodded, recalling my mother's reaction to Madam X. Maybe the matrons saw something neither Chauncey nor I recognized. Or perhaps it was merely maternal possessiveness. ("No one's good enough for my boy!")

"What is it you'd like me to do, CW?"

He stroked his bushy mustache with a knuckle. "I don't know," he admitted. "But everyone says you're so clever. I thought maybe you could give me a tip on how to handle this situation in a clever way."

"I'd like to help you," I told him. "But I can't come up with an instant solution this moment. Let me think about it awhile."

"Well, all right," he said grudgingly. "But not too long, Archy. I mean I don't want Theo to think I'm stalling her. You know?"

"Of course," I said, rising. "It's obvious you're very intent on marrying this woman."

"Oh God, yes!" he said with more fervor than I had believed him capable of. "I must have her!"

"Quite understandable," I said. "But meanwhile, CW, do not sign any paper, agreement, or contract. Is that clear?"

"If you say so."

"I do say so. Sign nothing!"

We shook hands and exchanged wan smiles. He unlocked his door, and I departed. I ambled back to the McNally Building suffused with a warm feeling of schadenfreude. But that, I admitted, was unkind and unworthy of the McNally Code of Honor, the main principle of which is never to kick a man when he's down. Unless, of course, he deserves it.

When I returned to my own office, which, after an hour spent in Chauncey's cathedral, had all the ambience of a paint locker, the first thing I did was phone Mrs. Jane Folsby again. This time she came on the line.

"Oh, Mr. McNally," she said, "I'm so glad you called. I know you've heard about Marcia Hawkin."

"I have," I said. "Sorrowful."

"Terrible," she said with some vehemence. "Just terrible. She had her faults as we all do, but she didn't deserve to die like that. It wasn't suicide, was it?"

"I really don't know the details," I said cautiously.

"I know it wasn't," she said decisively. "And I have my suspicions. That's what I want to talk to you about."

"Mrs. Folsby, if you know anything relating to Marcia's death, don't you think you should speak to the police? Sergeant Al Rogoff is handling the case. You've met him."

"No," she said determinedly. "This is something I don't want to tell the police. Because then they'll want a sworn statement and I'll get all involved and might even be forced to testify in court. And I really don't have any proof. But I know what I know, and I've got to tell someone. Please, Mr. McNally. I'll feel a lot better if I tell you, and then you can do whatever you think best. At least my conscience will be clear."

"This sounds serious," I said.

"It *is* serious. Will you meet with me?"

"Of course. Would you care to have lunch someplace or come to my office?"

"Oh no," she said immediately, "that won't do at all. Could you possibly come over here to my sister's home in West Palm Beach?"

"Be glad to," I told her, and she gave me the address. We agreed to meet at eleven o'clock on Friday morning.

"Thank you so much," she said, and the chirp came back into her voice. "You don't know what a relief it will be to tell someone. I haven't been able to sleep a wink since Marcia died."

And she hung up. Al Rogoff accuses me of overusing the word "intriguing." But at that moment I couldn't think of a better one.

I had absolutely no idea of what Mrs. Jane Folsby wished to reveal to me, so I discarded that topic instanter. I would learn on the morrow.

As for CW's admission that his marriage depended upon his signing a five-million-dollar agreement with his bride-to-be, I could only conclude that Mrs. Gertrude Smythe-Hersforth might not be as witless as I had assumed. And further, the senior McNally had been his usual omniscient self when he had described marriage as a contractual obligation.

What was perhaps most astonishing to me was my own ingenuousness. When I first met Theodosia Johnson I was convinced her nature *had* to be as pure as her beauty. Then, after I had been privileged to view that blue butterfly, I became aware of her fiercely independent willfulness. And now third thoughts had superseded the second; she was apparently a young lady with a shrewd instinct for the bottom line.

But then my musing veered from the relations of Madam X with the Chinless Wonder to her relations with yrs. truly. It occurred to me that

Theo had been aware from the start that I had been assigned to investigate her bona fides. During that demented deli luncheon, her father had denied she knew of my role. But Hector, I now reckoned, was as consummate a liar as I.

And if Theo was cognizant of what I was about, perhaps the granting of her favors (with the promise of more to come) was her astute method of insuring my willing cooperation in her endeavor to snare the heir to the Smythe-Hersforth fortune. It's possible that was her motive, was it not? Naturally I preferred to believe she had succumbed to the McNally charm. But I could not delude myself by completely rejecting the notion that she had been the seductress and I the object of her Machiavellian plotting.

I simply did not know. And so I left immediately for the Pelican Club bar, seeking inspiration.

14

My parents were not present that evening, having been invited to dinner at the home of octogenarian friends celebrating the birth of their first great-grandchild. And so I dined in the kitchen with the Olsons, and a jolly time was had by all. Ursi served a mountainous platter of one of her specialties: miniature pizzas (two bites per) with a variety of toppings. Romaine salad with vinaigrette dressing. Raspberry sorbet on fresh peaches for dessert. (Please don't drool on this page.)

That delightful dinner numbed me, but I was able to work on my journal in lackadaisical fashion until it became time to depart for my meeting with Sgt. Rogoff. Obeying my mother's dictum—"Never visit without bringing a gift."—I stopped en route to pick up a cold six-pack of Corona. It is one of Al's favorites, but I must admit that when it comes to beers he has no animosities that I'm aware of.

Rogoff's "wagon" is a double mobile home set on

233

a concrete foundation and furnished in a fashion that would make any bachelor sigh with content. Comfort is the theme, and everything is worn and shabby enough so you feel no restraint against kicking off your shoes.

The barefoot host was wearing jeans and a snug T-shirt, and when he uncapped the beer I had brought he put out a large can of honey-roasted peanuts. I said, "Al, I speak more as friend than critic, but your waistline is obviously expanding exponentially. To put it crudely, pal, you're cultivating a king-sized gut."

"So what?" he said. "I've noticed you're no longer the thin-as-a-rail bucko you once were."

"Touché," I said, "and I hope it will be the last of the evening. I've been meaning to ask, did you ever get to see that portrait of Theodosia Johnson by Silas Hawkin in the Pristine Gallery?"

We were sprawled in oak captain's chairs at the sergeant's round dining table. He had put on a cassette of the original cast recording of "Annie Get Your Gun," and what a delight it was to hear Ethel Merman belt out those wonderful tunes, even if the volume was turned down low.

"Oh yeah," Rogoff said, "I saw it. Great painting. And a great model. She's a knockout."

"My sentiments exactly," I said.

He looked at me quizzically. "Taken with the lady, are you?"

"Somewhat."

"You're asking for trouble."

"Odd you should say that, Al. Priscilla Pettibone at the Pelican Club told me the same thing."

"Smart girl," he said. "But I don't expect you to take her advice or mine. You're a hopeless victim of your glands. But enough of this brilliant chitchat. I've got the skinny on Hector Johnson and Reuben Hagler. The agreement was that you tell me why you want it before I deliver. So let's hear."

"It's a long story."

He shrugged. "And it's a long night. We've got your six-pack and another of Molson in the fridge. Get started."

I told him everything relevant: my first glimpse of Hagler while I was with Shirley Feebling; learning that Hagler was one of Hector Johnson's bank references; his hole-in-the-wall office as an investment adviser; my luncheon with the two men; and my accidental meeting with Hagler when I had traveled to Fort Lauderdale to question Pinky Schatz.

"My, my," Rogoff said when I finished, "you have been a busy little snoop, haven't you. You figure these two guys are close?"

"Peas in a pod."

"And you think Hagler shot Shirley Feebling?"

"That's my guess."

"Motive?"

"Haven't the slightest," I admitted. "Pinky Schatz might know, but she's not talking. At least not to me."

"How did you get chummy with her in the first place?"

"Told her I was Chauncey Smythe-Hersforth."

The sergeant laughed. "What a scammer you

are! If you ever turn your talents to crime, Florida
will be in deeeep shit. Well, it's not my case but
I'll give Lauderdale Homicide a call and tell them
about this Reuben Hagler. I don't think I've ever
seen the guy. What's he like?"

"Dracula."

"That sweet, huh? And what was the name of
the woman you talked to?"

"Pinky Schatz. She's a nude dancer at the Leopard Club."

"Your new hangout?" he said. "Well, I guess it's
better than collecting stamps."

"Oh, shut up," I said. "Now tell me what you
learned from Michigan."

"Hector Johnson used to be a stockbroker.
Racked up for securities fraud. He was fined,
made restitution, and was banned from the securities business for life. He never did hard time but
apparently while he was in jail for a few weeks
he met Reuben Hagler. This Hagler has a nasty
file: attempted robbery, felonious assault, stuff
like that. He's done prison time: three years for
rape. He was also suspected of being an enforcer
for local loan sharks."

"Sounds like he'd be capable of killing Shirley
Feebling."

"I'd say so," Rogoff agreed. "And now he's an
investment adviser in Fort Lauderdale?"

"That's what the sign on his office claims. But
in view of Johnson's history, Hagler might be a
front and Hector is calling the shots."

"Wouldn't be a bit surprised. What do you suppose Johnson's angle is on all this?"

I shook my head. "Can't figure it," I confessed, "but there's obviously frigging in the rigging."

We sat in silence awhile, trying to imagine scenarios that made some loopy kind of sense. But neither of us had any suggestions to offer.

"Al," I said, "how did you make out this morning when you talked to Louise Hawkin?"

"You were right," he said. "The lady was totally befuddled. And you know what? I think Hector Johnson means to keep her that way."

I will not say his comment was the key to the whole meshugass. But it did start me thinking in a new direction. I began to get a vague notion of what might be going on.

"Do you believe that letter Marcia Hawkin gave me?" I asked the sergeant. "Do you think she really did kill her father?"

He shrugged. "Beats me. Maybe yes, maybe no. If he had given her motive, I'd be more certain one way or the other."

"Me, too," I said. "Any word yet on that stained sheet or whatever it was we saw in the back of her Cherokee?"

"Nothing yet. These tests take time; you know that."

I stared at him a moment, then decided to put my vague notion to the test. "Are you a betting man, Al?"

"I've been known to place a small wager now and then."

"Tell you what," I said. "I'll bet you ten bucks I can tell you what those stains on the sheet are even before the tests are completed."

"They're not blood," he said. "I told you she was strangled."

"I know they're not blood. But I know what they are. Is it a bet?"

"Okay," he said. "For ten bucks. What are they?"

"Acrylic paint."

He took a swig of his beer. "How the hell did you come up with that?"

"A swami told me."

"If you turn out to be right, tell the swami there's a job waiting for him in the PBPD."

"I think I'm right," I said, "but I don't want your ten dollars. I want a favor instead."

He groaned. "I'd rather pay the ten."

"A simple favor," I said. "Get back to your Michigan contact and ask if they've got anything on Theodosia Johnson, Hector's daughter. The last name may be different but 'Theodosia' is probably for real. What woman would use that as an alias? And you met her this morning, you can describe her accurately. Or send Michigan a photo of that Silas Hawkin portrait."

He looked at me a long time. "She's involved?" he asked.

"I would prefer to think not."

"Screw what you'd prefer," he said roughly. "Do you figure she is?"

"As you just said about Marcia Hawkin, maybe yes, maybe no. This is one way to find out."

"I guess," he said, sighing. "All right, I'll play your little game. I'll query Michigan just for the fun of it. But our sawbuck bet is still on."

I finished my beer, grabbed a fistful of peanuts, and stood up. "I'm going home," I declared. "It's been a long, tumultuous day, and bed beckons."

"Yeah," Rogoff said, "I could do with some shut-eye myself. Thanks for the beer."

"And thank you for the peanuts," I said politely. "Al, let me know if anything turns up."

"Sure," he said. "And Archy . . . "

"Yes."

"That Reuben Hagler sounds like a foursquare wrongo. Watch your back."

"I always do," I said blithely.

By the time I returned home my parents had retired. I ascended to my seventh heaven and prepared for bed. I had had quite enough mental stimulation for one day and decided to postpone adding recent revelations to my journal.

I awoke on Friday morning ready for a fight or a frolic—or perhaps both simultaneously. Again I had overslept and was forced to construct my own breakfast. It consisted of leftover mini-pizzas from dinner the previous evening.

Before leaving home I remembered to phone Consuela Garcia as I had promised. She was at work in her office and was already in a snit trying to answer the demands of Lady Horowitz. I was hoping for a lazy, affectionate chat, but Connie made it short and sweet. Well . . . not exactly. Just short. But she did agree to meet me for dinner that evening at the Pelican Club.

I then tooled over to the McNally Building to check my messages (none) and incoming correspondence (none). My business day was starting auspiciously. I finished my inventive expense account, signed it with a flourish, and dropped the completed document on the desk of Ray Gelding, the firm's treasurer. He glanced at the total.

"You've got to be kidding," he said.

I treated that remark with the silent contempt it so richly deserved, bounced downstairs, and vaulted into the Miata for a drive to West Palm Beach and my appointment with Mrs. Jane Folsby.

Her sister's home was located in a neighborhood I can only term bucolic and was more bungalow than South Florida split-level ranch. Rose bushes were plentiful and the front yard boasted two orchid trees that would have elicited gasps of awe from my mother. The house itself was freshly painted and had a semicircular stained-glass window over the front door. Very nice.

Mrs. Folsby answered my knock and seemed pleased to see me. She led the way to a small, brightly furnished living room in the rear with windows mercifully facing north. Everything was flowered chintz but not overpowering, and the white wicker armchair I sat in was comfortable enough.

She insisted on serving minted iced tea. I told her how delicious it was—which wasn't *quite* the truth. Then we agreed that South Florida was, indeed, hot in midsummer. We also concurred that crime rates were too high and youngsters today had little respect for their elders.

Then there was a pause in this brilliant conversation. "About Marcia Hawkin . . ." I prompted.

"Yes," she said, looking down and moving a gold wedding band around and around on her finger. "I don't know how to say this, Mr. McNally."

"Take your time," I said encouragingly. "I am not a policeman, you know, although Sergeant Al Rogoff is a close friend. But if you wish this conversation to remain confidential, I shall certainly respect your wishes."

"That's for you to decide," she said. "The only reason I'm telling you is that a crime has been committed, and someone should be punished."

I have previously described her as "old, large, creaky," and with a chirpy voice. But now I saw something in her I had not recognized before: strong will and stiff determination. Not a woman to be trifled with, and I wondered how she had endured the disorder of the Hawkin ménage. Economic reasons, I supposed; she needed the money.

"I hadn't been with the Hawkins long," she started, "before I realized something was going on."

Again there was a short lull. I didn't want to spur her with questions, feeling it best to let her tell the story at her own pace.

"Mrs. Louise Hawkin and Marcia . . ." she finally continued. "Always at each other. I thought it was because Louise was a stepmother. Sometimes daughters resent it. And her drinking so much," she added. "The missus, that is."

I nodded.

"But it was more than that," she went on. "I don't know how to tell this and I wouldn't blame you if you didn't believe me, but I've got to say it."

I waited.

She looked away from me. "Silas Hawkin," she said, and her voice was dry, "the mister, he was bedding his daughter. I know that for a fact."

I took a gulp of my iced tea. "You're certain of this, Mrs. Folsby?"

"I am," she said firmly. "There is no doubt in my mind. I don't know how long it had been going on. Years, I'd guess. Before Silas married Louise. She was his third wife."

"So I read in his obituary."

"And Marcia was his daughter by the first. Yes, I think it had been going on for a long time."

I drew a deep breath. "Marcia was very disturbed," I commented.

"She had every right to be," Mrs. Folsby said angrily. "What her life must have been like! So naturally Louise was her enemy."

"Naturally," I said.

"I can't tell you how poisonous they were to each other. They had a fight once. And I mean a *fight* with slapping and kicking. The mister broke it up."

"Dreadful," I said.

"They hated each other," she said sadly. "Jealous, you see. Louise knew what was going on. Marcia was her rival. And Marcia saw Louise as *her* rival. All because of that awful man. He came on to me once. Can you believe it?"

"Yes," I said, "I can believe it."

"So that's why I think she did it."

It took me a moment to sort that out. "Mrs. Folsby," I said, "are you suggesting that Louise may have murdered her stepdaughter?"

"It does not behoove me to accuse her," she said primly. "But I think the matter should be looked into."

"It shall be," I assured her. "May I have your permission to relay what you've told me to the authorities?"

"Will you give them my name?"

"Not if you don't wish it."

"I do not," she said sharply. "But if you want to tell them the other things—well, that's up to you. I've done all I can do."

"I understand completely," I said, "and I thank you for your honesty. And for your hospitality."

I finished that wretched iced tea and rose to leave. She accompanied me to the front door. Just before I departed I said, "Mrs. Folsby, do you think Marcia Hawkin killed her father?"

"No," she said, shaking her head, "she loved him too much."

I drove back to the Island in a broody mood. I figured that conversation with Mrs. Folsby had yielded one Yes, one No, and one Maybe.

The Yes was the information that Silas Hawkin was having an incestuous relationship with Marcia. After what Lolly Spindrift had told me of the man's sexual proclivities, I could believe it. And probably, as Mrs. Folsby had guessed, for many years.

The No was her accusation—or suggestion— that Louise Hawkin had killed her stepdaughter.

That I could not believe. Marcia had been strangled, and that is very, *very* rarely the modus
operandi of a murderess. Also, I did not think
Louise had the strength—to be crude, it takes
muscle to wring a human neck—and what could
possibly be her motive since Silas, the reason for
the two women's enmity, had been eliminated.

The Maybe was Mrs. Folsby's stout declaration
that Marcia didn't murder her father because she
loved him too much. Perhaps. But that unhinged
child had also described daddy to me as the
"horribilest" person in the world. Theirs could
have been a love-hate affair in which the second
verb finally triumphed over the first.

It was then a bit past noon and I lunched alone
at Bice, ordering a hearts-of-palm salad and a
single glass of sauvignon blanc. Feeling justifi-
ably virtuous at having put a choke collar on my
appetite, I returned to the McNally Building and
phoned Mrs. Trelawney. I asked if the seigneur
might be available for a short conference. She
was absent a moment and then returned to tell
me I had been granted a ten-minute audience
before the boss departed for lunch with a client.

I scampered up to the sanctum and found him
at his antique rolltop desk filling a briefcase with
blue-bound documents.

"Can't it wait, Archy?" he said irascibly.

"Just take a moment, sir," I said. "It's something I think you should be aware of."

I related exactly what Chauncey Smythe-Hersforth had told me of the prenuptial agreement
demanded by Theodosia Johnson. The sire halted

his packing to listen closely. And when I mentioned the amount requested, five million dollars, one of his tangled eyebrows rose slowly as I knew it would.

"A tidy sum," he remarked wryly when I had finished. "I am not too familiar with the precedents of prenuptial agreements, but I shall certainly research the subject. Why didn't Chauncey consult me on this matter?"

"Father," I said gently, "I think he's afraid of you."

He actually snorted. "Nonsense," he said. "Am I an ogre?"

"No, sir."

"Of course not. And he obviously requires legal counsel. I suspect Chauncey's actual fear is having to inform his mother of what his fiancée has requested."

"I'd say that's close to the mark," I agreed.

He pondered a moment. "That young man does have a problem," he finally declared. "He's of age, of course, and can marry whomever he chooses without his mother's permission. But I can understand his not wishing to endanger his inheritance of the Smythe-Hersforth estate in toto. Any suggestions, Archy?"

"Yes, sir," I said. "Let me stall him as long as I can. A few things have turned up in my investigation that lead me to believe the question of a prenuptial agreement may become moot."

He stared at me. "Are you suggesting the young lady may prove to be unsuitable? Persona non grata, so to speak?"

"Possibly," I acknowledged. "But not so much as her father."

He nodded. "In that case I concur with your recommendation. Delay Chauncey's decision as best you can and redouble your efforts to bring this rather distasteful business to a successful conclusion."

"Yes, father," I said, resisting an impulse to tug my forelock.

I left his office and returned home for my ocean swim, then labored on my journal. I showered, dressed, attended the family cocktail hour, and departed for my dinner date with Connie Garcia.

And, you know, during all that time I do not believe there was a single moment when I ceased glooming about Marcia Hawkin, her life and her death. The things we do to each other! Sometimes I think I'd rather be a cocker spaniel or even a hamster rather than a human being. But I did not choose my species and so I must learn to deal with it. And it would be nice if I could become a nobler example of Homo sapiens. But I know better than to hope.

When I arrived at the Pelican Club that evening Connie was already standing at the bar surrounded by a ring of eager young studs.

She was wearing a jumpsuit of burgundy velvet with an industrial zipper from neck to pipik. Her long black hair swung free and oversized golden hoops dangled from her lobes.

But I knew it was mostly her warm vivacity that attracted that pack of hopefuls. Connie is a vibrant young woman with physical energy to spare and a spirit that seems continually effervescing. Add to that a roguish smile and Rabelaisian wit and you have a complete woman who, on a scale of 1 to 10, rates at least a 15.

She saw me standing there like a forlorn bumpkin, excused herself, and came bopping over to grant me a half-hug and an air kiss.

"Hiya, hon," she said cheerily. "I was early so I had a spritzer at the bar."

"And why not?" I said. "You look glorious tonight, Connie."

"You like?" she asked, twirling for my inspection. "The tush isn't too noticeable?"

"Not *too*," I said. "Never *too*."

"Let's go eat," she said. "I'm starving."

I wish I could tell you the evening was an unalloyed delight, but I must confess that dinner was something less than a joyful occasion.

It wasn't the food because chef Leroy Pettibone scored with a marvelous special of fried rabbit in a cranberry-orange sauce. And it wasn't Connie's fault because she was her usual bubbling self.

No, the fault was totally mine. I knew it and was utterly incapable of summoning up the McNally esprit. I seemed unable to utter anything but banalities—mercifully brief banalities—and I realized I was behaving like a zombie on barbiturates.

Finally Connie's chatter faded away, and she reached across the table to squeeze my hand. "Archy," she said, "what's wrong with you tonight?"

"Nothing."

"Don't shuck me, sonny boy," she said angrily. "I know you too well. Is it because I've been dating other men, including your close friends?"

"Of course not. Positively not. We agreed that we can see whomever we please."

"Then what *is* it?"

I never ever talk to anyone but my father and Sgt. Al Rogoff about details of my investigations. I mean I head the Department of Discreet Inquiries at McNally & Son, and how discreet can they be if I blab? No, I am a closemouthed lad and fully intend to remain so.

But at that moment I had to tell someone. I think it was because I needed to share the awful burden. I could understand why Mrs. Folsby had to tell me. It was just too much for one person to bear alone.

"Connie," I said, "I know you love to gossip and so do I. I want to tell you something. I *need* to tell you, but I want your cross-my-heart-and-hope-to-die promise that you won't repeat it to anyone."

"Archy," she said, suddenly solemn, "do you trust me? I mean really trust me?"

"Of course I do."

"Then I swear to you that whatever you tell me will go no farther."

I nodded. "I believe you," I said, and I meant it. "Well, you've heard about Marcia Hawkin's death, haven't you?"

"Of course. Now the police say she was murdered."

"That's correct. But today I heard something else and it's been tearing me apart."

I told her Silas Hawkin had been intimate with his daughter, probably for many years, beginning when she was quite young.

Connie stared at me, her lustrous eyes widening. Suddenly she began weeping. Silently, but the tears flowed.

"Oh God," I said helplessly. "I shouldn't have told you."

She shook her head and held her napkin up to her face. Her shoulders continued to shudder and I knew she was sobbing soundlessly. I could do nothing but wait and curse myself for shattering her.

Finally she calmed, dabbed at her swollen eyes, blinked. Her mouth still quivered and I feared the lacrimation might begin again.

"The poor child," she said in an anguished voice. "The poor, poor child."

"Yes," I said. "Can we move to the bar now and have a brandy? I think we both could use a buckup."

We sat close together at the bar, held hands, and sipped our Remy Martins without speaking. I admit that telling Connie of the Hawkins' incestuous relationship afforded me a small measure of relief. Do you believe that sorrow is lessened by sharing? It must be so because old wisdom declares that misery loves company.

What is amazing is that the pain seems to diminish slightly as it is transferred to another. I had no doubt that eventually, when Marcia's murder was solved, her secret would become known to the public. Then the distress, shared by millions, would dwindle away to become just another of the daily outrages we read about and eventually forget because to remember them all would be too painful to suffer.

After a while we agreed it was time to leave. Connie didn't suggest I accompany her home, nor did I. Before we separated, we stood alongside her car locked in a tight embrace. There was nothing passionate about it. It was the trembling hug of two mourners surviving in a world that sometimes seems too cruel to be endured.

15

I awoke on Saturday and discovered my morosity had evaporated with the morning sun. What a relief that was! I don't mean to suggest I had totally forgotten Marcia Hawkin—I am not the froth-head my father seems to believe—but now I was able to accept her tragedy without reviling the human race or cursing fate.

The new day helped, of course. The sky was lucent, a sweet sea breeze billowed our curtains, the birds and my mother were twittering and, all in all, it seemed a lucky gift to be animate. I celebrated by eating eight blueberry pancakes—count 'em: *eight!*—at breakfast.

Then father departed for his customary Saturday morning foursome at his club, mother and Ursi went grocery shopping in our old Ford station wagon, and Jamie Olson disappeared somewhere on the grounds, muttering about the depredations of a rogue opossum he was determined to slay. And so I had the McNally manse to myself.

I went into my father's study and sat in his chair behind his desk. Anyone spotting me there might have thought I was contemplating a regicide so I could inherit the throne. Actually, all I wanted to do was use His Majesty's telephone directory. I phoned Lolly Spindrift's newspaper, knowing he worked Saturdays to meet his deadline for the Sunday edition.

"Lol?" I said. "Archy McNally here."

"Can't talk," he said shortly. "Busy."

"Too bad," I said. "And I have something so choice."

"Never too busy to chat," he said merrily. "What have you got for me, darling?"

"What are you working on?" I temporized. "Marcia Hawkin's death?"

"Of course. It's the murder de jour. All of Palm Beach is nattering about it. And now I'll give you a freebie, only because it will be in my column tomorrow morning. Did you know the unfortunate victim had twice attempted suicide?"

"No, I didn't know," I said slowly, "but I can't say I'm surprised. Where did you hear that?"

"Oh please," he said. "You know I protect my sources. Now what do you have for me?"

"I went first last time," I reminded him. "It's your turn."

He sighed. "What a scoundrel you are. Very well, what do you want?"

"About Theodosia Johnson, your Madam X . . . She's been in Palm Beach about a year. But only recently has she become the one-and-only of Chauncey Smythe-Hersforth. Do you know if she dated other men before meeting Chauncey?"

His laugh was a bellow. "Oh, laddie, laddie," he said, "do you think she sat home knitting antimacassars? Of course she saw other men. A horde. A multitude. *Very* popular, our Theodosia. I have the names of all her swains in my file and, frankly, sweets, I'm amazed that you're not included."

"I am, too."

"Perhaps it was because her taste seemed to run to older men of wealth. That would remove you from her list of eligibles, would it not?"

"Effectively," I said.

"And now that I've paid my dues," he went on, "what delicacy do you have for me? Tit for tat, you know—although my personal preference is somewhat different."

"I don't know how you can use this, Lol," I said, "but I'm sure you'll find a way. It concerns Hector Johnson, father of the beauteous Theo. He was racked up for securities fraud in Michigan. Spent some time in the local clink, paid a fine, made restitution, and was banned from the securities business for life."

"Love it!" Lolly shrieked. "Just love it! Yes, I expect I shall find an occasion to use that gem one of these days. Ta-ta, luv, and keep in touch."

I sat at father's desk a few moments longer, reflecting on what Spindrift had told me of Theo's social activities prior to her meeting Chauncey. It was easy to believe. A young woman of her multifarious charms would attract scads of beaux: single, married, divorced, or lonely in widowerhood.

I was certain she had many opportunities to
form a lasting relationship. But she had chosen
Chauncey Wilson Smythe-Hersforth. Her selection of that noodle, I thought, was significant.

I had intended to call a few pals and see if
anyone was interested in a few sets of tennis or,
in lieu of that, driving out to Wellington to watch
polo practice while gargling something exotic like
a Singapore Sling or a Moscow Mule. But instead
I phoned Theodosia Johnson. If my choice was
between tennis, polo, or her, it was strictly no
contest.

I was hoping Hector wouldn't answer, and he
didn't. But when Theo said, "Hello?" her voice
had the tone of sackcloth and ashes.

"Archy," I said. "Good lord, you sound low. Anything wrong?"

"A slight disagreement with daddy," she said,
"and I'm still seething. But I'll recover. I always
do. Archy, I'm so happy you called. I was beginning to think you had forgotten all about me."

"Fat chance," I said. "Theo, how *are* you, other
than suffering from the megrims."

"What are megrims?"

"Low spirits."

"I'm suffering," she admitted. "Cheer me up."

"How about this: I drop by around noonish and
we drive down the coast. It's a super day and it
would be a shame to waste it. We'll have lunch
outside at the Ocean Grand and talk of many
things."

"Of shoes—and ships—and sealing wax—" she
said.

"Of cabbages—and kings—" I said.

"And why the sea is boiling hot—" she said.

"And whether pigs have wings," I finished, and she laughed delightedly.

"The only poetry I know," she said. "Thank you, Archy; I feel better already. Yes, I accept your kind invitation."

"Splendid. See you at twelve."

I went back upstairs to take off jeans and T-shirt, shower, and don something more suitable for luncheon at the Ocean Grand with a smashing young miss. I settled on a jacket of plummy silk with trousers of taupe gabardine, and a shirt of faded blue chambray. Casual elegance was the goal, of course, and I believe I achieved it.

Then I set out for my luncheon date with Madam X. A duplicitous plot was beginning to take form in that wok I call my brain, and if all went well I intended to start the stir-fry that scintillant afternoon.

I had imagined Theo would wear something bright and summery, but that woman had a talent for surprise. She wore a pantsuit of black linen. No blouse. Her hair was drawn back and tied with a bow of rosy velvet. Very fetching, and I told her so.

"No bra," she said.

"I happened to notice," I said.

She laughed. "Chauncey never would. And if he did, he'd be shocked."

"Surely he's not that much of a prig."

"You have no idea."

Her obvious scorn of her fiancé discomfitted

me. She could think those things, but wasn't it
rather crass to speak of them to others? As I
soon learned, she was in a sharp, almost shrew-
ish mood that day.

For instance, as we drove southward along
the corniche I remarked, "I had the pleasure of
meeting your father's business associate, Reuben
Hagler, the other day."

"Rube?" she said offhandedly. "He's a boozer."

It wasn't her judgment that startled me so much
as her use of the sobriquet "boozer." She might
have said, "He drinks a little too much," but she
chose the coarse epithet. It was not the first time I
had noticed her fondness for vulgarisms. I hoped,
for her sake, that her speech was more ladylike in
the presence of Mrs. Gertrude Smythe-Hersforth.
That very proper matron, I suspected, would be
tempted to put trousers on the legs of a grand
piano.

And not only did Theo seem in a perverse humor
that afternoon but she made no effort to conceal
her lack of restraint.

"You were right," she said. "It's a super day.
Why don't we just keep driving."

"Where to?"

"Oh, I don't know. Miami. The Keys. Check into
some fleabag hotel for the weekend."

"Theo, I don't think that would be wise. Do
you?"

"I guess not," she said. "Just dreaming."

But I knew that if I kept driving and found a
hotel that accepted guests without luggage, she

would have happily acquiesced. Her unruliness was daunting.

We arrived at the Ocean Grand and she was suitably impressed by the elegant marbled interior.

"This is what it's all about, isn't it?" she commented.

"You've lost me," I said. "All about what?"

"You know, Archy. Money. Comfort. People to serve you. No problems. The lush life."

There was such fierce desire in her voice that I didn't even attempt a reply. She had a vision and it would have been brutal to explain that what she sought was a chimera. She wouldn't have believed me anyway.

We dined on the terrace of the bistro, overlooking the swimming pool. And beyond was a larger pool: the Atlantic Ocean. I suppose that setting and that luncheon came close to matching Theo's ideal. The omelettes were succulent, the salad subtly tartish, the glasses of chilled chenin blanc just right. And while we lived "the lush life," I initiated my intrigue.

"Theo," I said earnestly, "I have a problem I hope you'll be able to help me with."

"Oh?" she said. "What is it?"

"First of all I want you to know that I have no desire whatsoever to intrude on your personal affairs. Whatever you do or whatever you plan is no business of mine, and I don't want you to think I'm a meddler. But willy-nilly I've been handed a decision to make that concerns you."

That caught her. She paused in the process

of dredging a slice of smoked salmon from her omelette.

"Archy," she said, "what *is* it?"

"Well, Chauncey and I are really not close friends. Not buddy-buddy, you know, but more like casual acquaintances. However, on occasion he asks my advice on legal matters. I have tried to convince him that I am an ersatz lawyer—no license to practice—and he'd do better to consult my father, who not only has the education and experience but is the attorney of record for the Smythe-Hersforth family. But I think Chauncey is somewhat frightened of my father."

"Chauncey is frightened of many things," she said coldly.

"That may be, but I must admit Prescott McNally can be overwhelming at times. He is a stringent man of high principles. Unbending, one might say. Chauncey prefers to discuss his problems with me."

"And am I one of Chauncey's problems?"

I waved that away. "Of course not. Not you personally. Chauncey declares he is deeply in love with you and I believe him. He wants very much to marry you. What he is concerned about is the prenuptial agreement you have requested."

"Oh," she said. "That."

"Theo, I definitely approve of what you're doing to ensure your future, although I do think five million is a wee bit high."

"He can afford it," she said stonily.

"Perhaps not now," I said. "I don't think his present net worth could accommodate it. But he'd certainly be capable of a five-million settlement after he inherits."

"Yes," she said, "that's what I figured."

A cool one, our Madam X!

"But that's Chauncey's quandary, don't you see," I said. "I must tell you that Mrs. Smythe-Hersforth is not wildly enthusiastic about her son marrying. Not just to you but to any woman. You know what dominant mothers are like."

"Do I ever!"

"So if Chauncey tells her about the prenup, she may change her will and pull the plug on his inheritance."

"Can she do that, Archy? He's her only child, you know."

"True, and though I'm not too familiar with Florida inheritance law, I reckon Chauncey would be legally entitled to a certain percentage of her estate. I mean I doubt she could totally disinherit him. And if she tried, he could certainly contest the will. But what if she becomes so angered she decides to diminish her estate while she's still alive? Spend all her millions on a program for spaying cats, for instance. I'm jesting, of course, but it's her money and if she wants to give it all away, or most of it, to worthwhile charities while she's living, she's completely within her legal rights."

Theo took a gulp from her wine glass. "Jesus!" she said. "We hadn't thought of that."

Did you catch that "We"? I did.

She gave me what I believe she thought was a brave smile, but it looked rather tremulous to me.

"You don't think his mother will approve of a prenup agreement, Archy?"

"I don't. Do you?"

"I guess not," she said. "The old bitch doesn't even approve of *me*. I knew that from the start. What did you tell Chauncey to do?"

"I stalled him. Until I had a chance to talk to you about it and see how you felt."

She reached across the table to pat my cheek. "Good boy," she said.

We were silent while our emptied plates were removed. We both declined coffee, but I ordered bowls of fresh raspberries.

"You're a clever lad, Archy," Madam X said. "I'll just bet you've got an answer up your sleeve."

"There is one possibility," I admitted, giving her a straight-in-the-eye stare. "Have your own attorney draw up the prenuptial agreement for five million. My father doesn't have to know about it and Chauncey's mother doesn't have to know about it."

The simplicity of my solution stunned her and she took a moment to grasp it. "And you'll tell Chauncey to sign it?" she asked, almost breathlessly.

I switched into my enigmatic mode and didn't give her a direct reply. "Think about it," I urged her. "Talk it over with your father. Frankly, Theo, I think it's your only hope. But it's your decision. Now let's eat our raspberries. Don't they look delicious!"

"Archy," she said, "daddy is over at Louise Hawkin's place."

"Is he?" I said. "And when is he returning home?"

"Probably tomorrow morning," she said, and we smiled at each other.

I shall not attempt to apologize for my conduct during the remainder of that afternoon. I agree that "reprehensible" is as good an adjective as any to describe my behavior. But I do have an excuse: The devil made me do it.

We drove back to Theo's condo. Once again she led me to that appalling cretonne-covered couch, and once again I saw the blue butterfly flutter and take wing.

She was mystery incarnate. Ignoring her physical beauty—which I certainly did not—I sensed there was a fury in her convulsions. I do not believe I was the cause of her anger; it was her malignant destiny that enraged her, and she rebelled with puissance and a bravado that asserted her strength and independence.

I returned home exhausted and saddened, although if what I suspected was accurate, there was little reason for my sorrow. Still, I find it depressing when people with admirable attributes put their talents to wicked use.

I conducted myself with stately decorum during the evening routine of family cocktail hour and dinner. I do not believe either of my dear progenitors had any inkling of the deception I had practiced that afternoon.

After dinner I retired upstairs to work on my journal. I had hardly started scribbling when Sgt. Al Rogoff phoned.

"How many chukkers of polo did you play today?" he demanded.

"None," I replied.

"How many sets of tennis?"

"None."

"How many holes of golf?"

"None."

"Heavens to Betsy," he said, "what's happening to the primo playboy of Palm Beach? Then what have you been up to?"

"Investigating," I said. "I do work occasionally, you know."

"You could have fooled me," he said. "Hey, I told Lauderdale about Reuben Hagler and that Pinky Schatz. They can't locate him, but they've planted an undercover policewoman in the Leopard Club."

"Yikes!" I said. "Surely not as a nude dancer."

"Nope," Al said, laughing. "I guess she's not qualified. They put her in as a waitress. Her job is to buddy up to the Schatz woman and try to get her to spill."

"It might work," I said, "but I doubt it."

"Me, too," Rogoff admitted. "But one never knows, do one?"

"Al, will you stop stealing my line? You're infringing my copyright."

"Don't tell me you made it up."

"No," I confessed, "it's not original. I think Louis Armstrong said it first, or maybe it was Fats Waller. I don't remember."

"Talk about remembering," he said, "I just did. I owe you ten bucks."

"What?" I said, and then I recalled our bet and knew the real reason he had phoned. "You mean that sheet in the back of Marcia Hawkin's Jeep had acrylic paint stains?"

"Yep," he said, "but it wasn't a sheet. More like a drop cloth. Now tell me how you knew the stains were acrylic paint."

"Gut instinct," I said, and Al, who has as much contempt for that phrase as I do, roared with laughter.

"Bull*shit!*" he said. "You know something I don't know and you're holding out on me. This is a homicide investigation, you charlie, so let's have it."

"I really didn't *know,*" I said. "I was just guessing. Listen to this Al . . . "

I told him of my conversations with Luther Grabow, the art supply dealer, and how Silas Hawkin had purchased a palette of acrylics to paint a nude on a wood panel.

"Nice job, sherlock," Rogoff said when I had finished. "You figure the nude on wood was the painting Hawkin labeled 'Untitled' in his ledger?"

"Yes, I think so."

"Oh, boy," he said. "Bubble, bubble, toil and trouble."

"It's 'Double, double toil and trouble,'" I told him.

"Whatever," he said. "Got any idea who the model was?"

"Nope."

"Could it have been his daughter? She ices him like she said in that letter and then swipes the painting because she's afraid it might incriminate her."

"Could be," I said. "You reckon she had it in the car when she went in the drink?"

"A possibility," Rogoff said. "I'll send divers down to look around and see if they can spot it. Maybe it floated out of the Cherokee."

"If it floated out," I said, "it would be on the surface, wouldn't it?"

"Yeah, you're right. That scenario doesn't wash. But I still think she had the 'Untitled' painting in her possession sometime during the evening she was killed."

"And now someone else has it?"

"Sure," he said. "Unless she burned it or hacked it to splinters. That's what I like about my job: Everything is cut and dried."

"I know what you mean. Al, did you hear anything from Michigan about Theodosia Johnson?"

"Not yet. Archy, tell me something: Do you think the Shirley Feebling kill in Fort Lauderdale has anything to do with Marcia Hawkin's murder?"

I hesitated. "Yes," I said finally.

"Uh-huh," he said, "that's what I figured. Are the Johnsons involved?"

"It's all supposition."

"Sure it is," he agreed. "Like meat loaf; you don't know what's in it. We're tracing Marcia's movements the night she was killed and we've got what we tell the newspapers are 'promising leads.' Maybe they are, maybe they're not, but I'll keep working my end, old buddy, and you keep working yours. Eventually we may take the gold, though I'll settle for the bronze."

"Me, too," I said.

"See you," he said shortly, and hung up.

I sat there, stared at my open journal, and decided I didn't want to labor on a Saturday night. So I pulled on a nylon golf jacket (Day-Glo orange) and clattered downstairs to my wheels. I headed south on Ocean Boulevard to eyeball the Hawkin home, Villa Bile. I didn't have to stop to see that Hector Johnson's white Lincoln was parked outside.

Then I made an illegal U-turn and sped off to the Pelican Club. I was in dire need of a plasma injection, for what I envisioned had happened to Silas Hawkin, Shirley Feebling, and Marcia Hawkin seemed too awful to endure without Dutch courage.

It was still early so it was no surprise to find the club relatively quiescent. I tested Simon Pettibone by ordering an obscure cocktail from my antique Bartender's Guide.

"I would appreciate a Frankenjack," I stated.

He stared at me, rolled his eyes upward, concentrated a moment. Then he recited, "Gin, dry vermouth, apricot brandy, Triple Sec."

"You're incredible," I told him.

"Served with a cherry," he added. "You really want one, Mr. McNally?"

"No," I said. "A double vodka-rocks will do me fine, Mr. Pettibone. The good stuff."

"Sterling or Stoli?"

"Sterling, please."

He poured and placed the tumbler before me. "First of the night?" he asked pleasantly.

"First and last," I said. "I shall not be a problem."

"You never are," he assured me. "Until you start reciting Shakespeare."

"Dear old Willy," I said. "What would I do without him? Tell me something, Mr. Pettibone: Do you believe that money makes the world go 'round?"

"Not entirely," he replied. "I do not believe it is money itself. After all, that is just metal and paper. No, it is the power money confers that makes the world go 'round."

"Power," I repeated reflectively. "Ah. As in comfort, people to serve you, no problems, the lush life?"

"You've got it, Mr. McNally."

"No," I said, "but I wish I did. However, I wouldn't kill for it. Would you?"

"Kill? Another person?"

"Yes."

"No," he said, "I would not do that. I enjoy my sleep too much."

"Well put," I said. "But I suspect there are those who would kill for money and sleep as soundly as you."

"Oh yes," he agreed, "there are those. But they will get their deserts on judgment day."

"And when will that be, Mr. Pettibone? Next Tuesday?"

He didn't laugh or even smile, so I ordered another belt. I finished that and departed. The Pelican was beginning to fill up with a riotous Saturday night throng and I was in no mood for revelry.

I returned home, undressed, and donned a silk nightshirt. But before I took to the sheets I consumed a dollop of marc and smoked one cigarette. To insure a deep, untroubled slumber, you understand. I finally went to bed absolutely convinced I would awake the next day with a clear head, a settled tum, a sweet breath—and possibly five pounds lighter.

16

Of course my hopes were more than dashed on Sunday morning; they were obliterated. But I shall not weary you with a detailed account of my agonies. The only thing more boring than another person's dream is another person's hangover. Suffice to say that it was almost noon before the McNally carcass calmed to the extent that I ceased thinking of suicide as the only cure for my woes.

But my physical fragility was not the only reason I stayed at home that day; I was awaiting a phone call from Hector Johnson. I was certain his daughter had told him of our conversation during that luncheon at the Ocean Grand, and I was just as certain dear old Heck would gobble the bait.

A word of explanation is in order here. The reason for my scheming was that I had no proof. I had suspicions aplenty, but they might well have been skywriting, so ephemeral were they without a test of their validity and permanence. And the only way I could do that was by scamming the scammers. It may sound unnecessarily devious, but bear with me.

I was in my rooms and it was almost one-thirty before my phone rang. I grabbed it up.

"Archy?" he said. "This is Hector Johnson."

A surge of satisfaction dissolved the last remnants of my Katzenjammer. "Heck!" I said cheerily. "Good to hear from you."

"Likewise," he said. "Listen, Arch, I think you and I should get together for a little man-to-man."

"Oh? Concerning what?"

"I can't discuss it on the phone," he said brusquely. "It's about what you mentioned to Theo yesterday."

"Ah," I said, "that. Yes, I agree you and I should have a chat. Where and when?"

"I'm leaving in a few minutes for Fort Lauderdale. I've got some business down there and I'll be gone all day. But I should be home tonight. Is, say, ten o'clock too late for you?"

"Not at all."

"Suppose I come over to your place. I know the address. We can sit in my car and talk."

"Surely you'll come in and have a drink."

"No, thanks," he said shortly. "My car would be best. Private, know what I mean?"

"Whatever you prefer," I told him. "I'll be waiting for you."

"Just you and me," he said. "Right?"

"Of course."

"Good," he said. "See you at ten."

He hung up and I did everything but dance a

soft-shoe, thinking my plot was developing nicely.

Is it elitist to recognize there are cheap people? There are, you know. I don't mean "cheap" in the sense of stingy, but cheap as meaning shoddy, of inferior quality. I thought Hector Johnson was a cheap person, and so was his old buddy, Reuben Hagler.

But sleazy people can sometimes be remarkably clever and remarkably dangerous. I do not take their tawdriness lightly. And so I spent some time devising and rehearsing my dialogue with Hector that evening. I knew the role I had to play. I believed I knew his and could only hope I was correct.

I recognized there was a certain degree of risk involved. Good ol' Heck did not impress me as a man who would accept defeat resignedly. But if he became physical, I was breezily confident I could cope. A perfect example of my damnable self-deception.

But before we met there was something I needed to do. Not because it might aid my investigation but because it was simply something I felt necessary. I dressed conservatively and went downstairs to my mother's greenhouse. She and father were still at church, I could not ask her permission, so I stole one of her potted begonias. It was the Fiesta type with red flowers. I was certain mother would forgive the theft when she learned the purpose.

I drove south to the Hawkin home, slowed to make certain Hector Johnson's Lincoln was not present, then turned into the driveway and parked. I carried the begonia up to the front door and knocked briskly. Nothing. I tried again and there was no response. My third attempt brought results; the door was opened slowly and Mrs. Louise Hawkin stared at me dully.

Oh lordy, but she was a mess. I did not believe she was drunk but she seemed in a stupor, and I wondered if she was drugged. I wasn't sure she recognized me.

"Archy McNally, ma'am," I said. "I want to offer the condolences of my parents and myself on your stepdaughter's tragic death."

But she wasn't listening. She was staring at the plant I was carrying and I thought she brightened.

"Glads," she said.

"No, Mrs. Hawkin. It's a Fiesta begonia."

"The red flowers," she said. "My mother always had fresh glads in the house. She went to the market every three days. All colors but mostly she liked red. So cheerful. I should have bought fresh glads every three days."

"May I come in?" I asked.

She allowed me to enter and watched while I carefully placed the plant on a glass-topped end table. Then she came forward to touch the rosettes tenderly. It was a caress.

"So lovely," she murmured. "So lovely."

I feared she had been sleeping and I had awakened her. She was wearing a wrinkled robe of stained foulard silk. Her hair was unbrushed and looked as if it needed a good wash. Her makeup was smeary, the polish on her fingernails chipped and peeling.

"Mrs. Hawkin," I said, "is there anything I can do for you?"

"Do?" she asked, seemingly bewildered.

I looked around the littered room. Overflowing ashtrays. A spilled drink. A tilted lamp shade. Newspapers scattered on the floor. An odor of grease and mildew. Total disarray.

"Perhaps a cleaning woman," I suggested. "I can find someone for you."

Unexpectedly she flared. "Everyone is always picking on me," she howled.

"Picking?" I said, and then realized she meant hassling. "I didn't wish to upset you, ma'am, and I apologize. Would you like me to leave?"

She calmed as abruptly as she had exploded. "No, no," she said, then added coquettishly, "Sit thee down, lad, and I'll get us a nice drinkie-poo."

I should have declined, of course, but at the moment a drinkie-poo was exactly what I needed. Unfortunately, Mrs. Hawkin returned from the kitchen with two tumblers filled with a clear liquid. After a cautious sip I discovered it was warm gin.

"Have the reporters been bothering you?" I asked.

"Everyone," she said. "Everyone's been bothering me. Reporters, policemen, photographers, friends, strangers who park outside to stare at the house."

"Awful," I said.

"I can't stand it!" she shrieked. She threw her filled tumbler away from her. The contents spilled, the glass bounced on the shag rug without breaking. Then she fell to wailing, face buried in her hands.

Shaken, I did what I could to clean up the mess. Then I went into the kitchen, a pigsty. I poured about a quarter of my gin into a reasonably clean glass and added ice and water. I made another like it for Louise and brought it to her.

She had stopped keening. "Thanks," she said huskily and gulped down half. "I don't know what's happening to me."

"You've been through a horror," I told her. "First your husband, then your stepdaughter. It would shatter anyone. It's amazing that you're coping as well as you are."

She stared at me blankly. "Coping? Is that what I'm doing?"

I nodded.

"I'm not," she said. "I'm dead. I can't feel anything anymore."

I didn't believe that for a minute. I saw that strong, determined face sagging and the heavy body gone limp. Sorrow was taking its toll; she seemed to be shrinking. But there was something else in her expression besides grief. Something I could not immediately identify that I had recently seen and could not recall.

"Mrs. Hawkin," I said, "don't you think it might be wise to ask Jane Folsby to come back to take care of you and the house?"

"No," she said at once. "Not her. She knows too much and might talk."

Then I knew Mrs. Folsby had been telling the truth but I feigned ignorance. "Knows too much?" I repeated. "About what?"

"Things," Louise Hawkin said darkly. She finished her drink and held the empty glass out to me. Obediently I returned to that smelly kitchen, realizing I was no better than Hector Johnson. But if I didn't fetch her lethe she'd get it herself. Still . . .

I sat across from her, leaning forward, intent on keeping up with her fleeting moods.

"Mrs. Hawkin, I don't know if you're aware of it, but I met with Marcia the afternoon before she died."

I saw her stiffen. "Did you?" she said. "What did you talk about?"

"It was a rather disjointed conversation. I didn't clearly understand it. She was obviously disturbed."

"Marcia was insane!" she said forcibly. "I wanted her to get help but she wouldn't. What did she say?"

"Something about a business deal she was planning. Very vague."

"Oh that!" she said, and her laugh was tinny. "Marcia had mad dreams. She thought Hector Johnson would lend her enough money so she could get her own apartment."

"Oh, that's what it was all about," I said. I relaxed, sat back, crossed my legs. "So I guess it was Hector she was going to visit after she left me."

Then that expression I had previously been unable to identify returned more strongly and I recognized it. It was fear, and the last time I had seen it was during my talk with Pinky Schatz in Lauderdale.

"It might have been," Mrs. Hawkin said, shrugging. "It's not important."

"Of course not," I agreed. "That's police business, not mine."

She responded hotly. "Police business? What do you mean by that?"

"Why naturally they'll be trying to trace Marcia's movements the night she was killed. I suppose they'll be talking to all her friends."

She looked at me. "Marcia didn't have any friends," she said flatly.

That might have been true but it struck me as a cruel thing to say. I remembered that poor waif telling me that I was her best friend.

I finished my drink and rose. "I think I better run along," I said. "Thank you for your hospitality and I hope—"

"No," she said. "Stay."

"I'd like to," I said. "I really would. But I promised my parents to accompany them to a croquet match."

"Too bad," she said. "I hate to be alone, and Heck's gone somewhere for the day."

"Why don't you call Theodosia to come over and keep you company."

"That bitch?" Louise Hawkin said tonelessly. "I'd rather be alone."

I could not reply to that so I made my adieu and departed.

"Thanks for the glads," she called after me.

I drove home slowly, trying to nuzzle things out. My visit to Louise Hawkin had been planned as an ostensible sympathy call, but as I had hoped, it had turned out to be more than that. Nothing conclusive had been learned, you understand, but I was beginning to see things more distinctly— as I'm sure you are also, for I have faith in your perspicacity.

It was during a long, lazy ocean swim that I realized my scam's risks, initially treated with sangfroid, could very well prove to be heavier than I had first calculated. They might, in fact, endanger the physical well-being of your humble correspondent. In spite of what I had heard from Mrs. Hawkin I had no intention of abandoning my cunning scheme, but now I recognized its dangers. I am not, I trust, a craven coward, but neither do I claim to be Dudley Doright.

The perils of what I planned disturbed me. If I should, by evil chance, suddenly be rendered defunct, what I knew and what I suspected would be sponged forevermore. I decided to insure against that unhappy possibility.

During the family cocktail hour I confessed to the mater I had purloined one of her beloved begonias and had given it to the bereaved Louise Hawkin.

Mother beamed, kissed me, and said, "That was sweet of you, Archy."

It was indicative of my mood that a bit of wisdom—"A good deed never goes unpunished."—popped into my mind.

"Father," I said, "could you spare me a few minutes after dinner?"

"How many minutes?" he demanded. He can be something of a martinet at times.

"Fifteen," I said, knowing it would be thirty and possibly more.

"Very well," he said. "In my study."

Dinner that night was another of Ursi Olson's specialties: medallions of veal, breast of chicken, and mild Italian sausage sautéed with mushrooms and onions and served with a wine sauce over a bed of fettuccine. Father contributed a decent merlot from his locked wine cabinet, and he and I shared that bottle while mother sipped her usual sauterne.

After a lime sorbet and coffee I followed father into his study and closed the door. He seated himself behind his magisterial desk, and I selected a straight-back chair facing him. I did not want to become too comfortable.

Ordinarily my liege does not request, nor do I provide, progress reports during the course of my investigations. He tells me he is only interested in results. That may be true but I suspect it is also self-protective. He is well aware that my detective methods, while not actually illegal, might be considered unethical or immoral. And he doesn't wish to hear the gruesome details.

In other words, he wants no guilty knowledge. I don't blame him a bit; he has more to lose than I.

But my current inquiry, involving the Smythe-Hersforths, the Johnsons, Reuben Hagler, the Hawkins, Shirley Feebling, and Pinky Schatz, was a special case. I needed someone to share my information and my suspicions so that if I met my quietus (sob!) the investigation could continue and my labors would not be wasted.

I told him everything: what had happened, what I had learned, what I surmised, and what I planned to do. I spoke for almost twenty minutes and saw his face tighten. But he controlled himself; not once did he interrupt.

But when I finished, his wrath was evident. His courtroom stare was cold enough to chill all that merlot I had imbibed at dinner.

"If I thought it would do any good," he said in a stony voice, "I would absolutely forbid you to do what you contemplate. The potential hazards are too great. But I don't imagine you would obey my command."

"No, sir," I said, "I would not. There is no real evidence that what I suspect did, in fact, occur. The only way I can prove my hypothesis is to offer myself as a greedy dupe. If there was a less dangerous way of unraveling this tangle, I would happily adopt it."

"Archy," he said, genuinely perplexed, "what is your obviously intense personal interest in all this? It doesn't directly concern McNally and Son. It's a police matter."

"Not totally," I said. "There are connections to

our clients. And two young, innocent women have been brutally murdered during an investigation we instigated."

He looked at me a long time. "Lochinvar," he accused.

"No, father," I said. "Nemesis."

His anger was slowly transformed to a concern that affected me. "Is Sergeant Rogoff aware of all this?" he asked.

"Some of it, but not all. I intend to tell him more tomorrow after my meeting this evening with Hector Johnson. I'm going to ask Al to provide some measure of backup protection."

"Yes," he said, "that would be wise. Do you think you should be armed?"

"No, sir. If a concealed weapon is found or suspected, it might prove an irritant. A fatal irritant."

His smile was wan. "Perhaps you're right. You're playing a very risky game. I know you're aware of it and I won't attempt to dissuade you. All I ask is that if things become too hairy, you shut down your operation at once and extricate yourself. You understand? If there is no hope of success, give it up and withdraw immediately. Agreed?"

"Yes, father," I said. "Agreed."

I think we both knew that if I failed, a safe withdrawal would be most unlikely.

I went upstairs and spent the remaining hour rehearsing my role once again. I tried to imagine what objections might be made and what my responses should be. I reviewed the entire scenario and could see no holes that needed plugging. I felt I had devised as tight a scheme as possible. The only thing I could not be sure of was luck, and it was discouraging to recall Hector's remark that when you really need it, it disappears.

But then I comforted myself with the thought that his dictum applied to him as well as to me, and perhaps his disappearing luck would be my good fortune. It was a zero-sum game.

A few minutes before ten o'clock I went downstairs and stood outside the back doorway. The portico light was on and I placed myself directly below it so he'd be sure to see I was alone. I lighted a cig and waited. He was almost fifteen minutes late but that didn't bother me. I was certain his tardiness was deliberate; it's a common ploy to unsettle one's adversary. I've used it myself on several occasions.

Finally the white Lincoln Town Car came purring into our driveway, tires crunching on the gravel. It stopped, the headlights went off, flicked on, went off again, and I stepped down to join Hector Johnson.

The first thing I noted after I had slipped into the front passenger seat and closed the door was the mélange of odors: 86-proof Scotch, cigar smoke and, overpowering, his cologne, a musky scent I could not identify.

"Hiya, Arch," he said with heavy good humor. "Been waiting long?"

"Just came down," I lied cheerfully. "How are you, Heck?"

"If I felt any better I'd be unconscious," he said and laughed at his own wit. "Hey, the reason I'm late is that I stopped at Louise Hawkin's place to check on how she's doing. She tells me you dropped by today and brought her a plant. That was real nice."

"From the McNally family," I said. "To express our condolences on the tragic death of her step-daughter."

"Yeah," he said, "that was a helluva thing, wasn't it. First her husband, then Marcia. The poor woman is really taking a hit. Listen, would you object if I lighted up a stogie? If it would bother you, just tell me."

"Not at all," I assured him. "Go right ahead."

We were silent while he extracted a cigar from a handsome pigskin case. He bit off the tip and spat it onto the floor at his feet. He used an old, battered Zippo lighter, which made me wonder how much he knew about cigars. No connoisseur of good tobacco would use anything but a wooden match.

"I guess you and Louise had a long talk," he said, puffing away and blowing the smoke out his partly opened window.

"We did," I admitted. "She seemed in the need of a sympathetic listener."

"Uh-huh," he said. "That's what I've been try-ing to be. She tells me you talked to Marcia the afternoon before she was killed."

"That's correct."

"And that lunatic kid said she was going to ask

me for money so she could get her own apartment."

"Heck," I said, "if Mrs. Hawkin told you that, she's confused. I said only that Marcia spoke of a business deal she was planning. It was Mrs. Hawkin who suggested she was going to ask you for money."

"That figures," he said, showing me a warped grin. "Louise is a little nutsy these days. But that's neither here nor there. What I really want to talk about is Theo's prenuptial agreement. Let's see if I've got this clear. Chauncey comes to you and tells you about it. But he's afraid to tell his mother because then she might put the kibosh on the marriage. Have I got that right?"

"You've got it."

"And what did you tell him to do, Arch?"

"Not to sign anything until I had a chance to think about it."

"That was smart," Johnson said. "So you thought about it and figured Chauncey could sign the agreement without telling mommy. That's what you told Theo—correct?"

"Correct."

"Now I get the picture," he said. "He'll sign if you tell him to?"

"I think he will."

"Sure he will. We get a shyster to draw up the papers, Chauncey signs, and his mother and your father know nothing about it. It's our secret."

"That's right, Heck."

He turned slowly to look at me. "So why do we

need you?" he demanded. "You've already told us how to handle it."

"Two reasons," I said. "First of all, I could tell Chauncey not to sign."

"Wouldn't work," he said, shaking his head. "If he wants my daughter—and I know he's got the hots for her—he'll sign regardless of what you tell him. You're just not built right, Arch; you can't compete with Theo."

"That's probably true. But the second reason is that you're asking five million. A lot of money. I'd like a small piece of the action."

At least he had the decency not to express sorrow that his image of me as a "straight arrow" had suddenly been demolished. He just bit down hard on his cigar and stared grimly through the windshield at the night sky.

"For what?" he said. "So you won't tell Chauncey's mommy?"

"Let's call it a finder's fee," I said. "Just like you wanted for telling me about Mrs. Hawkin's intention to sell her property."

His laugh was short and not mirthful. "You got a great memory, boy. Okay, let's say you tell Chauncey to sign the prenup and you agree not to squeal about it to Mrs. Smythe-whatshername. How much do you figure that's worth?"

"A hundred thousand," I said brazenly. "Two percent. Very modest."

"Sure it is," he said. "Cash, I suppose."

"You suppose accurately."

He tossed his half-smoked cigar out the window. "Doesn't taste so great," he said. "Tastes like shit."

"Too bad."

He turned his head to stare at me. "I guess I underestimated you."

"Many people do." I smiled at him.

"A hundred grand," he said. "Is that your asking price?"

"No," I said. "I don't enjoy haggling. That's the set price."

"Like the song goes: 'All or Nothing at All.' "

"Exactly," I agreed.

"That's a lot of loot to raise in cash," he said. "You can't swing it?"

"I didn't say that. When it comes to my little girl's happiness I'd go to hell and back."

"Of course you would," I said approvingly. "She's worth it."

"Listen, Arch, let me think about this and make a few phone calls. Maybe we can work it out. I'll be in touch."

"When?" I asked.

"I should know by tomorrow. I'll give you a buzz."

"Can you make it early, Heck? I'm going to be running around all afternoon and wouldn't want to miss your call."

"I'll make it early," he promised.

I nodded and got out of the car. I stood at the opened door. "Sleep well," I said.

This time his laugh was genuine. "You're a nervy bastard," he said. "I'll say that for you."

I watched him drive away and then tramped up

to my digs. I was generally satisfied with the way our face-to-face had gone. I believed he had taken the bait. Now all I had to do was set the hook.

My most worrisome problem had been to determine how large a bribe to demand. If I had asked for a million, for instance, or even a half-million, I knew he would have rebuffed me instantly. But a hundred thousand sounded reasonable: not too outlandish, not too covetous.

Of course I was gambling that there was no way on God's green earth that Hector Johnson could raise a hundred thousand dollars in cold cash. I had an approximate idea of his bank balance, I didn't think Reuben Hagler was rolling in gelt, and Mrs. Hawkin would be on short rations until her late husband's estate was settled. I calculated Hector would make a counterproposal, and I could launch the second part of my scam.

I thought my plan was brill. But if, by any chance, Johnson handed over the hundred thousand bucks I'd be a puddle of chagrin.

17

There was a tropical depression moving slowly northward over the Atlantic about two hundred miles off the coast. It was no threat to South Florida, according to the weather wonks, but it turned Monday morning into a kind of soup. Well, consommé, at least. The air was choky, hard to breathe, and the sun gleamed waterily behind a scrim of clouds the color of elephant hide.

I awoke early enough to breakfast with my parents. It was an unusually quiet meal because a woolly day like that blankets the spirits and, if you're wise, you remain silent so you don't start snapping at other people or maybe tilting back your head and howling.

However, before father departed for the office he asked how my meeting with Hector Johnson had gone. I held up crossed fingers and he nodded morosely. That was the extent of our communication.

I returned to my journal, donned reading glasses, and began scribbling. I must confess that I mention my daily labors so frequently because the record I keep becomes the source of these published accounts of my investigations and brief romances. I just don't want you to think I'm making it all up.

I plodded along steadily, hoping for a morning phone call from Johnson. It didn't arrive until almost eleven o'clock, by which time I had begun to fear my crafty plan had gone awry.

"Listen, Arch," Hector said with mucho earnestness, "I know you're not an unreasonable man."

"No, I'm not unreasonable," I readily agreed.

"Well, to make a long story short, I can't come up with the total number you suggested. You capisce?"

"Yes, I understand."

"But I think I can swing half of it," he went on. "It should be available by tonight, and I was hoping we could work out a deal satisfactory to both of us. I'm ready, willing, and able to sign a personal note for the remainder to be paid over a period of time at regular intervals."

"You mean like an IOU?" I asked.

There was a brief silence. Then: "Well, yeah," he said finally, his voice tense, "something like that. How about us getting together and discussing this arrangement like gentlemen?"

"Suits me," I said.

"Hey, that's great!" he said, heartily now. "Let's do just what we did last night: I'll drive over to your place at ten o'clock and we'll sit in my car and crunch the numbers. Just you and me. And we'll both end up winners—right?"

"Right, Heck," I said.

I hung up and stared into space. I believed it extremely unlikely that he had raised fifty thousand in cash in such a short time. And I thought his offer of an IOU was a clumsy ploy. I reckoned he had another motive for wanting to meet with me and I suspected what it was. Definitely not comforting. So I phoned Sgt. Al Rogoff at police headquarters.

"What a coincidence," he said. "I was just about to give you a tinkle."

"Give me a *what?*" I said.

"A tinkle. A phone call. Ain't you got no couth?"

"I'm awash in couth," I told him, "but tinkles I can do without. Why were you going to call?"

"Good news for a change. The Lauderdale cops grabbed Reuben Hagler."

"That *is* good news, Al," I said. "You have no idea how happy it makes me. They're holding him?"

"Yep. He's in the slam."

"Very efficient detective work," I said.

Rogoff laughed. "I wish I could say the same but actually it was just dumb luck. He was beating up on that Pinky Schatz in her condo, and she was yelling and screaming so loud that neighbors called 911. That's how they nabbed Hagler. And the icing on the cake is that the Schatz woman is sick and tired of getting bounced around so she's talking."

"Wonderful," I said. "Did she identify Hagler as the killer of Shirley Feebling?"

"She can't do that, Archy," the sergeant said. "She wasn't an eyewitness and Hagler never told her that he had done it. But she's supplied enough to hold him on suspicion."

"Al," I said anxiously, "don't tell me he's going to walk."

"He probably will," Rogoff admitted, "unless Lauderdale gets more evidence. Like finding the murder weapon hidden in his closet wrapped in his jockstrap. Right now they haven't got enough to convict. Why did you call me?"

"Listen to this," I said, "and try not to interrupt."

I started repeating everything I had told my father: what I knew, what I surmised, what I planned to do. I was halfway through my recital when Rogoff interrupted.

"Why are you telling me all this horseshit?" he demanded. "I'm not interested in prenuptial agreements. What has it got to do with the PBPD?"

"Please," I begged, "let me finish. I need your help."

I described in detail the scam I had already set in motion and what I hoped to gain from it.

"That certainly affects your homicide investigations," I pointed out. "If my con works, you'll clear both the Marcia and Silas Hawkin cases."

He was silent a long time and I could almost see him, eyes slitted, calculating the odds.

"What you guess happened makes a crazy kind of sense," he said finally. "I can buy it. But what you're planning is strictly from nutsville. If you're right, you're liable to get blown away."

"And if I am," I said, "it'll prove I was right, won't it? Then you can take it from there."

"I always knew you were a flit," he said, "but I never suspected you were a total cuckoo. But if you want to take the risk I can't stop you. What do you want from me?"

"The showdown is tonight at ten o'clock. We'll be in Johnson's white Lincoln Town Car parked on the turnaround behind my house. He keeps insisting that just the two of us be present. I was worried he'd bring Reuben Hagler along, and then I'd really be in the minestrone. That's why I was so happy when you told me Hagler is behind bars in Fort Lauderdale. Now what I'd like you to do is park your squad or pickup someplace where Johnson can't spot it. Then be in our garage at ten o'clock—concealed, of course—in case I need assistance."

"Yeah," he said, "that's a possibility."

I ignored his irony. "If I need your help," I went on, "I'll give you a shout."

"Oh sure," he said. "But how are you going to do that if he's got his mitts clamped around your gullet?"

"He won't," I said with more aplomb than I felt. "I'm not exactly Charles Atlas, but I assure you I'm not a ninety-seven-pound weakling either. I mean brutes don't kick sand in my face on the beach without inviting serious retaliation."

"Cuckoo," Al chanted in a falsetto voice. "Cuckoo, cuckoo, cuckoo."

"Your confidence in me is underwhelming. Just

tell me this: Will you be hidden in our garage at ten o'clock tonight?"

"I'll be there," he promised.

I hung up, satisfied that I had done all I could to prepare to play Wellington to Hector Johnson's Napoleon.

I saw little reason to venture out into that scruffy climate so I decided to stay home, bring my journal up to date, futz around and wait for the great dénouement that evening. That plan evaporated, for my next phone call was from Theodosia Johnson. Southern Bell was having a profitable morning.

"Archy," she wailed, "I'm going cuckoo."

I laughed. "Two of a kind," I said. "What's the problem?"

"This miserable weather is suffocating me. And father has been a bear. He was bad enough last night but this morning he got a phone call—I don't know what it was about—and I thought he was going to blow a fuse. Ranting, raving, cursing. And he started drinking directly from the bottle. Have you ever done that, Archy?"

"Thirty-six years ago. But it had a rubber nipple on it."

It was her turn to laugh. "You always make me feel better," she said. "Listen, I'm going to drive daddy over to Louise Hawkin's place. He says he'll be there all afternoon. The two of them will probably get smashed—but who cares? Anyway, I'll have the car and I'd love to meet you for lunch at that funky place you took me to."

"The Pelican Club?"

"That's it. Tonight I'm having dinner at the Smythe-Hersforth mortuary so I've got to build up my morale, and you're the best morale builder-upper I know. So how about lunch?"

"Sure," I said bravely. "Meet you at the Pelican in an hour. Can you find it?"

"I can find anyplace," she said, and I believed it.

I didn't bother getting duded up, just pulled on a navy blazer over the white Izod and tan jeans I was wearing. The snazziest part of my ensemble was the footgear: lavender New Balance running shoes.

Madam X was already seated at the bar of the Pelican Club when I arrived. She and Simon Pettibone were engrossed in a heavy conversation. They seemed startled when I interrupted.

"Glad to see you've met our distinguished majordomo," I said to Theo.

"Met him?" she said. "I've already asked him to marry me, but he says he's taken."

"I think I've just been taken again," Mr. Pettibone said solemnly. "Mr. McNally, this young lady could charm the spots off a tiger."

"Stripes," I said. "And she could do it. What are you swilling, Theo?"

"Vodka martini on the stones."

"Oh my," I said, "we are in a mood, aren't we? I'll have the same, Mr. Pettibone, if you please, and hold the fruit."

I took the bar stool next to Theo and examined her. She was dressed as casually as I. Her jeans were blue denim and she was wearing a black T-shirt under a khaki bush jacket. Her makeup was minimal and her hair swung free. Her appearance was enough to make my heart lurch.

"Mr. Pettibone," I said when he brought my drink, "do you recall the other day when you and I were talking about money?"

"I remember," he said.

"You stated that money in itself isn't important, it's the power that money confers. Is that also true of beauty?"

"Oh yes, Mr. McNally," he said, looking at Theo. "Beauty is power. And even in our so-called enlightened age, it remains one of the few sources of power women have."

"You got that right, kiddo," she said to him. "If a woman's not a nuclear physicist she better have elegant tits. Archy, I've got to pick up daddy in a couple of hours. Can we get this show on the road?"

"Sure," I said, and glanced around at the almost empty bar area. "Slow day, Mr. Pettibone."

"It's the weather," he explained. "The boys and girls don't want to get out of bed."

"Lucky boys and girls," Theo said.

I carried our drinks and we sauntered into the dining room. We were the only customers, and when no one appeared to serve us I went into the kitchen. I found Leroy Pettibone, our chef, seated on a low stool in his whites. He was reading a copy of *Scientific American*.

"Hey, Leroy," I said, "where's Priscilla?"

"Malling," he said. "She'll be in later. You wanting?"

"Whatever's available. For two."

He thought a moment. "How about a cold steak salad? Chunks of rare sirloin and lots of other neat stuff."

"Sounds good to me," I said. "Heavy on the garlic, please."

"You've got it," he said.

I returned to the dining room and told Theo what we were having for lunch. I suggested a glass of dry red zin might go well with the steak salad.

"Not for me, thanks," she said. "You go ahead but I'll have another marty."

I went out to the bar and relayed our order to Mr. Pettibone. He nodded and prepared the drinks.

"Dangerous lady," he commented. It was just an observation; there was no censure in his voice.

"Yes," I agreed, "she is."

I toted the fresh drinks back to our lonely table. It was not the one at which Connie Garcia and I usually dined. I had deliberately avoided seating Madam X there. Don't ask me why. Probably dementia.

We raised glasses, sipped, said, "Ah!" in unison, stared at each other.

"Archy," she said, "I'm caught."

"Caught?"

"In a pattern," she said. "My life. And I can't get out. Don't you find your life is a pattern?"

"More like a maze," I said. "But I must like it because I have no desire to change."

"You're fortunate," she said wistfully.

I wanted to learn more about her being caught but then Leroy brought our salads and a basket of garlic toast.

"Looks delish," Theo said, giving him one of her radiant smiles. I could see he was as smitten as I.

"Plenty more," he said. "If you folks want seconds, just yell."

It was as good as it looked: Boston lettuce, cherry tomatoes, hunks of cold steak, radishes, shavings of feta, cucumber, thin slices of red onions, black olives—the whole schmear.

"Garlicky dressing," Theo said.

"My fault," I confessed. "I asked for it."

"I'm not complaining," she said. "I love it."

I snuck glances at her as she ate. Mr. Pettibone was right; beauty *is* power. I mean she was so lovely that one was rendered senseless. I could understand why the Chinless Wonder would sign *anything* to win her, to have and to hold, till divorce doth them part.

"Do you think I'm wanton, Archy?" she asked suddenly.

That puzzled me because I thought she had said *wonton* and I couldn't see how she could possibly resemble Chinese kreplach. Then I guessed she had said *wantin'* as Leroy had just asked, "You wanting?" Finally I decided she had really meant *wanton:* lustful, bawdy. I think my confusion is understandable. *Wanton* is a written word. Have you ever heard it spoken?

"No, Theo," I said, "I don't think you're wanton. Just a free spirit."

"Free?" she said with a crooked grin. "Don't you believe it. It costs."

Did she mean it cost her or cost others? I didn't know and couldn't guess. This woman never ceased to surprise and amaze. I was no closer to kenning her essential nature than I was the first time we shook hands at the Pristine Gallery.

"Theo," I said, "something is obviously troubling you. Would you like to tell me about it? Perhaps I can help."

"No," she said immediately. "But thanks. I can handle it. I always have."

"You're very independent," I told her.

"Yes," she agreed, "and I think that's my problem. It just kills me to have to rely on other people. I know I have to do it, but I don't like it."

"You're referring to Chauncey?"

"Chauncey. His mother. My father. You."

"Me?" I said, astonished. "What on earth do you rely on me for?"

"A four-letter word beginning with F."

I pondered. "Fool? Fuss? Fill?"

She laughed. "You know what I mean. I wish we had time this afternoon. But there will be other afternoons. Right, Archy?"

She was more riddles than I could count but the largest made me groggy when I tried to solve it. Was she aware of my role in her affairs and enlisting my support by letting her blue butterfly soar? Or was she genuinely attracted to me and needed my enthusiastic cooperation as an antidote to the numbing company of CW and his forbidding mama?

The enigma I faced was hardly original or unique. It faces every man when a woman acquiesces. Is it from profit or desire? The Shadow knows.

We sat quietly in that deserted room for another half-hour. I had a second glass of wine, but Theo declined a third martini. I don't recall what we spoke of. I have a dazed memory of murmurs, small laughs, a few sad smiles. I had a feeling, totally irrational, that this afternoon in a waning light was a farewell. I can't explain it but I had the sense of a departure, a leave-taking.

I believe Theo had the same impression, for just before we rose to leave she reached across the table to pat my hand.

"Thank you, Archy," she said softly, "for all you've done for me."

I was grateful for her sentiment, of course, but it did nothing to unravel the mystery of Theodosia Johnson.

I signed the tab at the bar and we went out to our cars. I think there was much we both wanted to say and neither had the courage. But perhaps I was fantasizing. There's a lot of that going around these days. I wondered if we would kiss on parting but we didn't; we shook hands.

I drove back to the beach in a dullish mood. It seemed to me that our luncheon conversation had been inconclusive to the point of incoherence. I had to admit I simply didn't know Madam X. And so, when I arrived home, I reacted as I customarily do when confronted with a world-class brainteaser: I took a nap.

It was an uneventful evening at the McNally manse. Casual talk during the cocktail hour and dinner was mainly concerned with Lady Cynthia Horowitz's buffet on Tuesday night. Her engraved invitation had specified informal attire, and I declared that permitted Bermuda shorts and no socks. Naturally my father objected strenuously to such an interpretation. His idea of "informal attire" is appearing in public without a vest.

I returned to my cell after dinner to prepare for my ten o'clock brannigan with Hector Johnson. I was tempted to phone Sgt. Rogoff and remind him of his assignment as a confederate concealed in the McNally garage. But on further reflection I decided not to call. Al hates to be nudged. He said he'd be there and I knew he would.

I spent the remaining time rehearsing my lines, attempting to imagine Hector's responses, and devising my rebuttals. It all seemed so simple, so logical and neat, I saw no way he could escape the trap I was setting for him. I might as well have pledged allegiance to the Easter Bunny.

When my phone rang about nine-thirty I plucked it up, hoping it was Rogoff calling to confirm our arrangement. It was Hector Johnson.

"Arch?" he said. "Listen, I think we better change our schedule."

"But you—"

"I just don't feel comfortable driving around at night with this much cash in the car."

"We could—"

"Too many outlaws on the road these days," he charged ahead, ignoring my attempted interruptions. "The best thing is for you to come over to my place. Theo is having dinner at her guy's home so we'll be able to have a one-on-one and maybe a few belts to grease the wheels of commerce, if you know what I mean. So you just drop by at ten o'clock."

"Heck, I don't—"

"I'll be waiting for you," he said and hung up.

I sat stunned, my battle plan reduced to shredded wheat. I now had no doubt whatsoever that Hector had never intended to replay our first meeting. His last-minute change of setting was made to insure that he would not be caught in a snare, which was exactly what I had planned for him. No dummy, our Mr. Johnson.

It appeared to me that I had few options. I could phone him back immediately and postpone our get-together. But to what avail? We could set a different time, a different place, but Hector would surely make yet another revision at the last moment. I might curse his strategy but I had to admire it. Skilled one-upmanship.

Naturally I phoned Sgt. Rogoff. I tried his home first and received a curt reply from his answering machine. I left a message. Then I called police headquarters. He wasn't in his office and the duty officer informed me his present whereabouts were unknown. But if he called in, I was assured, he would be told to contact yrs. truly at once.

Snookered.

Deep, deep thoughts. Pros. Cons. The odds. The risks. Did I dare? Reuben Hagler was in the Fort Lauderdale clink so Johnson would be my sole antagonist. Could I take him? Could he take me?

I suspect you may think me an epicene lad with an overweening interest in wine, women, and song. (Not too heavy on the song, and I could live without wine.) It is true I am something of a coxcomb but I am not completely incapable of self-defense or violent physical action should it become necessary. I have played lacrosse at New Haven and rugby in South Florida. What I'm trying to convey is that my muscles are not spaghettini even though my brain may be Silly Putty.

And so I sallied forth to dance a pas de deux with Hector Johnson, papa of the unknowable Madam X.

The first thing I did after exiting was to search our three-car garage, hoping to find Al Rogoff lurking in the shadows. He was not. And during the early moments of my drive I tried to spot Al's parked squad car or pickup. No luck. I was on my own.

The Johnsons' condo was brightly lighted and Hector opened the door before I knocked. He was grinning, and he grabbed my arm and pulled me inside with a great show of boisterous good-fellowship.

"Glad you could make it, Arch!" he shouted. "Sorry about the change of plans, but I figure it's better this way. Am I right?"

"Sure, Heck," I said.

He practically pushed me onto that cretonne couch of recent fond memory.

"Hey," he said, looming over me, "I'm having a Chivas. How about you?"

"No, thanks," I said. "I've been drinking wine and it's instant blotto to mix the grape and the grain. But you go ahead."

"I was just pouring a refill when you pulled up," he said. "Be right back."

He went into the kitchen. I didn't think he was sozzled, but he wasn't stone sober either. I wanted him to keep drinking, figuring it might impair his coordination if things turned nasty. He returned with a full glass and no ice cubes that I could see.

"Your daughter is having dinner with her fiancé?" I asked.

"Yeah," he said, plopping down in an armchair facing me. "She drove the Lincoln. That guy of hers is a real stiff, isn't he? What Theo sees in him I'll never know."

"Maybe she sees five million dollars," I suggested.

His expression didn't change, but he took a deep gulp of his Scotch. "I'm glad you brought that up, Arch," he said. "Listen, I got bad news. I know I told you I had fifty grand and I did, but now I don't. I was depending on a pal to help me out, but he's in a bind and can't come up with the gelt. Arch, I'm really, truly sorry about this, and you have every right to be pissed. I mean I think you're in the right to ask for a finder's fee and if I had it I'd be happy to hand it over with a smile. But like they say, you can't get blood from a turnip. I only wish there was some other way we could work this out."

The opening I had hoped for . . .

I was silent a moment, looking at him thoughtfully. "There may be, Heck. And it won't cost you any cash."

He took another swig. "No money?" he said. "Then what do you want?"

"That painting you bought from Marcia Hawkin."

"What painting?" he cried. "What the hell are you talking about?"

"Heck," I said, "let's stop playing games. I know Marcia sold you a painting."

"Are you calling me a liar?" he said menacingly.

"Of course not. I just think you're making a very chivalrous attempt to protect the reputation of that poor, unfortunate girl."

He suddenly switched gears. "Yeah, you're right," he said. "That's exactly what I want to do. Louise has enough problems without that. How did you know?"

Then I went into my rehearsed spiel, speaking slowly in a grave voice. Don't let anyone tell you that you can't con a con man. His ego is so bloated that it never occurs to him that anyone would even try to swindle him. Bankers have the same fault.

"Heck, when I spoke to Marcia the afternoon before she was killed she made a confession. I didn't ask questions; she just wanted to talk. You know what a flake she was.

"She told me she arrived home while the house-keeper, Mrs. Folsby, was on the phone reporting to the police she had just discovered the body of Silas Hawkin. Marcia went directly to the studio and saw that her father was dead. Murdered. She said he had been working on a nude portrait of her, acrylic on a wood panel, and she was so proud and happy that he wanted her to pose because it was the first painting he had ever done of her.

"So, she admitted, she stole it. Just wrapped it in a drop cloth, carted it away, and slid it under her bed in the main house before the cops arrived. What she did was unlawful, of course: removing evidence from the scene of a crime.

"But Marcia said she didn't care. She felt the painting belonged to her. Not only had she posed for it but it would be her only remembrance from her father. You can understand how she felt, can't you, Heck?"

"Yeah," he said, finishing his triple Chivas. "Sure I can."

"But then the hostility between Marcia and her stepmother became more venomous. After the death of her father Marcia had no money of her own; her only asset was the last painting by Silas Hawkin. So she decided to sell it. To you. Because she thought you were wealthy and would be willing to help her out. I tried to convince her that what she planned was illegal. She really didn't own the painting; after her father's death it became part of his estate and

Louise was his beneficiary. But Marcia insisted on going ahead with it. How much did you pay, Heck?"

The direct question shook him. He gripped his empty glass with both hands and leaned forward tensely. "She told you the painting was a nude of her?"

"That's what she said."

Then he relaxed, sat back, nodded. "I paid her twenty thousand," he said. "A bargain."

"It certainly was," I agreed. "And now I'm going to offer you another bargain. I'll take that painting as a finder's fee instead of the hundred thousand dollars I asked. A nice profit for you, Heck."

He rolled his empty tumbler between his palms while he stared at me closely. "You're so generous," he said, not without irony. "Why?"

"Because I like Silas Hawkin's work. I already own some of his watercolors. And I want to own his last painting, especially since it's on wood, something he hadn't done since he was a student in Paris."

Johnson kept staring and I still wasn't certain he had bought my fairy tale. I added more.

"If you're afraid of getting involved in the police investigation of Marcia's murder, forget it. I figure you paid her and she went out to celebrate with some of those crazy dopers and bikers she knew. They partied, things got rough, and she ended up dead."

"Uh-huh," he said. "That's the way I figure it, too."

"Another consideration is this . . . What we're

talking about is stolen property. Marcia started by stealing the painting from her father's studio. You committed an illegal act by purchasing stolen property. But you get out from under by turning it over to me. Then I have the hot potato. Do you think I'm going to hawk it, lend it to an exhibition, or even show it to anyone else? No way! That nude goes into my private collection and stays private for the rest of my life."

He was silent and I knew it was his moment of decision. Snowing him as I had was the only way to uncover the truth. And if what I suspected was correct, he would be forced to react.

He pondered a long time, not speaking, and I didn't know which way it would go. Finally he said, "Clue me in on this, Arch. What's my downside risk?"

That was Wall Street jargon and I remembered he had been a stockbroker cashiered for securities fraud.

"Your downside risk," I told him bluntly, "is that the cops question me and I repeat what Marcia told me of planning to sell you a painting. The stained drop cloth was found in her Cherokee when they hauled it out of the lake. That implicates you. Also I'd feel it my duty to inform Chauncey's mother that her darling son intends to sign a five-million-dollar prenuptial contract with your daughter, contrary to my advice. There goes Chauncey's inheritance.

"Your upside potential is that the cops never learn from me what Marcia said, and I advise Chauncey to sign the prenup immediately. And everyone lives happily ever after. *If* I get the painting."

He twisted his features into more grimace than smile. "I don't have much choice, do I?" he said.

"Not much," I agreed.

"I need a refill," he proclaimed hoarsely, hauling himself to his feet. "Be right back."

He went into the kitchen. I waited patiently, satisfied that I had given it my best shot. If it didn't work I'd be forced to consider enrolling in a Tibetan monastery.

It worked. Hector came slowly out of the kitchen, not with a drink but with a revolver. It looked like a .38 but I couldn't be sure. I don't know a great deal about firearms. Badminton rackets are more my speed.

I rose to my feet. "Judgment day," I said. "And it's only Monday. I suggested to Mr. Pettibone it might be tomorrow."

"What?" Johnson said, completely bewildered.

You may not believe this but the sight of him carrying a handgun was a source of exultant gratification more than fright. For I knew I had been right, and what is more pleasurable than saying, "I told you so," even if they're your last words.

He was holding the weapon down alongside his leg, not brandishing it, you know, but gripping it tightly. I took one small step toward the outside door.

"Is that the gun that killed Shirley Feebling?" I asked him.

Oh, but he was shaken! His face fell apart.

Emotions flickered: disbelief, consternation, fear, anger, hatred.

"You're a real buttinsky, aren't you?" he said, his voice an ugly snarl.

"A professional buttinsky," I reminded him. "I get paid for it."

I took another small step toward the door. He followed as I hoped he would. He was my sole assailant but little did he know that I had two allies: Desperation and Adrenaline.

I took another step. He came much closer, raising the gun and pointing it at me. When I saw the muzzle I realized it wasn't a .38; it was the entrance to the Lincoln Tunnel.

"Don't try to make a break for it," he warned harshly. "I'd just as soon drop you right here."

"And stain your beautiful shag rug?" I said.

I took a deep breath and made my play, a fast feint toward the door. It was a singularly adroit move if I say so myself, and I do. His gun swung to cover my anticipated departure. I whirled back and rushed, knocking the revolver aside and embracing him. We hugged, straining, tighter than lovers. He was heavy and he was powerful. It was like pressing a grizzly to one's bosom.

I feared this monster was capable of collapsing my ribs or snapping my spine, and so I craned and fastened my teeth, uppers and lowers, onto his nose. Of course I had no intention of amputating his beezer. That would have left me with a mouthful of nostrils, an unappetizing prospect. No, I merely hoped to cause him intense pain.

And I succeeded admirably. His roars of anguish were sweeter to my ears than Debussy's *Clair de Lune.*

I increased the pressure, hearing the creaking of cartilage in his beak. His groans became gasping whimpers. I opened my mandibles, disengaged myself from his clutch, and stood back. He fell to his knees and I stooped and plucked the revolver from his nerveless grasp. He put both hands to his bleeding proboscis and continued to moan.

I looked down at him and was tempted to utter a dramatic proclamation, such as *"Sic semper tyrannis."* Instead, I just said, "Tough shit," and rapped him on the occiput with the butt of his gun. It seemed to have little effect so I slugged him again and this time he slid face down onto the carpet. Kaput.

I began my search, starting in the bedroom at the rear of the condo. Only one bedroom: that perplexed me but I continued to toss the entire apartment. Every few minutes I returned to see if the comatose Hector was stirring. If so, I'd give him another sharp tap on the noggin and he would lapse into deep slumber again.

I was beginning to ransack the living room when I heard a heavy pounding on the front door. I rushed to the window and saw a police car parked outside, roof lights flashing. I yanked open the door to find Sgt. Al Rogoff with a young officer behind him. Both men had hands on their open holsters.

"You okay?" Al asked anxiously.

"Dandy," I assured him. "How did you find me?"

"I was a few minutes late getting to your garage. I stayed in there for almost half an hour. When neither you nor Johnson showed up I knew something had gone wrong. His condo was the obvious place to start looking for you. Did everything go like you figured?"

"Pretty much," I said. "Come on in."

They followed me into the living room and looked down at the prone Hector Johnson. Rogoff knelt and rolled him over.

"What happened to his nose?" he asked. "Did you bop him?"

"No," I said, "I bit him."

Al looked at me sorrowfully. "And I thought you were a gourmet," he said.

The two cops hauled Johnson to his feet. He regained a groggy consciousness, but they had to hold him upright. The sergeant cuffed him and they hustled him outside and thrust him into the back of the squad car. Rogoff returned, leaving the front door of the condo open. I handed him Johnson's revolver.

"This might be the gat used to kill Shirley Feebling," I told him.

"*Gat?*" he said. "I haven't heard that word since Cagney died." He examined the gun. "It could be," he admitted. "It's the right caliber. I'll send it down to Lauderdale for tests. What about the painting?"

"Haven't found it yet," I said. "I was just starting on this room when you showed up."

We searched and came up with zilch. Rogoff went into the kitchen and came back with two tumblers of Chivas and water on the rocks. He handed me one.

"Drink it," he advised. "You look a little puffy around the gills, and Johnson will never miss it."

He sat on the couch and I fell into the armchair recently occupied by mine host.

"Maybe he burned the painting," the sergeant said. "Getting rid of incriminating evidence."

I shook my head. "I don't think so, Al. That nude is valuable, and I can't see Johnson destroying anything that might prove profitable."

"Then what the hell did he do with it? Put it in storage?"

"Maybe he left it at Louise Hawkin's place," I suggested.

"That's a possibility. Or maybe—hey, why are you grinning like that?"

"I know where it is," I said. "Not exactly 'The Purloined Letter' but close to it."

"Cut the crap," Rogoff said roughly. "Where is it?"

"You're sitting on it."

"*What?*"

"The one place we didn't look. Under that ghastly couch."

I flopped down on my knees and dragged it out. I propped it up in the armchair and we stared at it. It seemed in good condition, a bit smeared but easily restored. The composition was classic, the colors vibrant, the pose almost lascivious. Perhaps wanton would be a better word: The model was more naked than nude. I looked for the tattoo of the blue butterfly and there it was.

"Sensational," Al breathed. "Better than that portrait of her at the Pristine Gallery. She was making it with Silas?"

"Whenever it pleased her," I said. "She's a free spirit. But she admits it costs. Naturally Silas was eager."

"That's why his daughter did him in?"

"Motive enough, wouldn't you say, Al? Marcia was a woman scorned. Daddy had brief affairs before, but Madam X was an obsession. I can understand that."

"Who?" he said, puzzled. "Madam X?"

"That's what I call her. So Marcia killed him, just as her letter said, and swiped the painting that infuriated her. But then she needed money and realized she had the perfect blackmail bait. If she showed the nude to Chauncey and Mrs. Smythe-Hersforth, the marriage would be canceled. Hector didn't have the cash she demanded so he had to put her down and grab the painting. I imagine Reuben Hagler helped him. It would be a two-man job to strangle Marcia and push her Jeep off the pier into the lake."

Rogoff took a deep breath. "All because of a beautiful broad," he said.

I was about to quote, "Beauty is power," when, as if on cue, we heard a car pull up outside. We moved to the open door to see Theodosia Johnson slide out of the white Lincoln. She paused a moment when she saw my Miata and the police car. She went over to peer in at the manacled Hector. Then she came marching into the house and confronted us. How I admired her! She was erect, shoulders back, eyes angry.

"What's going on here?" she demanded fiercely.

The sergeant showed his ID. "I'm afraid I'll have to take you in, miss," he said.

"Do you have a warrant?" she said stiffly.

"No, ma'am," Al said, "but I have probable cause coming out my ears. Do you wish to resist?"

She considered for the briefest of moments. "No," she said, "I'll come along."

Rogoff took her arm lightly, but she turned to me.

"Archy," she said, "I'm very fond of you."

"Thank you," I said faintly.

"And if you feel sorry for me I'll never forgive you."

I felt like weeping but a cliché saved me. "You're a survivor," I told her.

"Yes," she said, lifting her chin, "I am that."

She gave me a flippant wave and Sgt. Rogoff led her outside to join Hector. Eventually he returned. By that time I had finished my drink and his as well.

"What are you going to charge her with?" I asked him.

He shrugged. "Enough to convince her to make a deal. You had eyes for her, didn't you?"

"I did," I said, "and I do. I can't see where she did anything so awful. I think her father was the main offender."

Al didn't look at me. "Archy, Hector isn't her father. I heard from Michigan this afternoon. Her

real name isn't Johnson; it's Burkhart or Martin
or Combs or whatever she wants it to be. She was
a cocktail waitress in Detroit. Model. Party girl.
Arrested twice for prostitution. No convictions.
She's been Hector's live-in girlfriend for the past
three years."

"Oh," I said.

18

I arrived home shortly after midnight. Lights were still glowing in my father's study. That was uncommon; usually m'lord is abed by eleven o'clock. He met me at the back door.

"You're all right, Archy?" he asked.

"Yes, sir, I'm fine."

"Good. Did things go as you hoped?"

"Mostly."

He nodded. "Let's have a nightcap."

We went into his study. I was hoping for a cognac, but he poured us glasses of wine. That was okay; any port in a storm. We got settled and he looked at me inquiringly.

I started with a brief description of the murder of Silas Hawkin.

"Marcia actually killed her father?" the patriarch said, aghast.

"Yes, sir. But she had been sexually abused from childhood. Now I think she was more than disturbed; she was psychotic. Understandable.

314

Her father's affair with Theodosia Johnson was, in Marcia's raddled mind, his final act of cruelty and betrayal."

"What about the Johnsons? What was their role?"

"I think the three of them—Theodosia, Hector and Reuben Hagler—came down to Palm Beach from Michigan about a year ago with a definite plan. Their financial resources were limited but their main asset was Theo, her beauty and charm. The idea was to marry her off to a wealthy bachelor and take him for whatever they could grab."

"An intrigue as old as civilization."

"Yes, father, it is. The only difference was that these creatures were willing to murder to achieve their goal. I believe they thought of Shirley Feebling and Marcia Hawkin merely as impediments to their success. Shirley threatened to make Chauncey's love letters public unless he married her, and so she had to be eliminated. I suspect it was Reuben Hagler who shot her. And Marcia Hawkin threatened to show her father's nude portrait of Theo to Mrs. Smythe-Hersforth. That would have resulted in the marriage being called off or Chauncey being disinherited. And so Marcia also had to be eliminated. I have the feeling that Hector Johnson was guilty of that homicide."

"Despicable!" father said and rose to refill our glasses. When he was seated again I told him of the personal history of Theodosia Johnson.

The pater looked at me keenly. "You were attracted to this woman, Archy?"

"I was," I admitted. "Still am."

He sighed. "It never ceases to amaze me when talented people, intelligent people, imaginative people turn their energies to crime. One wonders what they might have achieved if they had devoted their talent, intelligence, and imagination to legal pursuits. The waste! When virtues are put in the service of vice it becomes not only a societal tragedy but a personal disaster."

I nodded gloomily. I was really in no mood for his philosophizing. We sat in silence for several minutes, sipping our port, and I could see he had gone into his mulling status. I wondered what was stirring in the dim recesses of his mazy mind. Finally he spoke.

"I think you have done an excellent job, Archy, and you are to be commended."

"Thank you."

"Not only have you cleared up a disagreeable mess but I believe it quite likely you have prevented one and possibly two homicides."

I stared at him in astonishment. "Prevented? Homicides? How so?"

"Hasn't it occurred to you that if Chauncey had signed the prenuptial agreement and married the young woman he might have suffered an early demise, perhaps in an accident craftily planned by this gang of miscreants. Or, in lieu of that, they might have plotted to arrange the death of Mrs. Gertrude Smythe-Hersforth first. Chauncey would inherit, and *then* he would be exterminated."

I sucked in my breath. "Leaving Theodosia

Johnson with the Smythe-Hersforth millions."

"Exactly."

"Do you really believe they planned that scenario, father?"

"I do," he said decisively. "From what you have told me, I am convinced these people are sociopaths. They are totally devoid of any moral sense. Nothing is good—except money—and nothing is bad. Things just *are*. And if you believe that, you can commit any heinous act carelessly without a twinge of guilt or remorse."

I finished my wine and rose. "I think I better go up," I said. "It's been a long, tiring night."

"Of course," he said, looking at me sympathetically. "Get a good sleep."

But it was not a good sleep; it was fitful and troubled, thronged with visions I could not identify except that I knew they were dark and menacing. My bed became a battleground on which I fought demons and constantly looked about for hidden assassins.

It was no wonder that when I finally slept I did not awake until almost noon on Tuesday morning. I staggered to the window and saw the sky had cleared, the sun shone and, I presumed, somewhere birds were chirping.

I took a hot shower, shaved, and dressed with special care. Not because I had important social engagements that afternoon but I needed the lift that nifty duds always give me. I went downstairs to a deserted kitchen, inspected the larder, and settled on a brunch of a garlic salami and cheddar sandwich (on pump) and a frosty bottle of Heineken. The old double helix began twisting in the wind.

I went first to my father's study, sat at his desk, used his phone, and called Sgt. Rogoff.

"What's happening?" I asked him.

He laughed. "It's finger-pointing time," he said. "Hagler, Johnson, and the bimbo are—"

"She's not a bimbo," I protested.

"Whatever," he said. "Anyway, the three of them are all trying to cut deals. Johnson says Hagler shot Shirley Feebling. Hagler says Johnson strangled Marcia Hawkin. These are real stand-up guys. Not!"

"What do you think they'll draw?"

"You want my guess? I don't think they'll get the chair. The evidence isn't all that conclusive. But they'll plea-bargain down to hard time."

"And Theodosia?"

"She'll walk," he admitted. "She's being very cooperative. And she agrees that she'll get out of Florida and never come back. Good riddance."

"Yes," I said.

I wanted to tell him that I thought Madam X was a self-willed, undisciplined woman who just didn't give a damn. But she was smart, sensitive, and fully aware of her excesses and how they doomed her. I didn't say it, of course; Rogoff would have hooted with laughter.

"Al," I said, "thank you for your help and keep me up to speed on this magillah. Okay?"

"Sure," he said.

I hung up and sat a few moments in the guv's chair, reflecting. I shall not claim I was wading barefoot through the slough of despond. It wasn't true and you wouldn't believe me anyway. Instead, I found myself in a remarkably serene mood. Which made me wonder if I had truly been in love with an associate of killers, a woman soon to be banished from the sovereign State of Florida.

I had been enthralled by her and still was. If she had used me, where was the harm? I had enjoyed it. I knew I did have and still had a strong affection for her. Was that romantic love? I didn't know.

I went outside into a brilliant noonday. I decided to drive down the coast and let the sun shrivel and the wind blow away all complexities. I wanted my life to be simple, clear, easy to understand. I really enjoy a broiled lobster more than paella. And that jaunt did rejuvenate me. Except that I found myself touring past the Ocean Grand and through Mizner Park, places where Theo and I had memorable luncheons. But I didn't stop.

I drove directly back to Palm Beach and arrived in time to visit the Pristine Gallery before it closed for the day. Silas Hawkin's portrait of Madam X was no longer displayed in the front window nor was it displayed within. The proprietor was wandering about disconsolately.

"Mr. Duvalnik," I said, "what happened to that beautiful painting by Hawkin?"

"Haven't you heard?" he said. "Theodosia Johnson has been arrested, the marriage is off, and now Chauncey Smythe-Hersforth refuses to pay. He commissioned it and I suppose I could sue, but I don't want the hassle."

"So it becomes the property of Mrs. Louise Hawkin?"

"I suppose so," he said glumly. "I talked to the widow and she really doesn't want it. Told me to sell it for whatever I could get. One of the tabloids offered a thousand dollars but that's ridiculous. I end up with three hundred? No thanks. I spent more than that on Hawkin's exhibition."

"I'd be willing to pay ten thousand for the portrait," I told him, "if you'd sell it to me on time, perhaps ten or twelve monthly payments."

"You're serious?"

"I am."

He brightened. "I'll speak to Mrs. Hawkin. I'll tell her of your offer and urge her to accept."

"Thank you, Mr. Duvalnik," I said. "I admire the painting and would be proud to own it."

"And why not?" he cried. "It's a masterpiece!"

"It is indeed," I agreed.

I tooled homeward, convinced that eventually I would become the legal owner of Silas Hawkin's painting of Madam X. Not the nude. I knew that wood panel would remain in police custody as evidence during a criminal investigation. I had no interest in its final disposition. I didn't want it. Too many bad vibes.

But I wanted the formal pose: Theo seated regally in an armchair framed by crimson drapes, her lips caught in an expression so mystifying that it made Mona Lisa's smile look like a smirk.

I would not hang the portrait on the wall of my bedroom, of course. That would be a bit much. I would hide it in a closet, and occasionally I would take it out, prop it up, and look at it fondly while remembering and perhaps listening to a tape of Leon Redbone singing "Extra Blues."

I had time for a curtailed ocean swim, then returned home to shower and dress in a slapdash fashion for Lady Cynthia Horowitz's informal seafood buffet. We skipped the family cocktail hour that evening, and at seven o'clock the McNallys set out. My parents led the way in father's black Lexus. I followed in my flaming Miata, feeling more chipper than I had any right to be.

The Horowitz estate was all aglitter with ropes of Chinese lanterns, and a goodly crowd had already assembled by the time we arrived. Tables had been set up around the pool and the buffet was being arranged by caterers, pyramiding seafood onto wooden trenchers lined with cracked ice. A small outdoor bar was already busy, and in the background a tuxedoed trio played Irving Berlin.

I sought out our hostess. Lady Cynthia was an old friendly enemy and she gave me a warm welcoming kiss on the lips.

"My favorite rogue," she said, tapping my cheek. "Have you been behaving yourself, lad?"

"No," I said, "have you?"

"Of course not," she said. "At my age naughtiness is a necessity—like Fiberall."

"At my age, too," I said, and we both laughed as she drifted away to greet newly arriving guests.

I looked about for Consuela Garcia but couldn't immediately spot her. So I ordered a kir royale at the bar and joined the gossiping throng of friends and acquaintances. You must understand that you are required to pass a Gossip Aptitude Test before you are allowed to live in the Town of Palm Beach.

That evening the only topic being bandied about was the Chauncey–Theodosia affair. There were many reports, rumors, hints, insinuations, and much ribald laughter. I listened but contributed nothing.

Finally I espied Connie. Zounds but she looked a winner! She was wearing a mannish suit of white linen, fashionably wrinkled, and a choker of black pearls I had given her. With her bronzy tan and long ebony hair she made the other women at that soirée look like Barbies. I hastened to her side.

"Hello, stranger," she said with a bright smile.

"Connie," I said, "you look marv. May I have the first dance?"

"I'll be too busy getting the place closed up after dinner."

"Then may I see you home, later?"

"I have my own car," she said and looked at me speculatively.

I interpreted that look to be half-challenge, half-invitation. "Suppose I tailgate you to make certain you arrive home safely," I suggested.

"If you like," she said. "Now go eat before all the prawns are gone."

I dined at a table for four with my parents and Mr. Griswold Forsythe II, a superannuated bore who had depleted his repertoire of anecdotes fifty years ago, which didn't prevent him from repeating them ad infinitum. The only things that saved me were that piscine buffet and the bottle of chilled sancerre on each table, replaced as needed.

After that yummy feast was demolished, dancing commenced on the pool verge and the cropped lawn. I watched affectionately as my parents waltzed to a fox-trot, and then I lured mother into joining me for a sedate lindy. We did beautifully, and it was a moment to treasure.

The night spun down, Mr. and Mrs. McNally departed, other guests shouted their farewells and were gone. The caterer cleared up, spurred on by Connie Garcia, and the trio packed up their instruments and left. The bar closed, lanterns were extinguished, and quiet took over. The hostess was nowhere to be seen and, knowing Lady Cynthia, I suspected she had retired to her chambers with the pick of the litter. And I assure you he would not be the runt.

Finally, only Connie and I remained. We met at our cars in the driveway and, giggling, she displayed her loot: two bottles of that sharp sancerre.

"Bless you, my child," I said gratefully.

She drove back to her condo and I followed closely. We arrived without incident and within fifteen minutes were lounging on her miniature balcony, gazing down at a shimmering Lake Worth and sipping sancerre. What more, I wondered, could life hold for a growing boy.

"Tell me, Archy," Connie said lazily, "what have you been up to?"

"Busy, busy, busy," I said. "Dinners, parties,

dances, and licentiousness. And you?"

"More of the same," she said, and we both burst out laughing.

"Actually," I said, "it's been sluggish."

"A drag," she said.

"Nothing," I said.

"Zip," she said.

We were contentedly together.

"Must you go?" she asked in a wispy voice.

"No," I said, "I must not."

"Promise not to snore?"

"I never snore," I said indignantly.

"Perhaps not but you do burble occasionally."

"I'll promise not to burble if you promise not to kick."

"I never kick," she said firmly.

"Do so."

"Do not."

"Then you sometimes jerk in your sleep. You convulse."

"Convulse?" she said. "Is that fun?"

"It can be," I said. "Under the right circumstances."

She refilled our glasses. "I've missed you, Archy," she said casually.

"And I've missed you, Connie," I said, just as casually.

"It's been silly-time," she added.

"Too true," I concurred.

"Right now?" she asked.

"Barkis is willin'," I told her.

"Who's Barkis?"

"A close friend of mine."

"I think I've had enough of your close friends," she said.

I skinned down and had popped between the sheets before Connie finished locking up and dousing the lights. She left a single bulb burning in the bathroom and when she came out starkly naked I almost swooned with longing. What a delight she was! And no tattoos.

She climbed into bed and we moved close.

"Let's go for it," she said.

I still refuse to believe romantic love is a myth. But an intimate friendship between a man and a woman is better.

I think.